DEATHSCAPE

Broslin Creek, book 2

Dana Marton

With contribution from A.G. Devitt

"... sucked me in from the beginning and kept me guessing... the characters are real people--with histories and motivations and interesting quirks. Add a scary killer, some romance and you have a perfect read!" *Susan Mallery, NY Times bestselling author*

DEDICATION

This novel is dedicated to my wonderful family who support me through thick and thin, and put up with the occasional missed dinner when I'm on deadline. My most heartfelt appreciation also goes out to my readers who keep me going day after day. Thank you!

Chapter One

The fox behind the hundred-year-old Pennsylvania farmhouse inched forward in the withered grass as it stalked the meadow vole. Gray winter clouds rolled above, forcing their way across the sky, large brutes that had been twisted into violent shapes by the winds of the troposphere. The fox paid little mind to the weather, its eyes on its prize.

At the other end of the farmyard loomed a dilapidated barn, filled with the scent of moldy hay and rotting wood—the sweet scent of decay. A man crouched in the shadows of the hayloft, looking out through a gap in the boards to watch the fox.

Some hunters stalked their prey; others baited their trap, then lay in wait for the ambush. He preferred the challenge of setting up the right trap, drawing his victim to him. He liked to think his way, since it required more finesse, was the nobler way.

Anyone could follow a guy into a dark alley and shoot him in the back. But a quick death was not what he had in mind for today. Detective Sullivan had dogged him for too long, had caused too much trouble. Outsmarting the guy over the years might have provided some amusement, but not enough to let him live. He'd reached too close this time.

The man glanced at the tool case at his feet. He couldn't allow the detective to jeopardize his legacy. His masterpiece had to be preserved for all the ages, for the generations that would be evolved enough to understand and appreciate it.

Outside, the fox pounced; then, a second later, it allowed the wriggling rodent to escape for a few staggering steps before pouncing again. A quick kill left no time to savor, gave the hunter no chance to improve his skills. Then the fox's ears flicked, and in the next instant, it snatched up the vole and darted into the stand of barren bushes.

Sullivan's black sedan rolled down the dirt road at last.

The detective had come alone. He would. He was that cocky.

A good hunter knew his prey and used its weaknesses.

The man in the hayloft pushed to his feet as the car rolled to a silent stop. Sullivan got out, surveyed the buildings and the surrounding barren fields, his right hand staying close to the weapon in his holster. He started for the house, crossing the yard in careful strides.

He almost walked past the chunk of bone, damn near tripped over it before he froze mid-step. Judging by the way his expression darkened, he realized pretty fast that the broken section of femur was human.

He squatted and bagged the piece of bone as evidence, by the book, called it in just as the first heavy, half-frozen raindrops crashed out of the sky. Instead of going back to wait in the safety of his vehicle for reinforcements, he kept going.

Jack Sullivan waited for no one. He worked with no one. He trusted no one. He asked for no quarter and didn't give any.

Anticipation of the pleasure of taking down a man like that, taking him apart piece by piece, gave flavor to the hunt. The man in the hayloft adjusted the rubber gloves on his hands.

He had at least twenty minutes before Sullivan's backup would show—he'd driven the distance on a half-dozen occasions in various traffic conditions and measured the time.

They would be too late.

* * *

3 days later.

"Can I stay?"

The question broke Ashley Price's heart as she crouched in her messy foyer with her daughter in her arms. She clutched her five-year-old tighter as skinny little arms wrapped around her neck.

"Very soon, okay?"

4

Maddie—pink coat, pink boots, pink hat, pink gloves—pulled back and put on her poor-lost-puppy look. "Mo-om, you always say that. I'll be good. I'll be quiet when you paint. You won't even know I'm here."

And it broke Ashley's heart a little more that her daughter thought she couldn't come home because she wasn't good enough.

"I know, Peanut. It's not about that. You could talk all you want." She missed her daughter's sweet chatter, had come to dread the dead silence of the house. "I'll be better soon, and you can come home. I promise."

"You don't look sick. You look better now." Maddie pouted.

Ashley forced a smile. "Would you like to take your picture back to Grandpa's place?"

They'd spent part of their day together making art, putting thin paper over various textures and making graphite rubs, then cutting and fitting the pieces together to create a new image. Maddie loved searching for different surfaces: a rough tile, sandpaper, money, the lemon grater, whatever she could find. They'd turned the rubbings into dolls and flowers and even did a giant, scaly dragon.

"You can keep them," her daughter said, the pout quickly disappearing. She wasn't one to keep grudges. "Then you won't be sad when I'm gone."

Ashley blinked hard. She wasn't going to cry in front of her daughter. And not in front of her father either.

William Price was coming back into the house, wiping his Italian leather shoes on the mat. He was tall and handsome, in his late fifties and in excellent shape. He played both tennis and golf weekly, belonging to some fancy club in Philly where he and his business partners gathered to conduct informal business.

If he was more comfortable at his club than with a five-year-old drenched in pink, he didn't show it. He doted on Maddie in a way Ashley didn't remember him doting on her when she'd been little. Of course, back then the man had still been in the process of building his empire, while now he had the luxury of making time for family.

"Come on, young lady." He waited by the door. "You've kept your grandfather waiting long enough. Car's nice and toasty."

"Can I stomp in the snow? It's not dirty here."

Pristine white snow was one of the advantages of living in the country.

"Of course." Ashley squeezed the little hand in hers one last time before letting go.

She waited until Maddie skipped out of hearing range, leaving the front door open so she could keep an eye on her, ignoring the icy blast of cold blowing in.

"When?" She spoke the single word in a low voice.

"Do you have everything you need? Can I do anything to help?"

"Thanks. I'm okay." To ask for anything would have been a sign of weakness, an indication that she hadn't gotten her life together yet, an excuse for delaying Maddie's return to her. "I'm fine. Really." Everything was a negotiation with William Price, head of Price Financial Consulting, a successful center city brokerage firm.

"She should be able to finish out the school year. It would be best." The what's-best-for-Maddie trump card. And how could Ashley fight that?

The end of the school year dangled four unbearable months away. Her eyes burned. *Show no weakness*. She drew a deep breath and prepared to fight.

Her father spoke first. "Will you come to see us next weekend, or should I bring her out again?"

The final thrust of the knife.

Her throat burned. Her hands clenched into fists. *I'll come to Philly*. The words were on her tongue.

"You could come here," she said instead, defeat tasting bitter in her throat. "If you don't mind."

She'd been tested and had failed. Again.

The implication was, if she wasn't well enough to drive into Philadelphia, then she wasn't well enough to take care of her daughter. She swallowed, knowing she truly wasn't, letting any misguided jealousy and anger dissipate.

Her father didn't know the half of her problems. Nobody did. Nobody ever would. She couldn't let anyone find out just how crazy she was, the secret she kept. She would fight her way out of that dark hole somehow. She had to, or it would swallow her for good.

Her father glanced up at her loft studio, at the H-frame easel and the nearly complete painting on it. "Glad to see you're making progress," he said before he walked out the door.

An acknowledgment to give her hope. He was a hard man, but not cruel. He wouldn't keep Maddie from her forever.

She went after him. "I'll see you next Saturday?" The time until then stretched in front of her, interminable.

"Bright and early." He strode to his new BMW, elegant in his camel-hair coat, a distinguished gentleman of means who lived an orderly life, in a different world from hers.

Maddie hopped around the car, making a giant circle with her boot prints. When she spotted Ashley, the little girl ran back into her arms again. "You'll call tonight to tell me a story?"

"Would I ever miss calling my sweetest peanut?"

Maddie smiled. "About the princess and the unicorn?"

"If that's want you want." She would have done anything to make her daughter happy, to keep the darkness from touching her in any way.

Which was why back when she'd been released from the hospital and had come home, Ashley had agreed for Madison to stay on with her grandfather. She'd thought it would be a short-term arrangement, but she hadn't been able to shake the darkness. So even if she wanted to pick her baby up and carry her back into the house right now, she didn't.

She would regret that decision from the moment the car pulled away until it appeared at the end of her driveway again a week from today. But when one of her spells came, she would know she had done the right thing, even if Maddie living away from her was killing her inside.

Until the end of the school year. Then her daughter would come home–if Ashley could fix herself by then. She had four months to get her act together, wrestle down her demons, and prove to her father that she was back to normal.

No more depression, no more paralyzing anxiety. She knew what brought them on. If only she could stop that.

She stood in the open door, waving until the car drove out of sight, disappearing behind the trees. She was all alone then, with nothing but gray sky, the empty road, and the barren, snow-covered fields that lined it on either side. She blinked hard a couple of times, then stepped back inside, suddenly cut off at the knees. No feeling in the universe compared to that of a mother watching her child being taken away.

She turned the old-fashioned brass key in the lock. She used to love its warm patina, the way it perfectly complemented the deep color of the hundred-year-old oak door. Braided wool rugs covered most of the wide-paneled floor that matched the door. The narrow stained-glass window above the door painted the walls with color and light in the foyer.

When they'd first moved in, she'd spent hours walking around the house, drinking in the colors and textures, the play of light and shadow, absorbing the visual feast through her skin. Maddie and she had giddily sketched every interesting nook, their way of taking possession of their new home.

For a moment, she could clearly remember that deep sense of contentment, the pure joy. Then it slipped through her fingers and she was left with longing and a sharp ache in her chest.

She glanced up to the loft, to the waiting easel. She'd started a project early this morning when she couldn't sleep. She needed to paint as much as possible, needed to catch up a little.

She owned the old farmhouse outright, but her heating and electric bills were a month overdue, and she didn't dare to be late with her health and home insurance. She needed to catch up and then set some savings aside. She had to regain solid footing by the time school ended.

She climbed the stairs. *Through the nose, breathe in—calm, creative energy. Through the mouth, breathe out—release all bad and negative thoughts.*

Her studio loft, designed by her, was her favorite place in the house. She'd had one wall taken out so it could be open to downstairs; another wall, on the north side of the house, had been replaced with windows for the perfect light.

The same oak planks covered the floor as below, the walls painted in something called "gallery white," so she could correctly judge her colors. She'd even had a sink installed so she could clean her brushes here.

Since the painting she'd been working on hadn't dried enough yet for the next layer of color, she set up another canvas that she'd already stretched and prepped herself, gessoed to a smooth finish.

The prepping process, her small rituals, helped her relax. A prefinished, frame-stretched canvas couldn't give her that.

She opened her sketchbook and picked a composition she'd been playing with, laid out her favorite brushes, then uncapped the first color, cerulean blue, and squeezed some onto her stained palette. Then the next color, then the next.

There had been a time when the scent of paint had filled her with euphoria. Now the blue smelled like the sharp chunks of crushed ice on the reservoir, the brown dark and threatening, the odor of wet earth, the smell of a grave.

She unloaded her chosen colors, what she would need for the first layer, adding crimson the very last, no more than was absolutely necessary. Of all the shades of red, she hated the wet, sticky brightness of crimson the most.

Her muscles drew tight as she dipped the brush into one color, then the next, the right amount from each, loaded the brush just so, then dabbed off the excess. Her hand trembled as she lifted brush to canvas. Beads of sweat formed on her forehead. When the first rolled down, she blinked. *Not today. It's not going to happen today.*

Through the nose, breathe in...

She'd painted that morning, and everything had been fine. But now, suddenly she didn't dare touch color to all that white.

Lately, every new painting began like this—with fear. The reason why she rarely painted anymore. Which had led to her dismal financial situation. Which had to end.

She made herself relax her death grip on the brush.

When the phone rang, her sense of relief at the delay was tangible. She didn't even look at the caller ID as she reached for the receiver. At this stage, she would have been happy to take a call from a telemarketer.

But instead, she came close to a smile when she heard her agent's voice.

"Hope I'm interrupting a mad work session," Isabelle chirped into the phone, a vibrant and successful twenty-four-year-old with a client list even industry veterans envied. She had energy to spare, instincts that rarely failed, and a personality that meshed with just about anyone, a big plus in an industry where divas and prima donnas abounded—both in her circle of artists and her circle of clients.

Ashley trusted her implicitly.

"I'm starting a new project. Two, actually. I already have another partially finished."

"When can I see them? Some top galleries are still asking about you." The still was said with undertones of, *they won't forever.*

"You have to keep producing to keep your momentum."

They both knew her momentum was gone. Her last solo show at a big-name gallery had been over a year ago. But Isabelle was a cheerleader through and through who'd never met a lost cause.

"I could come down next month to see what you have. Do you need an advance?"

She bit her lip. Even to Isabelle, she couldn't admit the full truth. "I guess I should order some supplies online." She no longer drove into the city to pick up her own supplies.

"I'll wire the money today."

"Thank you."

"What are you painting?"

"An abstract."

Ashley glanced to the back of her loft studio, at the five-foot-by-six-foot landscape she'd been working on before the accident. The image waited unfinished, frozen in time. She thought of some of her signature pieces with longing for a split second before she shook off her nostalgia. She no longer painted people or landscapes, if she could help it.

Her abstracts did well too. She'd been earning a couple of grand a piece. That much money could keep her afloat for a few months before she had to touch a brush again.

Professor Mathew Daniels-Roderick's lecture flashed into her mind. A celebrated artist in his own right, Roderick had been the best mentor she'd had the good luck to study with. "At the beginning, if you could draw a picture others recognized, you were considered an artist. Then came a higher form of art that showed emotion. Then, even better, made you feel emotion. You cried with the woman losing her lover, despaired with the revolutionaries in front of the firing squad."

"What about abstract art?" she'd asked, a first-year student who'd never really understood the abstract, had no intention of ever painting it.

The professor had focused on her with the full intensity of his lively gaze, instantly making her regret that she'd spoken up. "When you paint a scene of great joy, a mother finding her long-lost child, and that same joy shines on the people who view your painting, if that joy shines in their hearts, you've created art. But if you can call forth that joy with two triangles and a circle, if you can use the movement of the lines, the emotion and rhythm of the colors in a way that connects to another human being on a level so profound…" The professor paused. "That is great art."

So she'd been trying lately, sporadically, to create great art—without letting the darkness claim her. Sometimes she succeeded, and sometimes she went to hell.

"I'm flying to Philadelphia in a couple of weeks to meet the owner of a new gallery on South Street," Isabelle said. "I have to go to Baltimore to see a client after that. I could stop in to catch up. It's been a long time since you came up to New York."

Ashley hesitated as long as she could without being impolite, possibly longer. "Okay." She could give no other answer, really.

"Jeez, don't be so enthusiastic." Isabelle laughed on the other end. "It might go to my head."

"I'm sorry, I didn't—"

"I get it. Artists are introverts. If you were out there socializing all the time, you wouldn't have time to contemplate and create. I have artists who are social butterflies. I'm not making a lot of money off them." She paused.

She was probably reflecting on the fact that she hadn't made much money on Ashley lately either.

"Graham called again," she said after another second. "He keeps trying to convince me he'd be the perfect person to give you the right start. I'll give up agenting before I let you hang anything in his two-bit gallery. You don't need a start. You already made it. You just have to keep on producing."

"I'm working on it," she said, appreciating the vote of confidence.

"Graham called me too, by the way. A couple of weeks ago."

Graham Lanius was one of the local gallery owners. He fancied himself the godfather of local talent, a Maecenas, but had trouble with boundaries. You worked with him and sooner or later he would try to tell you what and how to paint, which rubbed a lot of artists the wrong way.

Still, he had plenty who went to him, the insecure who fed on his direction and grudgingly doled-out approval, and those who were happy to have their paintings in a gallery, period, and weren't too choosy what they had to put up with.

"Just keep telling him your agent schedules all your shows," Isabelle said.

"Exactly what I did."

"Is this about Andre?"

"Probably."

Andre Milton, descendant of famous Pennsylvania artist Franklin Milton was the big local talent. He had a good eye, and his famous last name didn't hurt either. He sold exclusively at a local gallery that was Graham's biggest competition. Which was why Graham wanted Ashley.

"Listen, somebody just walked in. I'll give you a call when I know what day I'll be down your way," Isabelle said. "I can't wait to see what you have." She sounded warm and cheerful as always. If she felt concerned about Ashley's recent lull in production, she didn't show it.

Ashley fidgeted around for a few seconds after they hung up, then walked back to her easel. She had to work now. The paintings were already promised. The money would be wired, and Isabelle would be here soon, wanting to see how far along the projects had progressed.

She picked up the brush again and lifted it to the canvas, except now the colors seemed all wrong. The light had changed too. She looked through the row of oversized windows that stretched from floor to ceiling, taking up the whole north end of the loft. Moody snow clouds had drifted in, casting a fatigued gray tint on everything.

Her hand jerked, leaving an angry slash in the middle of the canvas.

A headache drummed to life in the back of her skull.

It's not going to happen today.

She ignored the shiver that skipped down her spine.

This is a normal day. I'm painting a normal composition.

But it was too late. It was happening already. She squeezed her eyes shut against the images flooding her brain, but no resistance would help now. She couldn't escape.

This time, the body—a man, midthirties—lay in a shallow grave surrounded by low brush. A distinct rock loomed nearby, blocking the view of a creek beyond.

The image stirred faint memories that refused to come into focus. Her headache intensified.

She could walk away, had done so in the past. But if she did, neither the pain nor the image would go away; they would pound at her mercilessly. The only way to be rid of the pain was to get the image out of her head, put it on a canvas that she could pick up and hide later.

So she gritted her teeth and remixed her colors. Then she grabbed a brush.

Background first. She went as fast as she could, needed to be done so she could curl up in her lumpy armchair in the corner of the loft and find some numb place inside to escape to. Darkening sky in blue and gray, big, sweeping brushstrokes. The rock cast a wreathing shadow in the clearing. She picked and discarded brushes without conscious thought, mixed colors on instinct.

She delayed painting the body for as long as possible, pressing her lips together as she finally drew the shape. When she had that right, she used a fan brush to complete the see-through, drape-like material he'd been wrapped in—shower curtain?—before reaching for a soft sable brush for the face. She'd always hated this part the most, even before she'd realized that the bodies were real.

She drew the main outline, keeping her fingers on the ferrule—the metal piece that clamped the bristles to the handle—and created a nose, mouth, and eyelids. For a moment, she wondered what color his eyes might be, then shoved aside the macabre thought. He had a strong, square jaw, his hair pushed back, looking sticky from the dirt that had been thrown directly onto his face.

She shadowed the man's skin and added smudges of dirt to his cheeks and closed eyelids. Her real art, the paintings she sold, had a completely different feel from this monster. This looked as if the artist had X-ray vision, portraying the landscape along with what lay hidden beneath the ground. She hurried but had enough skill to have the face done well even with those few strokes.

13

Then the gruesome image stood completed, her headache ebbing. She could draw her lungs full for the first time in the past two hours. Her pulse slowed. The room came back into focus, seemed lighter all of a sudden.

But still that terrible sense of emptiness lingered inside her, and she knew it would stay with her for days.

It's over.

Breathe.

The brushes needed to be cleaned, so she did that, careful to avoid looking at the picture as she moved around. After the paint dried, she would wrap the canvas up and stack it in the garage with the others. And if she were lucky, she would have a long reprieve before the next dark compulsion to paint another vignette of horror.

Her muscles that had been clenched the whole time went weak with relief, and she walked away from the sink on wobbly legs. But as she passed the easel, the odd boulder that sat in the middle of the painting drew her eyes and the vague memory took shape at last in her mind.

Cold, disbelieving shock sucker punched her.

She knew that boulder, had painted it before, albeit from another angle, from the creek side. The creek that ran at the far end of her hundred-acre property, land she had bought after her first major art show.

Before she had time to consider the implications, her gaze slid lower. She broke out in cold sweat as her eyes zeroed in on the face of the man who occupied the lower right quadrant of the canvas.

He stared at her.

She blinked. She could swear she'd painted his eyes closed. She had meant to. But she had thought about the color...

Goose bumps prickled her skin. His face had less gray than the other victims she'd painted in the past. His body too lay differently—limp but not frozen in death with the stiff angles of a corpse.

As her breath hitched and her heart slammed against her rib cage, terrible thoughts clamored in her mind.

This one was on her land.

And he was still alive.

Fear pushed full force against the thought that she should help. She was all alone. Twilight was falling. Her land was impassable—back when she'd bought the property, there had been some tractor trails through it, but she'd left them to be overgrown long ago.

She could drive down Hadley Road until she reached the right spot, then walk in.

Would have to drive by the reservoir.

She didn't drive that road anymore.

But even if she could, she wasn't going to chase some imaginary dead man, or almost dead man, around the countryside.

Feel normal. Act normal. If she couldn't do that, she would never get Maddie back. Normalcy had become her holy grail, the thing she ceaselessly sought, fought for, dreamed about. Going off like some madwoman would be the very opposite of that.

She watched the man watching her from the painting. Just more of her craziness. She was always imagining stuff—noises in the night, things moving behind the house in the woods. Which always turned out to be deer, or teens sneaking around for a smoke.

Yet she whispered, "He's alive," to the empty room without meaning to.

No. She turned her back to the easel.

But the next moment, she was running down the stairs, not just away from the painting but toward the door.

Because what if saving a life would make up for the one she'd lost? Maybe then the dead would finally leave her alone. What if this single act could end the nightmare she was living?

She swept up her keys and coat. And ran into the mailman on her front stoop.

He smiled his usual, cheerful smile, a man without a care. He was so profoundly…normal, it was like looking into a parallel universe. "Brought the mail up. Last delivery for the day. You got a package."

Pete Kentner was in his midforties, wearing regulation hat and coat with hunting boots. More often than not, he brought her mail to the door when the temperature dropped to below freezing, so she wouldn't have to walk to the mailbox. He was a nice guy, helpful to everyone, took care of his mother.

"Thanks. Hope you had a nice break." She tried for normal conversation, her mind spinning. She rubbed her hands over her arms, shivering. "Wow, it's cold. What was it this time?" Could she ask him for help? And say what? He'd think she was crazy.

"Good hunting weather. One fox, a half-dozen woodchucks, a couple of raccoons. Didn't get a bobcat permit this year. Didn't see any, anyway. That's all the excitement until deer season next year." Disappointment crept into his tone, but he perked up as he gestured at the package she held. "Late Christmas present?"

She glanced at the return address. "Samples from one of the online art-supply stores, I think." They sent those from time to time to frequent customers, nudging artists to give new brands a try. A treasure on any other day, but right now, she was jumping with impatience.

She gave Pete a strained smile, willing him to leave.

But he chatted on instead. "Been ice skating yet? Saw a bunch of folks down by the reservoir earlier—" He snapped his mouth shut. "Sorry. Wasn't thinking. Don't know where my brain is today." He adjusted his hat. "Better get going."

He gave a cheerful wave, shuffled back to his mail truck, and backed out of her driveway.

She put the box on the hall table just inside the door, then locked up behind her and hurried to her own car.

His bringing up the reservoir and skating didn't help. She sat behind the wheel for a moment, fighting the urge to go back inside. But those cerulean eyes were burned into her brain and drew her forward.

Turn the key in the ignition. Put the car in drive. Step on the gas. Pete had turned left onto the main road, toward town. Broslin sat just a few miles from the Maryland border in one direction and about the same distance from Delaware in the other, a quaint little town with a history of art, a large Amish population, mushroom farmers, a lot of mom-and-pop stores still, nice, regular people. It had been paradise to her when she'd moved out here, a place to live in peace and create.

Then everything had fallen apart. But she was about to fix that, even if panic bubbled in her stomach as she reached the end of her driveway. Deep breath. She yanked the steering wheel right, away from town and toward the reservoir, not allowing herself to hesitate.

Her gaze skimmed the abandoned Miller farm at the corner. Hadley Road came too fast, another right. Blood rushed loudly in her ears as she turned. She stared straight ahead. *Don't look at the reservoir.* She hadn't been out this way in a year.

She focused on the two cars a few hundred yards ahead on the side of the road: a pickup in the front, a police cruiser in the back. Her heart beat a mad rhythm.

In her mind, she saw another evening like this with police at the reservoir, cops and other emergency personnel. All the more strange because she couldn't possibly have seen anything at the time. She shivered as she felt the bone-splitting cold of that day all over again. She let go of her death grip on the steering wheel long enough to crank up the heat.

"Can I help you, ma'am?" The police officer looked at Ashley through the side window of her SUV.

Of course, it had to be Bing.

She bit her lip. She'd gotten distracted by her memories to the point of forgetting to keep her foot on the gas pedal. She hadn't realized that she'd slowed to a stop.

The police made her uneasy. God, so many things made her uneasy these days. No, uneasy didn't begin to describe how she felt. Half the time, she was scared to death.

The captain watched her. She knew most of the local police, had been interrogated over and over about Dylan's death. She swallowed, not wanting to sink into those memories.

She cracked the window an inch. "I'm okay. Thank you, Captain." She shivered again as cold air swept into the car. She rolled the window up and stepped on the gas, watching in her rearview mirror as Bing turned after her.

She drew her gaze from him and focused back on the road, glancing at her land on the right. Her hundred acres stood unused: some trees, some brush, some abandoned fields. A lot of farms lay fallow these days. Closer to Philadelphia or Wilmington, developers were buying up land to put in cookie-cutter housing for freshly minted yuppies who couldn't afford the existing, expensive suburbs. This far out, commuting would be a major drag, so developers left the area alone.

Farming as a lifestyle was no longer economically feasible for most, and the new generation didn't have the same dreams as their grandfathers anyway. A hundred-acre farm could still be bought here for a reasonable price.

Not many people were thrilled at the prospect of a hundred neglected acres, but she'd bought the place specifically for untouched nature. She loved painting that, loved the views she had of the woods from her studio window, had once loved the proximity of the reservoir she had painted a hundred times.

She didn't even look at the frozen water now, grateful when the pine forest started on her left and blocked the view. She drove slowly, not wanting to miss her spot. In her mind, she could see the man in the shallow grave, those cerulean eyes.

She pulled over when she thought she was in the right place and dashed forward into the waist-high brush. Her feet sank into the snow, frozen branches tugging at her midcalf-length wool skirt.

The police cruiser drove by, slowed, and stopped.

"You need any help, Miss Price?"

"I, uh, I'm looking for a place to paint."

"It's cold out here."

Right. She had no hat or gloves on. "Just ran out on a sudden idea. I won't be long." She glanced down at her bare feet in her house slippers, nearly swallowed by the snow. At least, the captain couldn't see that.

He watched her. "It's going to turn dark soon."

She should have brought a flashlight. "Just the dusk I've been looking for." She attempted a smile and stood on the spot until the captain drove away.

Then she ran toward the creek, a couple of hundred yards from the road. *I can't be late. I have to save him. If I save him, everything is going to be all right.* She needed that hope, because she wasn't sure how much longer she could live the life she had lived this past year or so since the accident.

She trudged around a clump of larger bushes and finally spotted the small clearing in the twilight. She circled the boulder, judging the distance as it had been on the painting, looking at the creek to orient herself to the correct angle. Dead weeds and low brush grabbed after her with every step, getting tangled in her long skirt, scraping her legs.

"Where are you?" Frustration had her yelling out loud.

She searched in a random pattern, then finally saw the patch of disturbed soil and fell to her knees, attacking the loose dirt with her bare hands.

Small stones scraped her skin, frozen dirt packed under her nails. She dug harder, her fingers becoming stiff with cold within seconds.

"I'm here," she whispered as she clawed at the ground. But along with the urgency in her mind, on a parallel plane loomed the doubt that none of this was real, that she had finally gone truly and irrevocably mad.

Snow began to fall, the only sounds her fingers scraping the frozen ground and the way she gasped for air from the effort. But she uncovered absolutely nothing. Anger had her slapping her hands into the dirt.

She shrieked when she touched russet strands of hair caked with bloody mud.

Chapter Two

Jack Sullivan stared at the bright light at the end of the tunnel. He looked straight into the damn light, walked toward it, and was so glad to be rid of the pain, he couldn't have cared less that he was dying.

Time stood like seawater trapped in a tidal pool, disconnected and unmoving. But after a while, he realized he wasn't alone in the void.

Shannon?

No, not his sister. But someone definitely there. And the fact that he wasn't alone brought him some peace.

Until he was yanked back—by the cold and the pain and his unfinished business—and realized that he wasn't dead yet after all, but close to it. He couldn't lift his hands. He tried to blink and got an eyeful of dirt.

Something heavy sat on his chest, on his whole body. Seconds passed before he understood that he'd been packed into some cold, tight space—then another second before he realized he was buried. If there'd been anything in his clenched stomach, he might have thrown up and choked himself to death. As it was, he only heaved as disjointed memories floated back, vignettes from hell—the worst torture man could devise, and no food or water, no clothes.

His head swam. *Buried alive and too weak to do anything about it.* He was going to pass out again.

No.

He was a tough bastard cop, dammit. He willed himself to live.

He heard whispers—probably hallucinating. But then fingers touched his face. He wheezed for air, and then he could finally see at last. It was night, or nearly so. He had no idea what day. His eyes burned as he tried to make out the shadow that loomed over him.

Blackwell.

Fear gripped him now harder than the cold. The pain would begin again.

He couldn't take more torture. When his hands popped free, he fought back with what little strength he had, trying to blink the dirt and blood away. The sharp smell of paint thinner hit his nose as he grabbed an arm and held it tight, twisted it, pulled the bastard down to the ground.

Wrong shape. Whoever he held felt slighter than Blackwell. This one couldn't have gotten him the way Blackwell had. Jack held the man from behind, seeing only the back of his head and his stringy hair, some of which was stuck between them.

"Let me go!" she screamed.

What the hell?

He wouldn't have figured Blackwell for having a partner, let alone a woman. But it all made some sick sense to his fevered mind. Some women nurtured serious obsessions for criminals. Some women struck up correspondence with murderers in prison and married them. Not impossible that Blackwell could use his sick mind to tie a woman like that to him.

He spat dirt and held on tight as she flailed. She looked a few years younger than him, dirty and ready to run, fighting him wide-eyed. "Who are you?" He sat up, not letting her go, not giving an inch. He could barely feel his body, just enough to know that he'd been bound. No, not bound. He shrugged off the plastic, then struggled to standing, bringing her up with him.

He had no clothes on but could barely feel the cold. "How—" He cleared his raw throat. "How did you get here?"

"Car." The single word squeaked out in a panicked whisper as she tried in vain to tug herself away. "I can't breathe."

And he could? In the grave?

"I couldn't care less." He spat again. "Which way?" He'd been blindfolded on the way here, and before, during the days of torture. He shook her as she struggled. "Stop it."

She stilled, trembling, and reluctantly gestured with her head. He dragged her forward. In a few hundred yards, they burst out of the woods and he could see the older model Chevy Blazer, blue. Still no sign of Blackwell.

"Where is he?"

She didn't respond, just gave a long whimper.

He dragged her along, ignoring the pained and pleading noises she made, ignoring the blackness that hovered at the edges of his vision. He was too weak to carry himself let alone somebody else, but he made it to the vehicle on sheer will. The keys dangled from the ignition.

He opened the passenger-side door and shoved the woman in, pushed her over before getting in after her. "Drive," he growled. "Up the road, toward Broslin. You try anything, I swear to God, I'm going to kill you."

Wishful thinking on his part. He probably couldn't kill a fly at this stage. Hell, he wasn't in good enough shape to drive. But by some miracle, the woman looked suitably terrified. Good. She must have seen a thing or two from Blackwell.

Her hand shook so hard, for a moment it looked chancy whether she could start the car. Since he knew his hand would shake harder, he didn't even try.

"Go!" he shouted, not sure how long he had before Blackwell returned.

She managed at last, did a three-point turn in about a dozen jerky moves. But as darkness narrowed his peripheral vision, Jack realized he'd made a mistake. He was too far gone. He wouldn't make it to Broslin. "Give me your phone."

She kept her terrified gaze on the road. "I don't have it with me."

A quick look around netted no purse, nothing usable in the glove box either, just a sketchbook and a couple of sticks of graphite. He reached over and patted down her coat, ignoring when she shrieked and nearly landed them in the ditch.

He searched the falling night around them, desperate for help, and caught sight of a farmhouse with lights in the windows in the distance. He could call for backup from there.

"The house." He gestured with his head, then regretted it when everything before him went swimming. "Take me there."

Tears rolled down her face. "Please."

"Do as I say."

She drove to the house, shivering, and pulled up the driveway. He dragged her up the two steps and held her in front of him as he knocked on the front door. If someone looked out the window next to it, they might not open up for a naked man covered in blood and grime.

But nobody answered the door, not even on the second try. Maybe they were out. His body awash in pain, he rammed the wood with his shoulder. When the door didn't budge, he rammed it again.

"Wait." She drew him toward the car, and he went because he no longer had the strength to stop her.

She was too scared to notice, too terrified to realize that if she knocked him down, he wouldn't be able to rise. She grabbed the keys from the car, hobbled back to the door with him as he did his best to keep his hold on her arm.

She unlocked the door, and he pushed her in, went after her. He was about to ask why she had a key when it all clicked into place in some distant recess of his pain-fogged brain.

She lived here. Which meant Blackwell probably lived here, was probably in the house. Jack swore under his breath at the irony. He'd escaped death just to fall back, defenseless, into the hands of his worst enemy.

He let her go and turned, his vision swimming. *Get back to the car. Keys first.* He grabbed after her, but she was running away.

He blinked against the darkness that closed in on him. By the time he hit the floor, he was too far gone to feel a thing.

* * *

A naked, possibly dead man lay in her foyer.

Now what?

Ashley peeked from the kitchen, shivering against the cold that poured in the open front door. When she'd rushed off to save him, she hadn't thought this far ahead, what she would do once she found him. She hadn't thought he would attack her.

Maybe she hadn't been supposed to save him. Maybe he was the same kind of man as whoever had put him into that shallow grave, one criminal taking out another, eliminating competition.

She held on to the broom she'd grabbed as the first possible weapon she could think of and inched toward him. When she reached close enough, she poked him in the side. He didn't move.

23

Whoever he was, he was well built, had seen either plenty of physical labor or regular exercise. He had a well-proportioned body she might have been tempted to paint another time and place, under different circumstances. He hardly looked ready to be painted just now.

His face was swollen and bloody, like the rest of him. An arrangement of open cuts formed patterns on his skin, accented with burn marks, blue-black spots, and welts. Three of his fingernails had been ripped off; the rest were packed with blood and dirt.

A gust of wind hurled snow through the front door. When he didn't stir even from that, she lifted the broom a few inches and pushed the door closed behind him.

"Who are you?" She didn't expect an answer, and he didn't give any, just lay where he'd fallen—skin and muscles and dirt and blood.

No, he shouldn't be painted, she thought then. He was a completed work of art already—a human canvas painted with violence. Some people equated art with beauty. She knew, better than most, that wasn't always true.

His chest rose slightly.

Oh. She didn't know if she should be scared or relieved.

She had to call the police. Her lungs shrank. If she called, she would have to explain finding him.

At least he was still alive. Explaining a corpse in her house would be even more difficult. She stared at the slow rise and fall of his chest, backed up a few steps to grab her tartan wool throw from the couch, and draped it over him. "Here."

His lips were grayish blue where they weren't too dirty to see the color. She had no idea how long he'd been out there, but long enough for hypothermia, apparently.

She backed away again, still holding the broom, all the way to the kitchen phone. But once she got there, she hesitated.

The cops didn't like her. They hadn't forgiven her for Dylan; nobody in Broslin had. But if she didn't call, the man would die, and she couldn't handle another lost life on her tally sheet. Dylan's death had about broken her.

Don't think about Dylan now.

She leaned the broom against the wall but kept it within reach, and grabbed the phone to dial 911.

"My name is Ashley Price. I need an ambulance and the police." She gave her address. "I found an injured man on my property. I'm an artist. I was out looking for a place to paint." She'd told the captain that. She needed to keep her story consistent.

"How bad is he hurt?" the dispatcher asked.

"He lost blood. Unconscious. I think hypothermia too."

"Are you keeping him warm?"

She could hear the keyboard clicking on the other end. "Yes."

"Do you know his name?"

"No."

"He doesn't have any identification on him?"

"He was— He's naked."

A small pause from the dispatcher, then, "All right, ma'am. Help is on the way. Please stay on the line."

But as Ashley glanced around, she caught sight of the easel up in the loft and her painting still on it. "I can't. I need to put more blankets on him." She hung up and ran for her last dreaded creation.

She wrapped up the damn thing, then dragged it out to the garage, and hid it behind the others. Was that good enough? Would the police look there?

She stood staring at the pile for a moment, unsure what to do, unable to think of a better hiding place. Panic rose in her throat. She swallowed it. They had no reason to search her home, no reason to think she was involved in any of this. She hadn't done anything.

But she would have to destroy that painting. She had to get rid of all of them. Just not at this moment. She didn't have the time. She couldn't allow the cops to catch her in the process.

So she locked up the garage, then rushed back into the house and piled more blankets on the man, and could hear the sirens by the time she finished. She lived only a few miles outside Broslin.

She skirted the man to open the door, happened to glance at her feet as she stepped carefully around him. Streaks of mud covered her legs, and blood where the frozen brush had scratched her skin. How was she going to explain why she'd been out there barefooted?

25

She dashed into the laundry room, grabbed the first pair of knee-high socks she could find in the basket, and was yanking them on as cars pulled up her driveway outside.

Act normal. She hurried back to the door to open it. *Just act normal.*

"Miss Price." Captain Bing hiked up the steps first.

Tall, trim, and somber, he was married to his job, from what she'd heard. Local gossip had it he'd lost his wife to murder a few years back, a murder he hadn't been able to solve. That had to grate on a man like him.

And he grated on others in return, which didn't bode well for her.

"Captain." She stepped back to let him in, her heart slamming against her rib cage so hard it hurt.

Two younger officers came up the stairs behind him, a couple of EMTs in the back. He didn't pay them any attention, his gaze snapping to the body.

He squatted next to the unconscious man and swore, reaching for his radio. "Officer down. I repeat, officer down. It's Jack." Then he glared at her, black thunder on his face. "What the hell happened here?"

A cop? She stared. She didn't know this one. He hadn't come around with the rest last year.

She scrambled for something to say, but the paramedics shuffled her out of the way before she could answer.

Captain Bing herded her toward the kitchen. "Where did you find him?"

"At the back of the property, not far from where we talked."

One of the other policemen, Joe, she seemed to remember the name, loped over. He had the lean body of an athlete, different from Bing's more built strength. He didn't have any shadows in his eyes yet, hadn't been on the force for long. He'd just started back when they'd lost Dylan.

"Joe, you go out with Miss Price," Bing ordered." She'll show you where she found Jack. I'm staying with him."

She didn't dare leave the cops alone in her house.

"You won't need me." She swallowed as nerves shot through her. "Turn right at the corner, a hundred feet maybe before you get to the next intersection, you'll see my tracks in the snow. The spot is by the creek a few hundred yards in, next to a six-foot rock. It's the only boulder on the property. Can't really miss it." She held her breath.

Bing narrowed his eyes as he looked at her but then nodded, and Joe took off.

"Seen anyone else nearby?" The captain pulled out a notebook and a pen. He had a thing about taking meticulous notes. She remembered that.

"No."

"When did you find him?"

"Fifteen minutes ago. Maybe twenty."

"Why didn't you call sooner?"

"I didn't have my cell phone with me."

He flashed her a look full of suspicion. He'd probably be happy if he could make her pay at last, for anything, since she hadn't had to pay for little Dylan. He'd made it clear how he felt about that. He was fourth-generation local, his family deeply connected to farming.

He didn't like outsiders coming in, buying up land, then letting it go to seed. He'd let her know that as well. He had a bleak opinion of city folks, all of whom he viewed as having come here specifically to give the locals grief and cause trouble.

When she'd been involved in the death of the child of one of his friends, Ashley had shot straight to the top of the captain's shit list. She did her best to stay out of his way, give no excuse for as much as a speeding ticket. And she'd managed until now.

He looked at her dirty, bloody fingers. "How did you find him, exactly?"

She crossed her arms to hide her hands. "Saw some disturbed ground. Saw the corner of the shower curtain." She swallowed. "I thought maybe someone was burying garbage on my land. When I tugged on the plastic, a hand came out."

"What were you doing out there?"

"I was looking for a good spot to paint. I painted the creek before." Her response stopped him for a second. He seemed unsure how to ask an insinuating question about that. Then he found his footing. "Do you know Jack Sullivan?"

She glanced at the unconscious man by her front door. The paramedics were loading him onto a gurney, an IV bag hooked to each arm.

"No."

"You still live alone?"

"Yes."

"Any visitors in the last couple of days?" He was taking notes. On what? She hadn't given him anything. "My father and my daughter."

"Seen anyone around, back in the woods?"

"No."

"Have you seen or heard anything suspicious at all earlier, anything out of place?"

She shook her head.

"And you just went out there to look at trees?" He seemed to have a problem with that part of the story.

"It's like—" She grasped for an artsy explanation that would discourage further inquisition. "Paul Klee said that when he was drawing, he was just taking a line for a walk. Works the other way around too. Sometimes my lines take me for a walk." A walk straight to hell.

He wrote the name Paul Klee in capital letters, then tapped pen to paper.

She opened her mouth to tell him he didn't need to worry about Klee, but then changed her mind. If Bing wanted to run the Dutch artist who'd been gone for almost seventy years through the system, let him.

"Anything else you want to tell me at this point?"

"I already told you everything."

He huffed, watched her for a long moment, his eyes, the color of burned sienna, narrowing. "All right. I'm going to see what Joe found out there. I'll be back in a while. You stay right here."

She knew that tone. The captain blamed her for all this. She couldn't bear the thought of more interrogations to come. If her father found out...

The thought about stopped her heart.

Her father couldn't find out. Whatever she had to do, she had to keep her new batch of troubles secret. She had to find a way to clear her name and make this all go away, and she had to do it in a hurry.

* * *

Jack Sullivan saw the bright light again. This time, he wasn't about to march blindly ahead. Screw the light. With superhuman effort, he willed himself awake. His eyelids going up felt as if someone was dragging sandpaper over his eyeballs. It hurt to breathe.

"Welcome back, Jack."

Bing's face swam into focus.

"Captain." He cleared his throat, then tried for something better than the weak whisper. "What happened?"

"Do you know how much paperwork I have to fill out every time one of my men gets injured?"

He blinked at the hospital room around him—white walls, green sheets, strange-looking medical equipment—and wrinkled his nose at the smell of iodine. "I'll try not to make a habit of it. I'm fine."

"You might think differently when the painkillers wear off," the man said in a voice that leaned toward gentle. Not something Jack had heard from Bing before. He had to be dying.

He tried to sit up. Couldn't. What the hell?

"Take it easy, son."

Nobody had called him son in at least a decade. And Bing wasn't yet forty. They had less than a decade between them. Oh, hell. He had to be in even worse shape than he'd thought. Pain stabbed his side. He'd been hurt, badly, but couldn't remember how.

Bing leaned forward, the chair creaking under his weight. Not that he was fat by any measure, but solidly built with muscle. He put in his share of time in training at the station's gym. He required his team to keep in shape and would never ask anything of them that he himself wasn't prepared to do. "What's the last thing you remember?"

Jack forced his mind to focus. "Going out on an anonymous call. Suspicious activity reported at an abandoned farmhouse." At first he'd thought drugs. Then he'd gotten there and saw that chunk of bone.

Memories flashed across his mind suddenly, a horror movie on fast-forward. His teeth clenched. "It was Blackwell."

Bing went still. "You think too much about the man. You were in a lot of pain. Your mind came up with—"

"Blackwell," he said again. "I had time to make positive ID."

Bing sat up straighter, stared at Jack for a long moment. "They got some DNA from under a couple of your fingernails, but it'll be a

29

while before the results come in. Do you know if the FBI has DNA on him?"

"They don't." Adrenaline spiked through him. If they gained enough DNA, if it matched to something in the database...

Bing rubbed his hand over his knee as he watched him, that look of doubt still in his eyes. "Do you remember enough for a sketch? I can have someone here in ten minutes."

Jack shook his head. The images that had come back to him were only of the lower half of his own body, a cement floor stained with his blood, Blackwell's boots. He gritted his teeth. "He kept me blindfolded. But he talked about the others." The bastard had taunted him while he'd tortured him.

"I might recognize his voice." That he wasn't sure he would killed him. But there'd been a fan rattling the whole time, pushing the heat of the woodstove around the torture chamber. And his mind had been in a haze of pain, not exactly on full speed. "How long was I gone?"

"Three days." The captain's jaw clenched. "We were looking for you. Harper and Chase never went home. The rookies too. We were looking for you every hour of every day."

"I know. That kept me hanging on." A small cough sent stabbing pain through his midsection. "He knew who I was. He had a trap set up."

The captain swore, which was usually the worst of his temper. He was, for the most part, pretty even-keeled, not the type who got off on tearing his men down just to show who was boss. Although, at the moment, he didn't look too happy with Jack.

"I told you being obsessed with a serial killer was a dangerous hobby," he snapped.

He had. But Blackwell went way beyond a hobby. This went back to Shannon. But nobody needed to know that.

Machines beeped around them, various hospital noises filtering in the open door as Jack thought of all the people he'd looked for in the past, the ones he hadn't found in time. He figured Bing might be thinking the same. Except now Jack knew exactly how those victims had felt, what his sister had gone through before she'd died fifteen years ago.

Bile rose in his throat. "How bad is the damage?"

Bing waited a second before he answered. "Nothing to come crying to me about. Four broken ribs, blood loss, some internal bleeding, some burns, hypothermia, and a concussion, some nancy-ass lacerations barely worth mentioning. I pretty much figure you're only here to get out of mandatory overtime."

"When are they letting me out?"

"Some frostbite here and there," Bing went on. "I'm going to overlook it this time, but you've got to stop parading around buckass naked. You're scaring well-meaning citizens." He kept his tone as light as his words, but concern filled his eyes.

"I want to get on the case as soon as possible." Jack drew a shallower breath, testing if that might circumvent some of the pain. Not really. "You think you could pull some strings for me here?"

"We'll take care of Blackwell." The captain gave him a hard look.

Jack hardened his own gaze. "Blackwell is mine." He'd been after the man for most of his career. He wouldn't allow himself to think how close he'd come to having him.

"You're lucky to be alive. One of the broken ribs punctured your lung. If the Price woman hadn't been there, we'd still be looking for your body."

Price woman. For a second, he didn't understand; then more memories trickled back. The grave. There'd been a woman—a possible connection. He knew Blackwell now as he'd never known him before, and with an actual lead... "I want this case."

"Your body, Jack." Bing surged to his feet, his voice tinged with anger and exasperation. "Do you understand what I'm saying? You were that close."

He'd been closer than his captain thought. He remembered that light, the floating feeling, the out-of-body sensation. He remembered someone being there with him on the other side, how he had reached out to that presence. But it hadn't worked. Apparently, he hadn't been ready. The pain had returned. Then he saw the woman.

The Price woman. "I want to talk to her. She has to be in with Blackwell. How would she know where to find me? He sent her to check on me. Or she got nervous."

Bing shook his head. "She's a damn artist. I'm not saying I like her, but she's not a criminal. You have to stop thinking about this. You're on medical leave. And you're officially off the case."

Jack swore a blue streak.

"Forget Blackwell, dammit," Bing growled, but when he continued after a moment, he lowered his voice again. "You're losing perspective, Jack. I'm telling you this as a friend."

He had no friends. All he had was his badge and his mission to see Brady Blackwell dead. "You have to keep an eye on the woman for me."

Until he got out and he could do it himself. She would lead him to Blackwell. In his mind, she was all tied in with the pain. He'd about died of it on the trip from the woods to her house.

She hadn't looked like much—disheveled, hair plastered to her head, wet from the snow, eyes wild. She'd smelled like paint. And just thinking of paint made his body pulse with pain all over again. He felt the blood run out of his head. He drew a slow breath to steady himself as he blinked.

"Dammit, Jack—"

"What do we have?" he cut Bing off. "Doesn't being half-dead earn me the right to some answers?"

A bleak look settled on the captain's face. "The DNA, if the lab can make it work. A generic el cheapo sheer shower curtain with no other fingerprints than yours and Ashley Price's. Shoe-print casts, size twelve, men's. Pattern not in the shoe-print database. But we have a fair idea of the shovel used to dig the grave; standard-issue army-entrenching tool, triangle tip, one side serrated."

His lips narrowed for a second. "The kicker is, I was sitting just up the road, handing out a speeding ticket. I saw Ashley Price drive by."

"Who else?"

"The snowplow for one. And the mailman. Old Arnie Martin drove by too. Mrs. Smutzky. Couple of cars I didn't recognize. I was paying attention to the people I was ticketing." He rubbed his hand over his knee. "We canvassed the area as soon as you were found. Nobody reported seeing any strange cars pulled over in the hours before you were discovered."

Jack nodded while he gritted his teeth against the new wave of pain that washed over his body. Whatever drugs they'd given him were wearing off. Good. He wanted to be able to think clearly. He wanted to remember.

"Is someone watching the Price woman?"

"Forget her," Bing snapped. "She had nothing to do with this."

I'll be the judge of that.

He had a lead after all these years, a living, breathing, tangible link to Blackwell. He held on to that thought with everything he had. She might have fooled Bing, but she sure as hell wasn't going to fool him.

"Let it go. That's an order."

He looked his captain in the eyes, preparing for a shit storm as he said, "Shannon Sullivan, the third victim, was my sister."

A long, tension-charged moment passed as Bing stared at him. "So this hobby of yours is not a hobby. It's personal." His expression darkened as he put two and two together. "I don't believe in coincidences, not in one this big." His voice sharpened. "Have you followed Blackwell here? Is that why you showed up at my department last year, asking me for a job? You knew something?"

Jack said nothing as the man's hands fisted on his knees.

"You knew there was a damn serial killer in my town, and you said nothing to me?" Anger heated the captain's voice.

"I wasn't sure. I was trying to figure it out." He'd be damned if he apologized for it. "Blackwell killed my sister."

Bing pushed to his feet, jaw tight, eyes flashing, about as pissed as Jack had ever seen him. "I can't talk to you about this right now. I'm gonna strangle you if I stay. Hell, I liked you, Jack. You're a fine detective, one of the best I've ever worked with. But you crossed a line here."

He wasn't sure he cared at this stage.

The captain stalked to the door but then stopped to look back with a scowl. "You sure it was Blackwell?"

"One hundred percent."

A muscle ticked in the man's face. "Brady Blackwell, one of the most wanted serial killers of the decade, confirmed in Broslin. You know what this means? Freaking FBI all over my town."

Jack's jaw clamped tight. He needed to get the hell out of here before the FBI mucked up every clue and lead. Before Ashley Price could disappear.

He glanced around. "Where are my badge and my gun?" A sick cold spread in his stomach.

"He kept them," Bing said quietly.

The highest insult to a cop. That hurt more than all the injuries put together. Jack swore under his breath. When he got his hands on the bastard—

"Don't you worry about that now," the captain said. "You'll get a new set when you get better."

He watched Bing leave, then sat up experimentally and nearly passed out from the pain, sweat beading on his forehead. He might be able to walk out of here if he asked for some heavy-duty drugs, but with those drugs he couldn't think straight and, above all, he wanted to keep his mind clear.

He levered himself back onto the pillows and closed his eyes, ran through everything he knew about the man he hunted, from the very beginning, every case, every detail from the considerable file he'd put together over the years. And then he added every bit of new information, every impression he remembered from his three days of bloody torture.

He put everything in neat order first, then shuffled the puzzle pieces over and over again to see what might fit together, if he could see a clear picture emerging. Hours passed, awash in pain and trying to force his brain to work, to see something he hadn't seen before.

A nurse came around, a kind-faced black woman, and checked his chart. "How are you, Mr. Sullivan?"

"I need to get out of here." He struggled again to sit up, hoping to succeed this time, pulling on the tubes hooked up to him.

"You need to watch those." She pushed him down gently.

When he tried to resist, she frowned and did something with his IV. He wanted to protest, but his brain slowed and his tongue wouldn't turn in his mouth suddenly. And then darkness claimed him.

His dreams weren't happy. He was back in the cold and the dark, in the grave.

When he woke, the sun sat low in the morning sky outside. Long minutes ticked by as his brain slowly began clearing. Another nurse stuck her head in. This time, he didn't say anything. He didn't want to be put to sleep again. He closed his eyes, trying to work through the fog in his brain, come up with a plan. He was so focused on his thoughts, he didn't hear the man standing in the doorway until he cleared his throat.

"Detective Sullivan. I was told you were awake. I'm Dr. Beacon."
The doctor, wearing dress pants, a white shirt, and a lab coat,
strode into the room. He was meticulously trim and meticulously
groomed, right down to his fingernails, in his midthirties, his face
stretched into an artificial smile that matched the sense of artificial
serenity he carried.

"When can I be discharged?" Jack asked with all the impatience
that coursed through him.

The man sat in a chair next to the bed, not a hurried movement
there. "That will be decided by your attending physician. I'm the
psychiatrist the police department called in to help you deal with
your ordeal."

Jack's hands fisted at his sides as he cursed Bing. The captain
meant well, but no way in hell was some shrink going to poke
around in his head. "No, thanks. I'm fine."

The doctor tilted his head, regarding him with a smarmy calm.
"Here's the thing. While your discharge is up to your attending
physician, we'll both have to sign off on your returning to active
duty." He crossed his legs, gloating in his power as he took out a
small notebook from the pocket of his lab coat.

"Why don't you tell me everything you remember?"

At least he didn't ask about his personal connection to Blackwell,
which gave Jack hope that Bing had kept that part to himself. Not
that the captain owed him any favors. In his place, Jack would
have been just as ticked.

He gritted his teeth and sat up, the pain in his ribs a little better
than earlier. Or maybe he was just used to it. He slipped from the
bed, bracing himself on the side when the room spun with him.
When his vision cleared, he ripped the tubes out of his arms.

Dr. Beacon was on his feet by then. "What do you think you're
doing?"

"Checking myself out against medical advice."

The man stepped in to block the way, clamping a restraining hand
on his arm. "I realize it can be difficult to talk about a traumatic
experience—"

Jack put whatever strength he had into making sure his voice was
strong and clear, glancing down at the hand holding him back, then
back up into the shrink's pale eyes.

"Not as difficult as wiping your broken nose with a broken arm. Step aside," he said and didn't give a damn that his words would be quoted in his psychiatric evaluation.

Chapter Three

That Jack Sullivan still lived filled him with fury. He'd been careless. He wouldn't be careless with the detective again.

His art was more important than a handful of lives. Art at the level where he practiced it had to be protected.

He was living his dream at last, living to his full potential, and nobody was going to take that away from him. He'd always wanted to be an artist.

His father hadn't approved, had refused to pay for art school. And the art school hadn't given him a scholarship, unable to understand his art. He'd accepted then that they couldn't have taught him anything anyway.

In hindsight, the rejection had been lucky. Anyone could be trained to a fair level of competence in anything, but creative genius was born. Structured instruction would have imposed restrictions on his vision.

The old fan chugged on in its valiant effort to distribute the heat from the antique woodstove in the corner. He didn't really feel the cold. Creating always filled him with fire.

He manipulated the small engraving drill to draw his complicated design onto bone, working in his basement studio, pleased as his composition took shape. He didn't have to worry about the neighbors hearing the drill, or the hammer when he was assembling larger pieces. They hadn't heard Sullivan's screams. The basement was soundproofed.

He'd learned how to do that and all kinds of construction tricks from his father, who'd built houses for a living, the same path he'd chosen for his son.

His father had said art was for liberal loafers who lived on the government tit and did nothing but do drugs and fornicate with each other. Art was for the gays. Art was for the kind of women who would neglect their families for their own entertainment.

A real man built things with his two hands, big, sturdy things, manly things like houses. The family tree was full of carpenters. Yet even now, in the corner of the basement studio, stood his great-grandfather's walking stick with the whalebone handle he'd carved himself. Art.

Carving was the first art, practiced by the first men who first used tools and wanted to decorate them. The carving of bones was elemental, the highest form of art. It needed the highest-value medium.

He'd tried stone. He didn't like it. Stone was dead. Bone was alive. These days he no longer used cat and dog bones like he had for the art school projects that had been rejected. If they could see him now...

They still wouldn't understand him, he thought with irony as he worked, creating yet another piece for his latest installment, a statue of shards, every inch intricately carved, his skill bringing the pieces back to life. The beautiful bones of a beautiful woman, being made into something sublime. Women were special.

He hated his father, but he'd always loved his mother. Women were his connection to the elemental, to Mother Nature, to Mother Earth. Someday, a more enlightened world would understand the profound symbolism of his art.

He would never sell his work in his lifetime, he knew that, had accepted it years ago. This wasn't for some rich collector anyway, to lock away. He created for all humankind.

So he got a job that paid the bills, played the dumb everyday man people were comfortable with. Small-town folks, especially, didn't have the first idea what to do with true genius.

Someday his pieces would be exhibited in the finest museums. Someday he would be called the premier artist of the twenty-first century. Someday the rest of humanity would grow up to his vision.

All he had to do was keep creating and remove things that were a threat to his legacy, Jack Sullivan being at the top of his list.

But Sullivan would be wary now.

Which meant the next trap had to be even better thought-out with a better bait, something the detective couldn't resist.

* * *

Ashley added another small dab of white to the Prussian blue. No strange visions, no headaches—a good day. She mixed the paint carefully.

She had finished four works in the two weeks since she'd promised Isabelle the new series. Her loft was a good place to hide from all the police and FBI agents who'd been coming and going on her property.

She'd escaped into painting from sheer desperation, then kept up with the schedule even after they left.

She needed at least three dozen works for a decent show, and four dozen would be better. If she had a show, if it was well received, got good reviews, was written up in the papers—maybe that would convince her father that she was back to normal. Maybe then he would let Madison come back to her.

She missed her daughter. They hadn't come last weekend after all. Her father had some emergency board meeting, trouble at the company. She hated not seeing Madison, but in a way, the missed visit came at the right time. She'd still had the police on her land. This way, the latest mess she was in had at least remained her secret. It didn't become another weapon that could be used against her. And now that the police were gone, everything should be fine this weekend when Madison came. Things were back to seminormal again.

She let the brush glide across the canvas, let her arm relax into a sweeping curve reminiscent of the curve of a shoulder, then another one, smaller, the two twined together the moment before being torn apart. Each color she mixed turned out more profound than the one before as she painted her emotions onto the canvas, poured her heartbreak out with every stroke of the squirrel-hair brush.

"Painting is an attempt to come to terms with life." She murmured George Tooker's words to the shapes taking form.

For three hours, in the perfect morning light, she had soared. She existed in the elusive zone of creativity where no anxiety existed, just bliss. She felt the pain she painted, felt every ounce of despair, but differently from the darkness that assailed her at other times. At times, painting could be terror, but on days like this... pure healing therapy.

Not long ago, she'd been able to come and go from this place at will. Lately, she was lucky to find her way in, once in a great while, hacking ahead with sweat and desperation as an explorer in the deep jungle, trying to find a lost city.

The sun trekked across the sky, going around the loft windows, changing the light. She stepped back to inspect what she had so far. A few more days and the painting would be finished. She contemplated whether she could squeeze in another half an hour, even twenty minutes, glancing toward the window again. A movement in the hemlocks caught her eye.

Her muscles clenched as she felt her special place slip away. The wind, she told herself. But none of the other trees were moving. Maybe it had been a deer. It wouldn't be the first time deer strayed this close to the house. But her growing anxiety refused to ease. Her muscles tightened further as she cleaned her brushes and put them away, cleaned up the loft, glancing toward the window every couple of seconds.

She was probably getting cabin fever. She rolled her neck and headed downstairs. She hadn't left the house in the two weeks since finding Jack Sullivan. She hadn't liked all those investigators crawling all over her land.

They hadn't searched the house and the garage, at least. They probably wouldn't at this stage. Still, it would be better to get rid of those paintings out there. Not only as a symbolic act, the representation of hope that this part of her life was now over— she'd saved a man—but also because she didn't want Maddie to accidentally find them once her daughter moved back home.

Since the ground was frozen, she couldn't bury the canvases. Ice covered the reservoir, so she couldn't dump them into the water, even if she could make herself go near the place. Taking them somewhere far away and leaving them in a Dumpster seemed too risky.

That left burning, the only solution she could think of. But she hadn't dared burn them while the police and the FBI were still coming by.

She glanced toward the hemlocks again. All seemed serene in the yard. She had to fight her fears, not give in to the overwhelming anxiety that sometimes kept her housebound for weeks. She wanted her daughter back, which meant she needed to reclaim her life, starting now.

She could do it if she did it little by little, just as it had been taken from her. She could start with reclaiming her small backyard. She would go out there and do what she needed to do. She refused to worry every time a breeze moved a bush.

The temperature hovered on the freezing point, but no wind blew. She grabbed paint thinner for accelerant and padded down the stairs, swiping a box of matches from the kitchen counter where she'd been burning a scented candle earlier.

Boots, scarf, coat, hat, gloves.

Cold air hit her in the face as she stepped outside, making her draw a quick breath. Snow covered the landscape, an endless stretch of white. Up ahead, the town plow was hustling down the road. Eddie waved and turned into her driveway. The big plow pretty much cleared everything on the way in, stopping a foot or so from her car. That patch she'd have to do herself.

After she got a new shovel. The handle of the old one broke recently, which meant a trip to the hardware store. She didn't want to think about that right now. Hey, maybe they wouldn't get any more snow this winter.

"Thank you, Eddie, I really appreciate it," she called up to him. "Good to see the big plow fixed."

"Gave me plenty of trouble. Need a crane to take this damn thing apart. But, hey, at least there weren't any screws left over when I put it back together."

He drove the big plow in the winter and did whatever else needed to be done around the town hall the rest of the year. The fifty-something town handyman was the perfect guy for the job, a loner like her. When the town called, he went. He could fix a roof or fill a pothole and did it all with a smile.

"Everything okay?" Eddie called down from his high perch. "I see the police are gone."

"Thank God."

"They found anything?"

"I don't think so. Not that they share with me." But they looked just as gloomy leaving as they had coming.

"Mind if I come by in a couple of days to grab some wood?"

He had a woodstove in his workshop, and Ashley let him walk through her property and drag out whatever fallen timber he could find, chop it up and haul it away—the least she could do for him for keeping her driveway clean all winter.

"Anytime you want."

He gave a wave of thanks and backed the plow out of the driveway, getting back to work.

She waited until he was gone before she went around the house. The air was absolutely frigid, but at least no wind was blowing. She glanced toward the hemlocks as she opened the garage door. No movement back there now. Could have been a bird earlier.

To her right, floor-to-ceiling shelving held some old art supplies and sketches. Her gaze caught on a charcoal sketch of the spring landscape she'd made when she'd first moved here. And it hit her how much like the drawing her life had become, a shadow image of what she'd once been, all her colors reduced to shades of gray. She was going to change that. For herself and for Maddie.

She strode to the back wall and carried the paintings out by the armload, all wrapped in the paper bags from the local grocery store. Thank God for stores that stayed open around the clock. She braved a trip once every couple of weeks in the middle of the night, when she could be sure she would be virtually alone. During the times when she couldn't go as far as the store down the road, she lived on pizza and Chinese delivery.

That too would change, she thought as she tossed the first batch of canvases onto the ground in front of the garage, where the hard wind the previous day had blown a patch clear of snow.

When the phone rang in her pocket, she was tempted to ignore it. But what if it was the police? If they had another question, she'd just as soon answer it over the phone than have them come back here.

But instead of Captain Bing, the caller turned out to be Graham Lanius, the art dealer.

"Just checking in if you might have something for me. I'm going to do a big summer show this year. As one of my favorite local artists, I'd love it if you would participate."

He called every couple of months, trying to talk her into a show. But her agent, Isabelle, wasn't crazy about the man. Neither was Ashley, truthfully. He was smarmy, for one. And the few times she'd met him in person, she'd gotten the impression that while he made a living off artists, he looked down on them.

"I truly appreciate the offer. I'm working on a series, actually. But all my scheduling goes through my agent."

"Ah, yes, the lovely Isabelle." The words were still complimentary, but the tone had chilled a few degrees. "I'll be sure to get in touch with her as well. Would you mind if I just stopped by and looked at your new series in the meanwhile? We're practically neighbors."

The work wasn't ready. She didn't like strangers in her house. Living in the same town didn't make them neighbors. Yet she understood that since Broslin had three times as many galleries as the average small town, competition was rough. Although, her kind of art wasn't exactly what appealed to tourists who came to see Franklin Milton's birthplace and studio, his museum.

Milton had painted barns and fields and covered bridges, the cows, the horse farms, quintessential Pennsylvania countryside. His grandson, Andre, continued in that vein. But Graham didn't have Andre, and at least Ashley Price was a fairly well-known name in the contemporary art world.

She had broken in, after years of hard work. But what she had achieved could be lost in a heartbeat. Her gaze stayed on the small pile of canvases in front of her. She needed to deal with that now.

"I'm sorry. I'm in the middle of something. I really need to go."

"Sure. No problem at all. We'll be in touch," he promised.

She hung up and carried the rest of her dark creations outside. She'd never destroyed a painting before. But now, once her pile was complete, she lifted the paint thinner and poured. The liquid splashed onto the top package, immediately bleeding through the wrapping. She set down the bottle and pulled the matches from her pocket as she shivered, feeling as if she was about to commit murder.

But they weren't right, those images she'd created. Jackson Pollock had said that paintings had a life of their own; his job was to let it come through.

Her paintings had a death of their own. And her job was to destroy the dark images.

She was so focused on her thoughts that the question, "Need help?" coming from behind her, nearly made her jump out of her boots. Her heart broke into a mad rhythm as she whipped around. The man had appeared out of nowhere, his hands in the pockets of his black coat, his wiry frame standing in contrast to the white background. His cerulean gaze sharp, he focused his full attention on her, and she couldn't breathe for a second. She had pretty good color memory. She would have recognized that russet hair and those eyes anywhere.

But he did introduce himself.

"Jack Sullivan. I stopped by to thank you for what you did for me." He had been covered in mud and blood the last time she'd seen him. Now she had no trouble making out his features, the square jaw and the planes of his face. He looked gaunt, had probably lost weight from his ordeal and while recovering. Yet his aura was definitely not weak.

His unwavering focus and his intense gaze were complemented with a good dose of masculine energy. His sculpted lips made his face interesting. He would have made a great study for a painting. The edgy darkness in him made looking away from him difficult, something that would have come through in a painting if the artist did it right.

Another woman might have found him handsome. She found him, his presence at her house, terrifying. She would have preferred never having to see him again.

"Why don't we go into the house?" She moved forward out of sheer desperation, against instinct. She didn't want him in her house or anywhere near it, but she needed to draw him away from her paintings.

"I don't want to keep you from your work." His gaze slid to the pile. He stepped closer. "How about I give you a hand with this?"

* * *

She might have been shooting him a cool look, but she was hot. He'd missed that before.

44

Of course, the first time they'd met, he'd barely been conscious. And while he'd watched her nearly every day since he'd made his escape from the hospital, he'd watched her from afar.

She had large green eyes a man could fall into, with shadows at their depth that pulled at him. Her perfectly symmetrical face, beauty without artifice, was the face of a distressed angel. All that purity somehow accentuated her swollen lips that looked as if they'd been made to sin. Her body was mostly covered up by her coat, except for her legs that were long enough for a pole dancer. As he looked her over, he felt a responding tug at his groin, which he ignored. He hadn't come here for cheap thrills. He'd come to make her lead him to Blackwell.

And she probably knew it. She was as nervous as a king crab at an all-you-can-eat seafood buffet, although she tried to hide it. But she couldn't stop her feet from shuffling over the frozen ground, her hands grasped tightly together in front of her.

"I have a few questions about that night. I'm a police officer." Jack watched for her reaction.

His occupation set some at ease, carried a certain amount of respectability and trustworthiness, he supposed; others got decidedly nervous. Ashley Price didn't relax. Nor did his revelation surprise her. She'd known, and he wondered how. Bing had kept all details from the media. Of course, there was no way to stop gossip from spreading in a small town like Broslin.

"I was hoping I could ask you some questions." He laid his first card on the table, the only one he was willing to show her.

"I already told the police and the FBI everything I know."

Or everything she would admit to, he thought. He'd had his own tête-à-tête with the FBI, and given an official victim statement. He'd held back plenty. As nervous as she was acting, he had no doubt Ashley Price had done the same.

"It will only take a few minutes," he said in a tone that made it clear he wasn't leaving.

"All right, um… We should go inside." She moved forward but stopped after only one step.

He was standing between her and the house. She seemed reluctant to come too close to him.

"I'm sorry if I was difficult when you rescued me. I wasn't thinking straight."

Her gaze flew up to his. "You kidnapped me."

So he'd given her a fright. He couldn't rightly say he regretted it. "Sorry. Again," he apologized for form's sake.

She nodded, pushing thick auburn waves out of her face with the back of a gloved hand. The face of an angel, he thought again. Except, he didn't believe in angels, and he sure wasn't predisposed to believe anything Ashley Price was about to tell him.

He'd spent enough years on the force to know a person with secrets when he met one, and she was definitely hiding something. She wanted him gone and wanted it badly.

He glanced at the makings of her strange bonfire, the reason he had revealed himself. He wouldn't be a good cop if he stood by while a suspect destroyed evidence.

"What are you burning?"

"Some paintings of mine."

He tried for a light tone. "That bad?"

"Worse." She faked a ghost of a smile as she tapped her boot-clad feet. "It's colder out here than I thought." She made a move toward the house again.

But the more she tried to drag him away, the more his instincts prickled. He did want to see the inside of her house, but he was, for the moment, more interested in what she wanted to burn.

"It'll get better once you start the fire. Let me straighten this up for you." He stepped to the pile and shored it up, despite the protesting sound she made and the terrified look on her face.

He could actually bend over now; his ribs had healed some while he'd been going over his files this past week or so, calling around, trying to find out what the FBI had, sitting on fallen logs in the brush, watching her woods, watching her house.

She lived alone. He'd kept track of every man coming and going: Pete the mailman and Eddie the town handyman. He'd made a point to bump into both in town, but he didn't recognize their voices as Blackwell's. Still, he couldn't be one hundred percent sure. He hadn't been in his right mind. So he couldn't completely rule out either man.

He would have watched her house longer, put off a personal confrontation for another day or two in the hopes of catching someone else visiting her, if she hadn't come out and begun building her strange pile.

"Here you go." He worked the package he was holding so his finger would get caught in the folds of the brown wrapping paper and he could rip it, making it look like an accident. "Sorry."

He held the partially exposed canvas. Green trees. Brown grass. Legs. Red.

She dove for the painting, and he managed to rip more wrapping off as she pulled it away from him. He caught a glimpse of a prone figure before she snatched the painting away to cover it against her body.

Everything inside him went cold, and it had nothing to do with the temperature outside. He picked up another painting by his feet. There was a time he would have followed the rules and wouldn't have gone further without a warrant. Not today. By the time he could get back with one—if he could get one, considering he wasn't on active duty—the paintings would be a pile of ashes. He needed to know.

"Don't," she pleaded.

He tore into the wrapper.

A woman in a creek, pasty face, blankly staring eyes, the body bent at odd angles. Dark, insidious colors swirled in the water— except for the ribbon of red that looked violently vibrant. The scene pulled him in, pulled him under until he could feel the cold water on his own face. A shiver drilled down his spine.

The next painting depicted a man in a UPS driver uniform. The paint thinner had blurred this one, but he saw enough to remember the case even if he hadn't worked on it. The body had been found outside his jurisdiction, but this was rural PA and murder was big news. When something like that happened in any of the small towns nearby, all the cops in the area tended to know about it.

He reached for the next picture, then the next. She stopped protesting, looked as if she'd gone numb, clutching the one picture she had taken away from him. Just the same, he moved into a position from where he could grab her if she thought of running.

He ripped the wrapping from the next painting he picked up. Plenty of smudges on this one, but he had no trouble recognizing the scene—he'd spent enough time there in the last week or so. He blinked as he looked at an image of himself in the grave.

Air hissed out of his lungs. Rage filled the freed space. "How do you know Brady Blackwell?" His voice snapped.

She stood silent, shivering.

He grabbed up as many pictures as he could, tucking them under one arm, grabbing her with his other hand. "We need to talk."

She wouldn't move.

"Inside or you can come to the station with me." An empty threat, since he couldn't officially interrogate anyone. He was on medical leave, off the case. If Bing found out he came here—

"Please." She raised her luminous green eyes to his face.

If she thought she could soften him as easily as that, she had another think coming. "Let's go."

"I have nothing to do with what happened to you," she begged.

He very much doubted that.

He marched her into the house. He couldn't really remember much of it from before, little else but the pain. And when the smell of paint hit him, he could swear he felt that pain again. He shook it off and looked around.

She had a clean home with a sense of warmth, a place that contained a lot of natural wood surfaces and old-fashioned braided rugs. Not exactly a killer's lair. Then again, appearances could be deceiving.

He scanned the living room wall, covered with drawings and paintings that looked like they'd been done by a child. She had no other artwork on display, nothing that might have been her own save what he held.

As he stepped forward, his ribs ached, reminding him of those days of torture. "Do you have a basement? A root cellar?" He didn't see any sign of one from the outside but wanted to make sure.

"None of the houses have basements this close to the reservoir. The water table is too high." She shrugged out of her coat, looking dazed, as if she was moving on autopilot.

Could be an act, he thought as he watched her, making sure she wasn't planning on making a break for it. His gaze swept her from head to toe, looking for suspicious body language, but then he got distracted by other things.

Okay, he definitely hadn't remembered the breasts. They were a lot rounder up close and personal than from the distance when he'd been watching her through the loft window. Her body was the type to give men restless dreams. The wave of instant lust threw him for

a second, but for only a second. He was a seasoned investigator.
He could ignore his twitching dick, dammit.
"Take a seat." He motioned her to the sofa, not liking that he felt
the need to put some distance between them.
To start with, he asked a question he already knew the answer to,
an old interrogators' trick. "You have a daughter?" He nodded
toward the drawings, most of them signed Madison.
"Yes." She wouldn't look at him.
"Where is she?"
"She's temporarily staying with my father."
Not Madison's father? So nothing changed there. According to a
couple of old tabloid articles he'd found on her on the Internet, she
had claimed the father of her child was Dave DaRosa, a prominent
Philadelphia millionaire. DaRosa, twenty years Ashley's senior
and a reputed ladies' man, had publicly denied paternity, and
Ashley Price had never taken him to court. Could be she hadn't
been sure enough for a DNA test.
He knew DaRosa from the news. Everybody in the state did. The
man liked to throw around money and liked to do it publicly. An
image of the cocky bastard's signet-ringed hands on Ashley's long
thighs flashed into his mind and made him angry, which made no
sense at all. He was definitely off his game today.
He shrugged off his coat and draped it over the back of an
armchair, but he didn't sit. He kept one eye on her while he spread
out her paintings on the floor. When he reached for the one she
was still holding, she clutched it to her body.
"It's too late for that now." He tugged on the canvas, and she let it
go finally, her full lips pressed into narrow lines.
He lay the picture next to the others and looked over the bizarre
collection of disturbing images. He'd always wondered if
Blackwell might have had more victims, victims that had either not
been found, or found but not connected to him. He didn't
recognize a single person in the paintings from his Blackwell
victim files, yet some of the faces did seem vaguely familiar. He
racked his brain to place them, but nothing popped into his mind.
"How do you know these people?"
"I don't."
"Were you there when they died?"
"No."

"How long have you known Brady Blackwell?"

"I have no idea who he is."

Frustration pumped through him as he reviewed the paintings again. Something was off, but he didn't know what. Then it finally hit him. Blackwell's victims had all been found in pieces. All the corpses Ashley had painted were whole, without mutilation. Another killer?

His gaze snapped to her. Did she kill these people so she could paint them?

But Blackwell had definitely been the one to put him in the grave. Maybe they worked together; Jack circled back to his original thoughts.

Blackwell took young women, in twos and threes, chopped them up, kept some of the pieces. Whoever killed the people in the paintings had left them whole. Because she wanted to paint them? There had been a handful of boyfriend-girlfriend serial-killer teams, but they'd all hunted together, used the same MO. That a team like that would have a different murder profile didn't seem likely.

For the first time in a long time, he had a lead, dammit. He wanted it to make sense. He wanted a straight arrow pointing in the right direction, but confusion was all he was getting.

"Why do you paint these?"

She blinked rapidly, looking as if she was fighting tears.

He couldn't care less. He was too much of a hard-assed, cold-hearted bastard to be swayed by crying. Miss Price was about to find that out. Princess Price, the tabloids had called her back in the day. She came from major money, father a veritable tycoon, mother a nut, died over a decade ago in a mental hospital. Ashley, the only child, made herself a name in the visual arts.

He'd seen her police file as well. A four-year-old boy, Dylan Miller, had died while in her care, went under the ice of the reservoir last winter—ruled accidental drowning. He had to wonder now, didn't he, with all those paintings lying at his feet. Were the rest of those people Blackwell's victims like he'd been, or Ashley's? Maybe Blackwell was a killer with a split personality. Killed one set of victims one way, the other for a different purpose entirely. His jaw tightened. He didn't like the word "victim" applied to him.

From what he knew of Blackwell and what he'd seen of Ashley so far, his money was on Blackwell doing all the killing and Ashley doing only the painting. He didn't get a killer vibe from her. Yet she was involved, in up to her haunted green eyes.

"Did Brady Blackwell make you paint these?" Maybe they were something like trophies to the bastard. Ashley, the bodies, and Blackwell had to be somehow all connected.

"I don't know Brady Blackwell." She held herself together but not by much. Her hands, clasped tightly in her lap, were trembling.

"I'm going to bring in the rest. You touch any of these, you move an inch from that couch, and I promise you'll regret it."

He strode out, hurried back in with an armload two minutes later, laid them out and unwrapped them, examined them one by one. Then he asked the question he was most afraid of knowing the answer to. "Do you have others?"

He didn't know if he could stand looking at Shannon in the grave. It had been fifteen years, but the wound of losing his sister had never healed. He didn't breathe while he waited for the answer.

"No. This is it."

He exhaled. Of course. She couldn't have painted Shannon in North Carolina. Ashley Price was twenty-five, according to her file. She would have been only ten, living in Philadelphia with her parents, at the time of Shannon's disappearance. One of the tightly wound springs inside him marginally relaxed.

He stared at the images, and a faint memory popped into his head at last. The woman in one, lying in a dark alley, had been a rape/homicide case in West Chester six months back. The case belonged to a different police department, but Jack made it his business to look into cases of women disappearing, then turning up dead. This one he'd quickly ruled out as Blackwell's, and the West Chester police had gotten their perp within a few days, a rock-solid case. She'd been murdered by her ex-boyfriend.

No link to Blackwell. Yet there had to be a connection to Ashley Price, since Ashley had painted her. How and when?

"What do you know about these people?"

She shifted her gaze away from him. "Nothing."

"Stop lying." Frustration raised his voice, which made her jump in her seat.

"Just what I read in the paper."

Dana Marton

He drew up an eyebrow. "You only know them from the news?"
She nodded without looking at him.
He picked up the painting he'd been staring at and held it up for
her. "I don't remember the papers detailing the exact position of
the body when she was found. You need to come up with a better
story."
She paled, fighting more tears.
His cop instincts said she didn't have what it took to kill. Maybe in
self-defense, but not in cold blood and regularly. She seemed
messed up, granted, but cold, calculated murder wasn't in her.
He'd interrogated enough people to know when to go soft as well
as when to push hard. He could do bad-cop-good-cop all on his
own just fine.
"Look." He gentled his voice. "I've got all these paintings now. I
know you're connected. I don't think you harmed these people. We
both know who did. You have to tell me where he is so I can stop
him from doing this again."
She rubbed her arms, breathing erratically. "I don't feel well."
"You'll feel better once you get this off your chest. It's over. It's
the end of the line. You need to come clean."
Some strange energy seemed to zap into her then, and she shot to
her feet, vibrating with nerves. "I can't breathe." She gulped air.
Whatever her connection was to the people she painted, he knew
this: Brady Blackwell had put him in a shallow grave, and Ashley
Price had been there when he came to. For what purpose, Jack
wasn't sure yet, but he didn't think she'd just randomly wandered
the fields in the twilight and accidentally tripped over him as she
claimed.
And what about all these other people? They hadn't been on her
land. How had she come to see them dead? See them from close
enough and well enough to render the scene with accurate detail?
"Tell me, Ashley, where, when, and how did you come to paint
these?"
She moved to the kitchen and poured herself a glass of water.
Drank. Then, as if someone had taken out her battery, she
collapsed against the counter and slid to the floor, leaned forward,
her elbows resting on her knees, her face buried in her slim-
fingered artist hands as she hyperventilated.

"I see them in my mind." She choked up the words. "I don't want to. They are just there, and I have to get them out."

What she implied... Screw the good cop. Anger pumped through him. Did he look stupid? If she was going for this kind of bullshit, he seriously needed to work on his I-mean-business face. "So you're psychic?"

"No." The denial came between two gasps.

"What then?"

Her hands fell away, and she looked up at him, the desperation on her face gut-wrenching. "I don't know." Tears filled her eyes all over again. She blinked them furiously away.

A woman on the brink of falling apart. Good. Suspects usually told the truth when they came unhinged. Time to push harder.

"What is Blackwell to you?" he challenged. "Are you willing to go to prison for him? Is he your boyfriend?" While the idea of DaRosa's hands on her had angered him, the idea of Blackwell's hands on her disturbed him on a deeper level. "Is he worth a charge of accessory to murder? Is he that good a fuck?"

Her eyes widened with shock, and she recoiled from him as if he'd physically struck her. If her reaction made him feel like a bastard, he wasn't willing to acknowledge it.

"I don't know him," she protested in a voice filled with despair.

"So you just saw me in your mind?"

She nodded.

Judging by the look in her eyes, she hated him as much at this moment as he hated Blackwell. She was welcome to it. "And?"

"I recognized the rock and the creek. I knew where you were."

* * *

Jack Sullivan thought she was in league with a serial killer. And, stupidly, to convince him she was innocent, she had blurted out her darkest secret. *Oh God.* She would have done anything to undo that, to erase her words.

Soon everyone would know that something was seriously wrong with her. And then she would never get her daughter back. She wrapped her arms tightly around herself, dizzy with the anxiety and anger that gripped her.

She had to make Sullivan believe her, accept that she had nothing to do with the killer he was looking for. He seemed dead set on pinning a slew of murders on her. Or accessory to murder. Nausea bubbled in her stomach. She squeezed her eyes shut for a second. To think that she'd been scared of Bing. For Bing, the case was a job. For Sullivan, it was personal. He was aggressive and crass and relentless and—

"Have you tried to find any of the others?" He glanced back at the pictures, then at her again, his face hard, his eyes narrowed. He had a look of emptiness about him, as if he'd left his soul in that grave and brought only the darkness with him. He had no right to bring that to her house.

She wanted to curl up into a ball and howl with the unfairness of it all. "I didn't know where the others were. Only you. And I knew you weren't dead."

"How?"

She pointed at the painting with a frustrated gesture. It was so obvious. How could he not see it?

He picked up the painting, looked at it for a few seconds; then he looked at the rest of the canvases. "I don't look like the others." He paused. "Why did you come?"

If only she hadn't. She'd been scared out of her mind. "I thought..."

He waited her out.

"I thought if I saved you, maybe I wouldn't see another...vision, ever again." She had expected relief, some sort of absolution and an end to the nightmare that had kept her bound for over a year now. Instead, she'd gotten Jack Sullivan with all his disapproval and suspicions, and his ability to reach to the deepest, darkest core of her.

He kept his face inscrutable, leaving her no way to tell if he believed anything she told him. She wouldn't believe it if it wasn't happening to her.

The first time she had painted a lifeless body, she'd thought it some sort of a fluke, another symptom of the depression that had followed the accident on the reservoir. The landscape she'd planned on painting kept changing as she was compelled to change the location of the trees, add a road, take out the barn she'd meant to have as the focal point. She'd painted that first body, an older woman, in a trance, horrified when she'd stepped back at the end.

After the second time it'd happened, a black teenager, she packed up her paints and canvases and decided not to paint for a while until whatever was going on in her mind blew over. Her shrink upped her antidepressant. It didn't help, made her slightly manic, keeping her up night after night with nothing to do.

The third body she'd seen in her mind, a man in a UPS uniform, she'd been determined not to paint. But her hands moved on their own, dragging out her supplies. She'd been terrified enough after that to throw the rest of her blank canvases and paint tubes into the trash.

When the image of the fourth body invaded her thoughts, she'd been forced to paint on the back of an old kitchen cabinet with leftover household paints. After that, she'd accepted that she couldn't fight the curse and no longer tossed the odd canvases friends brought by or the paint and brush samples sent by companies she'd frequently ordered from in the past.

When the next terrible urge came, she simply painted the young woman, Megan Keeler, the first who had a name. Ashley had recognized her in the Inquirer a few days later. Missing College Student's Body Found in Southeastern PA.

She'd thrown up twice before she could finish the article.

With the next victims, she searched the papers obsessively until she found them. She didn't dare go to the police. What help could she be? They were already all dead. What could she say? I paint dead people?

The man with the cerulean-blue eyes, Detective Jack Sullivan, had been her ninth.

She was not going crazy. There had to be a way out of this. She would find it.

"When did it start?" he demanded.

God, not that. She couldn't go back to Dylan. But looking at the man's face, she finally understood that she wasn't going to get a choice. "An accident happened on the reservoir."

He nodded.

Did he know about that? Of course he did; everyone around here knew the whole sordid tale.

"We fell through the ice, Maddie and Dylan and I." She rubbed her hands over her arms, feeling the deadly chill all over again. "I was under for twenty minutes, but they pulled me out and revived me. I was in a coma for a week."

The cold water had slowed down her metabolism to the point where she didn't suffer any brain damage from the lack of oxygen, the doctors had explained later, declaring her a medical miracle. "And after that—" It killed her to have to think back to the accusations, the tremendous guilt, the depression.

The Millers, her neighbors, had lost Dylan. But she had lost her daughter too. Her father had taken Maddie while Ashley had been in the hospital. And considering the state she'd been in even after she'd gotten out, he'd been reluctant to give Maddie back.

She wanted her daughter more than she wanted anything. But she was scared to the bone that there was something seriously wrong with her, that she was going crazy, that she would never get better, would never get Maddie back, would end up dying in a mental hospital like her mother, strapped to the bed.

None of which she could share with anyone, not ever.

All she could give Jack Sullivan was the most basic truth, which he had already seen and had refused to believe. "And now I paint the dead."

Chapter Four

Jack smashed his fist into the boxing bag, the sharp slap the only sound that broke the silence in the small workout room in the back of the police station. The gym was utilitarian, nothing but the basics. He didn't need much. He just needed a place to build his body back.

He lost himself in the rhythm of his punches. He liked it when he was alone in here. He was still on leave—not by his own choice—but he could at least use the gym, part of his physical therapy. Maybe he was doing it a little harder than he was supposed to, but he didn't have time for a slow recovery.

So he came in, once a day, for the gym, and because he could usually sneak a few minutes at his computer, check on things, ask around about what progress the FBI was making.

None whatsoever.

Pretty much the same as he. His home visit a week ago with Ashley Price had netted more questions than answers.

He'd spent the intervening days with identifying everybody on the paintings he'd taken from her. Other than himself, he couldn't find a single link to Blackwell.

Punch, right, left. Forearms, right, left. Elbows, right, left. Knees, right, left. He exhaled sharply on each blow. He was focused on the bag, but not as deeply as he would have liked to be.

What did he know about her for sure?

She painted the dead.

People who died violently, to be more specific. Ashley Price, an untimely death, and geographical proximity were all the victims in her paintings had in common. Somebody coming in fresh and looking at those facts would have theorized that she was one of the rare female serial killers.

Except, he'd met her, and she wasn't a killer. She was a mess. And she hadn't been the one who'd put him into the grave.

But she was the one who'd dug him up.

He'd be damned if he knew what that meant.

He was almost puzzled enough to seriously consider her psychic tale. Almost.

Punch, right, left. Forearms, right, left. Elbows, right, left. Knees, right, left.

Maybe the FBI could make more sense of her. The four agents who'd arrived had taken over the single conference room at the police station and one of the offices. Bing wouldn't let Jack near them. But even if he had, Jack wouldn't have handed over the paintings. Ashley was his lead. He wanted to be the one who found Blackwell, dammit.

He danced around the bag, working it over as it swung on the chain. Left, right, back, forth. Everything hurt. He thought he'd learned long ago to shut out pain, both emotional and physical. Not quite.

Time to burn that pain out of his muscles. With every hit, he imagined Blackwell, let himself feel just enough to create a controlled flame burning in the dark. The sick bastard had left him alive even as he'd buried him, left him to die slowly so he would have time to think about how badly he'd failed.

The faces of Blackwell's other known victims played through his mind like a film on an endless loop, each one of the eighteen crying out for revenge. North Carolina, Virginia, Maryland, New Jersey, New York, Long Island, Connecticut. He'd made it his career to follow Blackwell up and down the East Coast, transferring from department to department over the years.

After a triple murder in Baltimore, he'd picked up on something in a forensics report the FBI had missed—spores at a crime scene, from some gourmet mushroom produced in only a half-dozen places in the country. He'd put six brown pins in the map on his wall at his rental, one for each location.

The line of eighteen red pins that marked the victims all concentrated in the middle section of the East Coast. The six brown ones were distributed randomly over the US, only one on the East Coast, Broslin, PA, in the middle of all the red. A state surrounded by victim states but where no victim had been taken. Why? Because it would have hit too close to home for Blackwell? So Jack took the first police job that came up in Broslin and had been damn proud of himself for getting another step closer. Except now it seemed Blackwell had caught on. The bastard had trapped him and nearly killed him.

Nearly.

His turn. But he couldn't let his revenge blind him. Every move had to be carefully calculated. They were in the endgame.

Jab. Cross. Elbow. Uppercut. Jack let the force of his legs explode through his hips, torso, and shoulders, sent the energy through his arms and into the bag.

Only when he was completely spent, covered in sweat, did he let himself drop to the mat. But even then, he couldn't rest. He reached for his phone and shuffled through the photos he'd taken of Ashley's bizarre paintings. He paused the screen at the painting of himself in the grave, eyes open but unseeing.

Blackwell's other known victims hadn't been buried alive. They'd been buried in pieces. The FBI had never done a full recovery. The bastard was keeping trophies.

But he hadn't cut Jack. Why? Why bury him alive?

He pushed back his rising anger. You go into a fight hot, you've already lost—one of the fundamental rules of combat he'd learned early on. He withdrew to the darkroom in his mind, as always when emotions threatened to get in his way. He liked the black, hollow space that let in no light. Except this time he wasn't alone. He'd somehow carried Ashley Price in there with him.

The woman carried a load of guilt, grief, and despair, along with some pretty dark secrets. They had that in common.

Hot as all get-out, but a basket case. Then again, anyone who would hook up with Blackwell had to be seriously messed up. He sure as hell didn't believe the psychic-vision bullshit. She was with Blackwell—either coerced or by choice. Probably the latter.

For one, Jack had given her a way out: cooperate with the police and be taken into protective custody. But she hadn't given up anything. Two, he didn't want to think of her as a possible victim. He needed an enemy he could reach to fight, and right now Ashley

Price was the only one within reach. He was going to bring
Blackwell down through her.

He'd rattled her before, had taken her paintings. She'd come close
to breaking. He would push her as hard and as far as he needed to,
to finish the job.

His phone rang. Always hoping for a lead, he took the call. Then
wished that he hadn't.

"Hi, this is Dr. Beacon," the shrink Bing had sicced on him at the
hospital said on the other end.

"I'm in the middle of something."

"We need to make an appointment."

"How about I call you back?"

"That's what you said the last time."

"I really don't have any problems."

"That'd be a miracle, after what you've been through. Denial is
normal. What do you know about Post Traumatic Stress
Disorder?"

"I don't have time to have PTSD."

"Insomnia, trouble breathing, anxiety, hallucinations, paranoia…
It's a long list, Detective. Why not let me help before things get
really bad?"

"How about this? I'll call you at the first sign of trouble." He hung
up on the man as Joe, one of two rookies, pushed through the door
and dropped his gym bag on the floor, heading straight for the
treadmill with a grin.

"Fallen and you can't get it up?"

He'd been the town football hero back in his high school days, had
gone to college on a sports scholarship. Never managed to turn
pro, although he'd spent time with a couple of the East Coast
teams before coming home and settling back into his small-town-
hero life.

"Odd that should be on your mind at your age." Jack rolled to his
feet. "Trouble in that department? You'll get better with
experience. Try not to worry."

"I don't know what you're talking about, old man. Hot stud is my
middle name." The twenty-something flashed another cocky grin
as he began running.

He was so full of hot air it was a wonder he didn't float to the
ceiling. But he was well-meaning, and he would watch a man's

back if needed, so pretty much everybody liked him around the station and overlooked his strutting peacock tendencies.

"What are you working now?"

Joe picked up speed on the treadmill. "The burglaries."

"Still?" There'd been a rash of burglaries in town over the last few months, a pushed-in back door here and there, small items taken, things that could be quickly sold online. Property crime like that usually picked up as the economy dipped.

Joe shrugged. "They stop for a week, then start again. I'll get the sucker."

Jack nodded as he passed by the treadmill, ready to hit the shower. "Bing in yet?"

"Came in, went out. Someone reported some hunting-camp bunker thing out by Spring Road. Filled to the rafters with guns and knives and axes and some weird shit. Chase went to pick up a flasher. Harper is at a tractor-trailer accident. I'm not sure where Mike is. Nobody's in."

Jack picked up speed, the parting jab he'd meant to throw at Joe forgotten. He rushed through his shower, and stopped by the front desk on his way out of the station. "You got that number I asked for earlier?"

"You bet." Leila slipped a piece of paper across the counter.

She was the sole admin support, a widow in her late forties with three boys to raise. She was competent and tough, wouldn't take flak from anyone. She had short hair that hadn't dared to gray yet, and the voice and demeanor of an admiral. Although the six men who made up the Broslin police often ribbed each other, nobody was fool enough to go up against her.

He glanced at the empty conference room. Looked like the FBI was out. He wished he knew what they were doing.

He pocketed the sticky note. "Thanks. You're the best."

She gave a bark of a laugh. "Stop kissing up, Sullivan. Christmas is over. I'm not bringing in any more cookies."

He put on his best crestfallen expression. "The thought of those cookies brought me back from death, you know that?"

"Your stubbornness brought you back. The same thing that's keeping you from being home and recovering like you should be. You need to take better care of yourself, Jack. Gain some weight back."

"That's exactly where the cookies come in," he said, straight-faced.

She was laughing as he walked out the door.

In less than half an hour, he was in the woods off Spring Road, walking up to Bing.

The captain's eyes narrowed. "What are you doing here?"

"Was driving by, saw the commotion."

"And I'm a woodland fairy. You know what sick leave means? You stay home and heal."

"You sound like Leila. So what do we have?"

"A hiker called the place in." Bing shrugged, then called out, "Anything back there, Mike?"

"Locked up tight." Mike, the other rookie who'd joined the team the previous year with Joe, came around the cabin, a round Irish kid, red hair sticking up all over, eyes green as shamrocks, and a grin that betrayed he hadn't spent too much time on the force yet. He'd barely seen anything.

"Who owns the place?" Jack asked. "You called it in?"

Bing nodded. "It's been for sale for a couple of years. Sold recently, but the new deed hasn't been put into the system yet. When we're done here, Mike will go to the county clerk's office to look through the paper files."

"You think it's connected to Brady Blackwell?" Mike asked Jack with a little too much enthusiasm.

"Jack is not investigating Blackwell." Bing stepped in and effectively ended that topic.

Mike's enthusiasm didn't dim any. "Are we going in?"

"What do you think?"

The rookie's shoulders slumped after a second of thinking. "No probable cause, no search warrant. We have to walk away."

"Heard that, Jack?" Bing turned to him.

Jack strode up to one of the front windows, cupped his hands around his eyes, and looked in. A row of gun cabinets stood against the back wall, all filled. In the corner, a stack of metal boxes nearly reached the ceiling, probably ammunition and who knew what else. Instruments of torture, possibly. His muscles tightened.

He glanced back at the captain. "Kids are out in these woods all the time. Some testosterone-flooded teenage boy gets his hands on this stuff…"

"Until they do, there's nothing we can do about it." Bing swore under his breath.

"And if it's really connected to Blackwell?" Mike wanted to know.

Bing glared at him. "Get a fingerprint kit from the car. Let's see if you can lift anything off the door. If you get something, we can run it against the database."

They walked out to the road together. Bing drove away, heading back to the office. Mike popped the trunk of his cruiser. Among all the other emergency response supplies, a standard-issue army shovel caught Jack's eye, brand-new, still in the wrapper.

"Where you get that from?"

"Sunday flea market, the old Polish guy in the back row. He's gotten some army surplus in." Mike caught on the next second. "Already checked him. He sold two dozen in the last month, but he keeps no record of his customers. No credit card record either. Place like that, most people pay cash."

Jack filed the information away. He'd go check out the flea market on Sunday. But that was two days away, and he had things to do in the meanwhile. He strode back to his car and got in but didn't put the key in the ignition just yet. He pulled out his phone instead, then the piece of paper Leila had given him, with the phone number he'd asked her to track down.

He needed ammunition to break Ashley, and he had a feeling her father, William Price, would have it. If he was raising Ashley's daughter, it could mean only one thing: he didn't trust Ashley with the kid. Why?

He dialed the number, lining up his questions, hoping that this lead at last would take him somewhere, give him some answers. He let the phone ring a dozen times before he gave up and tossed it onto the passenger seat.

He pulled a different piece of paper from his other pocket, this one well used and wrinkled, a list of buildings in town that had a somewhat isolated location. One could possibly be the site of Blackwell's "workshop" where the bastard had tortured him.

The farmhouse where he'd been trapped, tased by a rigged-up mechanism as soon as he'd opened the door, had already been inspected several times over but was spotlessly clean, not a speck of dust in the place, let alone a fingerprint. He needed to find the torture chamber Blackwell had taken him to from there.

He'd been going through his list of possibilities one by one, whenever he had time for a drive. He'd already checked a dozen homes repossessed by various banks and sitting empty, closed-down businesses in town, and an old, crumbling silo that had nearly collapsed on top of him.

If he found a place, he might find a clue that could lead him straight to Blackwell. The "workshop" was somewhere in or near town. He'd been conscious—if tied and blindfolded—for the trip from the torture chamber to the grave. While the ride, with all that pain riddling his body, had seemed to last an eternity, he didn't think it took more than twenty to thirty minutes.

He unfolded the list and looked at the next item that hasn't been crossed off yet, the old firehouse, abandoned when the new state-of-the-art facility had been built, just before the recession had hit.

He drove over frozen roads, traffic sparse, then sparser yet as he reached the back roads again. The old firehouse had been built on the edge of town, back when they used the creek to fill the trucks with water. The new bigger one sat in the middle of the town, within easier reach.

The township still owned the building that now housed road-maintenance equipment. The building stood deserted and locked up for the moment. Jack pulled up to the front and eyed the big padlock on the door of the single bay.

Eddie Gannon had access to the place. Eddie was friendly with Ashley. Eddie was about the same build and age as Blackwell. Yet the voice was off, Jack thought. But could he trust his full-of-holes memory?

He got out of his car and walked around, looking in windows. He saw no suspicious activity, and, more importantly, no door that could have led to a basement. The two inside doors were open, one to a bathroom, the other to the kitchen.

And he'd definitely been held in some sort of a basement, the only thing he was sure of. The place had smelled like a basement. He could see a small strip under the blindfold, saw the stained cement floor. The light had been on 24/7. So he was looking for a basement without windows, most likely, but not necessarily. Could be Blackwell kept the windows boarded.

He was looking for a place away from other buildings, in an area that was deserted. Nobody had heard his screams.

For a few seconds, he stared at the big snowplow that took up most of the place, its cheery yellow color mocking him. Then he went back to his car with a disappointed grunt and crossed the firehouse off his list.

Only two more places to go. Another abandoned farm and the old train station. He was almost sure the old train station didn't have a basement either, the place little more than a shack. He checked it anyway. But neither the train station nor the farm panned out.

He called William Price again. And when the man, once again, ignored his call, Jack decided to swing into Philly. He didn't feel like going back to his lonely rental. The sticky note Leila handed him with the phone number also contained an address, in the posh Art Museum district.

He had some time to think on the way. He went down the list of things he knew about Blackwell for sure, as he did several times a day.

Name: unknown. Blackwell was a name he'd used early on at a motel where he'd stayed. He would have used a number of aliases, Jack expected.

Age: midthirties to midsixties.

Body type: medium, fit. He'd been strong enough to drag Jack into his car after he'd tased him.

Occupation: possibly something that required travel.

Smart. He'd outsmarted everyone for a long time now, taking victims when he pleased, as he pleased.

Strong possibility for sociopathic or psychopathic tendencies.

A collector. That would make sense, since he kept parts of his victims.

No accent of any kind.

Jack turned all that information over in his head, plus the timeline, the victims, every single clue strong or weak that he'd collected over the years. He was close, so close he could taste it. But he wasn't seeing the big picture yet, no matter from what angle he looked.

That left him pretty frustrated by the time he reached William Price's penthouse apartment. The doorman let him up when he identified himself as a police detective. But the housekeeper, a middle-aged woman named Bertha with ridiculously curly gray hair and a goofy mess of elbow macaroni necklaces, tried to make him wait outside the door upstairs. He simply pushed his way in. Then all his bluster leaked away when he saw a little girl, a small replica of Ashley Price, watching him from the lavishly furnished living room with anxious eyes. All right, he was a hard-assed bastard but not at the point yet where he would have enjoyed scaring small children.

"Hi, Maddie." He did his best to soften his face. "I'm Jack. I'm a friend of your mom." He stretched the truth there, more than a little.

The kid's face lit up with a smile. "Is my mom here?"

"No. I came to talk to your grandfather."

The man in question appeared through a doorway, holding a phone and tapping his earpiece, probably muting it. He cut an impressive figure, clean-cut in a conservative suit, with a faint air of superiority. He could have passed for a politician. "What is the meaning of this?"

"He says he's from the police," Bertha rushed to say.

"Detective Sullivan. Broslin PD. Not an emergency. Nothing bad. But I need to talk to you in private." He looked toward the little girl, who was hanging on their every word.

The man nodded. "I'm in the middle of an important meeting. Let me wrap up. Give me two minutes." Then he turned and tapped his earpiece again, walking away, probably back to his home office.

"I'm playing princess," Maddie said.

Definitely. The million-dollar Persian rug in the middle of the elaborately furnished living room was smothered with dolls and horses and castles. Some small toy stores had a lesser inventory, he was sure.

"The drawbridge is stuck," Maddie prattled on." If Prince William can't get to Princess Lillian, they can't fall in love."

A tragedy.

"Bertha can't fix it." The little girl looked at him expectantly.

Kids were trouble. He wasn't good at relating to kids. But it was clear that this one expected something from him.

He cleared his throat. "I could look at it."

The smile that lit up her face was nothing short of angelic. She had eyes the exact shade of green as Ashley's, and hair the same color too, except with some waves to it.

He strode over and went down to one knee, and wiggled the drawbridge that had gone off track. He pulled out his pocket knife and popped the piece of brown plastic back in, sliding it up and down a couple of times while Maddie clapped her hands and made happy kid noises.

He stood as Prince William rode his white horse into the castle, slid from the saddle, then stumbled his way up to the tower room to have tea. Poor bastard.

"Did you see my mom today?" Maddie asked while the prince and the princess gazed blankly at each other over a pink plastic miniature table. They didn't look like they were having the time of their lives, frankly.

"Not today."

She jumped up, scrambled over to the marble coffee table, and grabbed a sheet of paper from the pile. "I drew her a picture. It's me and Bertha making cookies. Can you take it to her?"

Someone out there might have been able to say no to that face, but he sure couldn't. He took the picture, two stick figures playing with something that looked like dog doo-doo. Didn't look like the kid had inherited her mother's art genes.

She kept looking at him expectantly.

A few seconds passed before he figured out what she wanted.

"Very, um, pretty."

Her smile widened another inch. Her tiny teeth were going to fall out if she didn't watch it. He'd never seen anyone that happy.

In stark contrast to her mother, who had shadows all around her.

"Can you take her some cookies too?"

In for a penny, in for a pound. "Sure."

Whatever her grandfather's reservations were, the kid clearly loved Ashley. The thought that he was here to dig up enough dirt on her to put her behind bars left Jack slightly uneasy. Which was plain stupid, so he shook off the feeling.

He stepped back, but if he'd been hoping for some distance from the kid, he wasn't about to get it.

Maddie grabbed his coat sleeve and dragged him through a door into the kind of fancy kitchen he'd only seen on cooking shows when he couldn't sleep in the middle of the night and clicked through the channels. Gleaming hardwood and granite stretched everywhere, punctuated by stainless-steel appliances that were at the high end of high end.

Bertha followed them with a pinched look on her face, but she did help with obtaining a plastic container from the fancy cabinetry.

"Would you like a cookie?" Maddie offered him a lopsided plop of brown something.

On second thought, her drawing wasn't too off the mark.

"No, thanks."

The smile began sliding off her face. "I made it."

He took the darn thing and bit in. The perfect sweetness spread on his tongue. Whatever the cookie looked like, Bertha had clearly made sure all the right ingredients had gone into it. "I like it."

She beamed at him.

Even Bertha seemed to defrost a little.

"Can we give some cookies to Jack too?" the little girl asked the housekeeper.

As Bertha produced a second container, William Price appeared in the doorway.

"Detective Sullivan. I should be able to talk to you now."

So Jack left Maddie and Bertha to pack the containers and followed the man back to his home office. Mahogany-paneled walls, floor-to-ceiling bookcases, a sprawling desk, an antique globe bar—the place looked like a movie set from a period movie about the English aristocracy, the smoking room where the gentlemen withdrew for cigars after a dinner party.

The man pointed to a sprawling leather armchair. "Since you're from Broslin, I assume this is about my daughter. I wasn't aware that the accident was still under investigation. Isn't it time to close the door on that unfortunate event?"

Didn't sound like he knew about the latest trouble. Interesting. Jack sat. "I'm not here about Dylan Miller."

The man stayed standing, leaning against his desk. He seemed the type who would enjoy the position of authority. Jack didn't mind letting him have it if it would set him at ease and make him more talkative.

"I'm here about the recent incident on Miss Price's property."
The man shot him a blank look.
So Ashley had told her father nothing. Maybe they weren't close
enough to share things. Although, this was pretty big, and they did
see each other regularly. He knew Price took his granddaughter
nearly every weekend to visit her mother.
"What incident?" the man demanded.
So Jack filled him in, keeping to the basics, not mentioning the
paintings.
"You can't think that my daughter has anything to do with this,"
Price charged Jack when he was finished.
"How close are you to your daughter?"
"Close enough to know what she's capable of. You people
harassed her enough. I don't want you to talk to her again without
a lawyer present."
"That's her choice, I believe."
"If you think—"
"Why are you raising your granddaughter? Why isn't she with her
mother?"
The man flashed a grim look. "Ashley has had a hard time since
the accident. Anybody would. Look, she's struggling with
depression. She's taking medication, and she will get better."
"You believe that her being alone is the best thing for her?"
"I offered her to come here."
Another interesting tidbit. He wondered why Ashley hadn't
accepted.
"She has this…anxiety," the man said. "She doesn't like to leave
her house. She's mentally fragile at the moment. But not like her
mother," he quickly added.
"Her mother?"
He'd found the story of the woman's meltdown and subsequent
death in the online archives, society pages, but he wanted to hear
Price's version.
The man stepped to the window and stared out, shoving his hands
deep into his pockets. "My late wife was an actress. Broadway.
She pushed herself. Stimulants to work, depressants to sleep, other
drugs she thought would help her with emotions and creativity. I
didn't realize at the beginning, and then… She's…" His jaw

tightened. "I'm not sure what happened at the end. She began having hallucinations. And then her heart gave out."

"How old was Ashley?"

"A teenager. A bad time to lose a mother."

"I don't suppose there's a good time."

Price nodded as he turned back to him. "I suppose you're right, Detective."

They shared a moment of silence while Jack thought of his own mother. He barely remembered her. He remembered Shannon a lot more clearly; the big sister who'd stepped into the mothering role and had taken care of him. Only he'd been too much of a snot-nosed teen to appreciate it. And then she was gone. Taken.

"Is Ashley seeing anyone?" he asked, although, all that time he'd spent watching her house, he hadn't seen anyone go inside her place and stay.

"No. What does that have to do with anything?" Price strode back to the desk. "Is she in any kind of danger?"

"We don't believe so. Nothing in the killer's profile says that he would go after her. His victims have always been carefully selected, two or three at a time. Then he moves on to a whole other state. This time, he wasn't hunting. He just wanted me off his trail."

Price didn't look reassured.

Jack watched for his reaction as he asked, "Can I ask where you were during the first three days of this month?"

"Now, listen—" he blustered immediately, but Jack raised a placating hand.

"I'm asking everyone I talk to regarding the case. No suspicion implied. Standard procedure."

But the man shot him another dark look before he glanced at his calendar. "Thursday and Friday I was at work, then here with Maddie and Bertha. Saturday my granddaughter and I went to see Ashley in Broslin."

An alibi easily checked, so no point lying about it.

Jack asked the man some questions about his job, about his relationship with Ashley, then more questions about his daughter, her childhood, her career.

William Price was a type-A, dominant personality. Ashley wasn't, although she had fire inside her, part of her artistic passion. But crimes of passion were usually part of domestic violence. Being a serial killer required cold ruthlessness. She didn't fit a killer profile, he thought for the dozenth time. But would she allow herself to be dominated by one? After all, she let her father call the shots regarding her daughter.

Could she be manipulated or forced into some sort of twisted relationship with Blackwell? Did Blackwell need an audience? Mementoes of his crimes? Was he using her for that?

But none of her paintings, other than the one of Jack, were of Blackwell's known victims. A lot of those crimes had been solved, and he couldn't find cracks, no matter how hard he'd looked, in the convictions.

Nothing made sense.

Frankly, her tale of dark visions came closest to an explanation, the only possibility he refused to consider.

He thought about the absurdity of her claims all the way back to Broslin, with two batches of grossly misshapen cookies on the passenger seat.

He wanted to give the cabin in the woods another look.

He found nobody there this time, so he picked the lock, eased inside, inch by careful inch, ducking low and watching for a trap. He looked through the arsenal, opened the boxes—ammunition and water bottles, no instruments of torture, no Taser, no human remains. He could see nothing he could tie to Blackwell, dammit.

*　*　*

Ashley looked at the small chunk of cheese and wilted celery in her nearly empty refrigerator. She was going to have to brave the grocery store tonight. She needed bread and milk, cold cuts, some microwave dinners for herself when Maddie wasn't here, and the makings for a healthy, homemade meal for her daughter tomorrow. Her father and Maddie were coming, finally. Which meant she couldn't put off the shopping trip any longer. As much as she dreaded the store, the thrill of seeing her daughter again gave her strength to do it. Their way-too-brief visits were the only thing that kept her going.

She closed the fridge door, then tidied up the old-fashioned tile countertop a little. Not that her small kitchen was messy. She'd already mopped the ancient glazed-brick floor. Once she filled the fridge and her plain oak cabinets, she'd be ready for visitors.

She'd go shopping after midnight; by then the store was usually deserted. She wasn't looking forward to sleep anyway. The night before, she'd dreamt of Detective Sullivan, had awoken with a start, then dreamed of him again. And again, variations of the same dream over and over. Always the dream started with him coming for her. Sometimes he took her to jail. Sometimes he made love to her.

She really was going crazy now, she thought as her phone rang. Her father.

"I just heard about the incident on your property. Good God, Ashley, why didn't you tell me?"

Her jaw clenched; a headache blinked awake in the back of her head and quickly intensified. "It was no big deal."

"A Detective Sullivan came to see me about a serial killer."

"They don't know that for sure. And the...victim is fine. It's over."

"I don't know if I feel comfortable bringing Maddie out there."

Her throat tightened. "But I didn't see her last weekend either."

"You shouldn't be out there alone."

Her head pounded too hard suddenly to point out that Broslin rarely had any violent crime, while there were half a dozen murders on the average day in Philadelphia where her father lived. Nausea rolled in her stomach. Her palms began to sweat, and with a shock, she realized what it meant. She knew what was coming. So damned unfair.

She squeezed her eyes shut. She shouldn't have another stupid vision. She'd saved a man's life. Shouldn't that have bought her some sort of salvation?

She fought back her rising desperation and focused on keeping her voice steady. "The police and the FBI were here for days on end. They checked every ditch and bush." She stared out the living room window into the moonlit night but barely saw the road or the fields on the other side. "Everything is perfectly safe."

"Why don't you come to my place? You could stay with us for a while. I'll even have Bertha set up a second room as a studio so you can paint."

The first impulse was to say no. Half a dozen excuses sprang to her tongue. She swallowed them.

If she could somehow go... She would see Maddie every single day. And she would never be alone in her father's eight-room penthouse that overlooked the art museum. She wouldn't have to jump at every noise the wind made in the trees. Her father would be there in the evenings and at night. During the day, she would have Bertha and Maddie. Maybe she wouldn't have another spell if she wasn't alone.

But if she gave up her hard-won independence, she wasn't sure if she could regain it again. She needed to fight the anxiety, not give in to it, or her life would become smaller and smaller.

That was the truth, and she knew it, but she also knew that she was using that truth as an excuse because she was terrified of driving into the city. If she were well, going to stay at her father's for a few days would be no big deal.

Then Maddie came on the phone and said, "Mom, Grandpa said you could come here." The little girl squealed. "Can you come today?"

Her sweet voice reached inside Ashley and got hold of her heart. She drew a deep breath, pushing down on the nausea. "How about tomorrow?" Her forehead broke out in cold sweat as she added, "First, I have to pack."

"She's coming! She's coming!" Maddie's voice wobbled as she probably jumped around with excitement. "Grandpa says we'll be expecting you. We'll be right here."

A black car shot down the road, slowed as it reached the end of her driveway, turned, its headlights cutting through the dark. Ashley's stomach dropped as she recognized Jack Sullivan's Crown Victoria. Her headache kicked up a notch.

"I better go and find some bags." She smacked a kiss into the phone. "Tell Grandpa I'll see you both tomorrow, okay?"

"I can't wait to tell Bertha. I'll help her make a room for you next to mine."

"I love you, Peanut." She hung up the phone as her body screamed, invisible powers pulling her toward the loft. She needed to paint, get the darkness out, and get it over with. But first, she had to get rid of the detective.

She unlocked the door and yanked it open before he had a chance to ring the doorbell, the last thing her blinding headache needed.

"Miss Price." He gave a curt nod, his expression closed, his tall frame and his fighter's stance more than a little intimidating.

His face really did have some interesting lines, especially the strong jaw. And that cerulean gaze too drew the eye. She imagined that another woman, one he wasn't trying to pin any crimes on, would find his masculine energy attractive. She had, in her dreams. But not now. Now she was just pissed at him.

"You had no right to talk to my father."

He cocked his head as he watched her. "Interesting that you wouldn't share something as big as this with him. Why is that?"

"I didn't want to worry him."

"You hide too much," he observed coldly.

Part of her wanted to slink away, to hide from him. But she was done accepting defeat. She would face down her demons and Jack Sullivan today. Tomorrow, she would go and see her daughter.

He towered on her doorstep, ready to go at her.

She hadn't played much sports since college, but she figured the best defense still had to be a good offense. She stuck her chin out as she said, "I want my paintings back."

As much as she hated those monstrosities, she hated someone else having them even more. If he hadn't shown them to anyone yet, she wanted to keep it that way.

He raised an eyebrow, looking utterly unimpressed with her newfound assertiveness as he pushed by her. "I brought you something from your daughter." He handed her a plastic box and a piece of paper she hadn't even seen him holding.

She closed the door against the cold and took what he was offering.

Cookies and a drawing, with "I miss you MOM" scribbled on top. Warmth spread through her chest for a second, then a blast of cold as her gaze flew to his. "She doesn't know, does she?"

He gave her a hard look. "I don't entertain five-year-olds with tales of serial killers."

She relaxed a little, then snapped when he still kept the displeased look on his face. "What? You can assume the worst of me, but I can't do the same of you?"

"She's a good kid," he said.

Which, for some reason, got her dander up. "And that's a surprise because I'm a crazed criminal? Are you here hoping for a confession?"

He watched her carefully, his full attention on her. "Anything you want to tell me, I'll be happy to hear it."

"I don't have time for you. I'm in the middle of a project." She had been working on a new painting earlier but had not planned on doing more today. She didn't like working with artificial light. It messed up her colors.

"Make time. Because I'll be coming back as many times as it takes. Count on it. Hope you don't have plans to leave town."

"I was going to stay with my father for a couple of days." He reached up to unbutton his coat.

Oh God, he can't possibly mean to stay. Her gaze slipped to his hands, the scars that crisscrossed his skin, to the tape that covered his missing fingernails. His knuckles looked like they'd been busted a couple of times. His fingers moved stiffly. He'd never be able to paint, she thought for a weird, disjointed moment, and felt sorry for him. She shook that off. He was the enemy.

Which he proved by saying, "I don't think so. For the time being, you need to stay here where we can reach you with further questions as needed."

As his wide shoulders emerged from the coat, tense, she imagined every muscle in his body was coiled, the predator ready to leap at a moment's notice. And she was the prey he'd set his eyes on, God help her.

Her headache pulsed. She had to paint. She'd stood up to the detective; now time to get rid of him.

"I really do have work to do. You can let yourself out." She walked toward the stairs.

Instead of taking the hint and leaving, he followed her all the way up to the loft. "You can talk and work at the same time."

Not when she was like this.

She looked around, anywhere but him, her stomach rolling. Her abstracts lined the loft, a sign of progress that encouraged her. She could do what she had to. She faced the man and put some force into her voice. "This is harassment. You need to leave."

He stiffened, dark thunder crossing his face, anger tightening his jaw. He stepped forward and grabbed her by the shoulders. "When you let Blackwell into your life," he threw the words into her face, "you're letting in a killer. Whatever sick hold he has on you... He is a dangerous man. Don't you at least care about your daughter?"

Fury washed over her, and she shoved against him. "You know nothing about me and my love for my daughter!" She stabbed his chest with her index finger, pushed forward, went on the offensive. "Blackwell is a sick killer," she agreed. "Maybe I'm sick too. But so are you. You're so obsessed with the man you can't see straight. You're a no-good, messed-up, obsessed cop. Now get your hands off me."

She got right up in his face, rose to her toes so they were eye to eye and he could see that she meant every word, that she was done cowering before him.

"Fine. And you're a freaked-out, loopy artist." For a moment, raw heat flashed in his gaze and his hands tightened on her arms. He held her like that for a split second, their faces inches apart, both of them breathing a little hard with their own fury. Then he set her apart and let her go.

"I will get him, one way or the other." His tone carried warning. She wanted to point out that Blackwell was not here, so he should look elsewhere, but suddenly the dam broke and a torrent of images flooded her. Her headache intensified to the point of being unbearable, her peripheral vision darkening.

She strode to a shelf, grabbed a prepped canvas board, and slammed it onto an empty easel, hoping he would leave at last, now that he'd done his best to intimidate her. She couldn't fight him anymore, not right now. What she faced now, what dark force threatened to drown her was bigger than the detective and his accusations.

Dizziness swirled through her, too much to handle suddenly. She reached for the wall to steady herself but got the detective's arm instead.

"What is it?" His tone was cold and hard, his eyes full of suspicion.

"Bad headache." She rubbed her temple. "Migraine."

"A play for sympathy? I'm afraid that doesn't work with me. Why don't you just tell me the truth?"

"Why don't you leave?" She wanted the words to be an order but found herself nearly begging.

"Because I don't have yet what I came for."

For a moment, the pain that sliced through her head was blinding. Her stomach rolled. She squeezed her eyes shut. When she opened them, his face was once again just inches from hers.

His cerulean gaze held hers for a long moment, his thoughts undecipherable. He pushed her down onto her ratty old armchair, then crossed over to the sink and brought her a glass of water. "Do you have some pain pills you could take?"

She took the glass and drank, refusing to let her hands shake. "They don't make pills for what I have." The antidepressants hadn't helped either, so she'd stopped taking them a long time ago. He took the empty glass from her. "It's the stress. Once you confess, you'll feel better."

Hopelessness washed over her, a wave of misery, then anger, which she liked better. She'd painted him in the grave just a few weeks ago. She shouldn't have a spell again this soon. Sometimes she went months and months in between. She'd been hoping, damn him, that she would never have another gruesome vision.

"Has Blackwell threatened you?" he asked with concern that was probably pretend. "I can offer protection if you turn prosecution witness. The offer still stands."

She barely heard him as nervous energy pushed her to her feet. She walked to the cluttered table by the wall and reached for her palette. "Please leave."

She didn't want to let him see how bad it was, what it did to her. If he saw, if anyone ever saw, they'd stick her in the loony bin. And then she would lose her daughter forever.

But he stayed where he stood. And when she couldn't take the images in her head, the tension and the pain any longer, she squeezed a dab of soulless black onto the palette, then a row of other colors, leaving the crimson last.

And then she painted.

Chapter Five

Whatever had hold of her scared the spit out of her. But she stood her ground in front of the canvas and worked. While her posture was rigid, her hand moved in a fluid motion, concentration on her face.

The fire she'd attacked him with was gone. That had been interesting. Made him respond in more ways than one—his body was still buzzing with the sudden contact. She was such a study in contrast, fear and courage, fire and innocence. She had the looks, but layers too, and talent and depth. And one seriously sick friend.

"Talk to me, Ashley."

But she was no longer aware of him, creating in a trance, in the grip of a vision only available to her. Or doing a hell of a job faking it.

The artist in her studio. Except he'd imagined the creative process differently. He would have thought artists got joy out of creating. She clearly didn't.

"Ignoring me isn't going to work."

But she kept doing it.

For a second, he looked away from her to the wall of windows. Outside, the darkness seemed extra thick tonight, smothering the landscape rather than settling on it. Even the pale moon looked brittle in the sky. And there was something in the house too, some strange tension he couldn't identify that was separate from the tension emanating from her.

Jack moved a step closer to shield her, his senses on full alert, his body tightening as if expecting an attack. But from where? He was pretty sure they were alone in the house, had made a point to glance in every open door he'd walked by.

Yet he felt an odd need to protect her, although he couldn't have said from what. He shook his head to clear it. He was tired. He still wasn't himself yet, not fully. He was building his body back, but it took time.

A small gasp escaping her lips drew his attention to her. The expression on her face was pure torture.

A chill skated down his spine as he watched. The touch of that icy finger felt so real that he whipped around. Nothing behind him.

His jaw muscles drew tight. Great. Now he was going to start acting strange? The shrink had said something like this might happen. PTSD.

Like hell. He rolled his shoulders. He wasn't going to let Blackwell drive him crazy. He wasn't going to let Blackwell win.

Ashley guided the brush across the canvas. She looked haunted and in pain. He didn't like that he seemed to be responding to the despair she was drowning in. He didn't want to pity her.

And he definitely didn't want to want her.

Yet he'd thought about her. He'd thought about her in ways an investigator shouldn't think about a suspect. Her pinup-girl body and her haunted eyes were a pretty potent combination.

The smell of paint and turpentine filled the air. It brought back all those jumbled memories of being in her house for the first time, of having just escaped from the grave and every inch of his body screaming in pain.

He rubbed a hand over his healing ribs as he watched her mix more colors. Her face tight, she winced every couple of seconds, as if the very act of painting hurt her. Then her hand stilled, and for a moment, she stared off somewhere beyond the easel.

"What is it?" He looked at the same blank wall, then moved closer to the canvas that now held a preliminary sketch of walls closing in a small space.

She loaded her brush and began filling out the details, her eyes darting between the blank wall and the painting, as if copying something that remained hidden to his senses. One of those visions she spoke of? Or was she trying to con him?

If she was faking it, she was a better actress than he'd ever seen in any movie.

He could play along for a little while. "What do you see?"
She rubbed her forehead with the back of her hand, closing her
eyes for a second. "A face."
That didn't make any sense. It couldn't be real. Which didn't mean
she didn't think it was. According to her father, the accident on the
reservoir had messed her up pretty badly. Maybe her brain had
been affected.
She made no sound save for tapping the brush on the palette from
time to time. More shapes took form; objects materialized out of
color alone. The interior of a dark, confined place took up most of
the canvas. Clothes hung above a pile of boxes on the floor. Low
in the right corner, stroke by stroke, a human form appeared.
"Who is that?"
His words could have been gunshots for the shock they gave her.
As if she'd forgotten, in the space of a few minutes, that he was
standing behind her. Her shoulders dropped. "Someone who can't
be saved."
"How do you know him?"
"I don't."
Part of him responded to the strong emotions rolling off her—
horror, dismay, fear—and his protective instincts rose. He set that
ridiculous impulse aside. "How do you know where he is? How to
paint him? Did Blackwell show you? Did he bring you pictures?"
She whirled on him with tears in her eyes, anger tightening her
mouth. "The picture is in my head! Don't you think I would stop it
if I could? You really think I want this?"
He glanced back and forth between the canvas and the despair on
her face. No, she didn't look like she wanted any of this. For the
first time, he wasn't sure what to say. He didn't like it.
She turned back to the painting and lifted her brush again. By the
time she completed the last finishing touches, her shoulders hung
limp, fatigue rimming her eyes. She cleaned her brushes on
autopilot, barely looking, stuck them in an old, stained spaghetti
jar, then slumped into the lumpy armchair by the window, legs
pulled up under her, arms wrapped around herself, looking out into
the darkness without really seeing anything as far as he could tell.
"Go away," she whispered.
When he was ready.

He pulled his phone from his pocket and snapped a dozen pictures of the painting. Then he stepped away from the easel to walk around the room, paying little attention to the large abstracts he didn't understand, his gaze returning to the easel in the middle over and over again.

She sat with her eyes closed and her hands up to shade them from the light.

"Head still hurts?"

"It'll be better in a minute."

Not having the light in her eyes would probably help. He strode to the top of the stairs and flipped the switch. Some light still filtered up from downstairs, but the loft was lost in a twilight of semidarkness that surrounded them like a cocoon.

He could no longer see the painting clearly, but every detail had been etched into his mind, the entire image, and the way she'd created it.

His brain circled back to the same question over and over again. What had he just witnessed? A carefully choreographed performance was the only logical answer. He didn't believe in psychic phenomena.

The police departments he'd worked for over the years often received calls from psychics on high-profile cases. "I see a body near water." "A body near a cabin." All general predictions, bound to come true once in a blue moon in an area that was riddled with creeks and lakes, or in woods where hunting cabins abounded. Out of a hundred calls, one would hit close enough for the media to make a big deal out of it and it would be splashed all over the news as "proof." Even a blind squirrel found an acorn now and then— law of statistics—was his opinion.

And if Ashley Price wasn't psychic… Blackwell had to be somehow behind her convincing little play. He walked around, trying to figure out their game.

As he passed by the bank of windows, he caught sight of a dark figure outside, illuminated by moonlight at the edge of the trees, and the last small doubts he might have had disappeared. Blackwell.

Instantly, his entire body was alert. "I need some air. You stay inside."

She still had her eyes closed. She didn't even acknowledge him, too busy to be pretending to be off in her own little world of dire visions.

Had the bastard come to watch the performance? To make sure she was convincing?

Jack brushed past her and took the stairs two steps at a time. He ran through the house, burst through the door, nearly slipping on the slick steps outside. He caught his balance and set off across the snow.

The shadow man took off, slip-sliding on a patch of ice. Jack pushed forward, sucking in his breath against the cold. He'd left his gloves in his car. He shoved his hands under his armpits as he ran. He'd need his fine motors skills when the time came to go for his gun and squeeze the trigger.

Adrenaline filled him, and elation.

Now. He would have the bastard this time.

The man up ahead jumped a ditch and scrambled up a snowy incline. He slipped back. Jack put everything he had into an all-out dash, caught up, and vaulted on top of the rising figure.

"I didn't do anything!"

Not Brady's voice. Definitely, not. This one sounded much younger.

Disappointment slammed into him like a fist.

He flipped the gangly boy onto his back and held him by the front of his down jacket with both hands. "Who the hell are you? What are you doing out here?"

The kid, about fourteen or fifteen, stared up at him, wide-eyed and breathing hard from his dash, scared now. "They dared me…go out to the creek in the dark. Where that cop was buried."

"They who?"

"My friends."

Jack pulled both of them to standing, anger pumping through him. Every breath stung; the cold bit into his skin. "And where are your friends now?"

"They were right behind me. I think they took off when they saw you coming. I didn't do nothing wrong."

He gritted his teeth. "You were trespassing." But he let the boy go. Stupidity wasn't a crime.

He watched as the kid scampered toward the road without looking back. "And don't come here again! This is private property," he called after him.

The adrenaline had worn off, and his whole body ached, reminding him that he was far from fully recovered. He swore, hating the weakness. He couldn't afford aches and pains. When he caught up with Blackwell, he needed to be ready.

He hadn't been ready tonight. He'd seen the shadowy figure, rage had taken over, and he'd acted without thinking. What the hell was wrong with him, tackling that kid? But he could have sworn…

He took a slow breath, let his lungs fill with cold air.

Bing would warn him about becoming so obsessed that he was starting to see what he wanted to see. Good thing the captain hadn't been here to witness this.

He rubbed his hand over his face, then climbed out of the ditch and slogged back through the snow. Her front steps were covered in snow and ice, he registered again, and reached for the shovel leaning against the stairs before he realized the handle was broken. He kicked the snow off the steps the best he could, then walked inside, stepped out of his snowy boots, and padded up the stairs.

Ashley stood at her easel, arms wrapped tightly around her body, staring at the painting in the semidarkness.

He came to a stop behind her, trying to see what she saw when she looked at the macabre image. "There were some teenagers out back."

"What?" She turned, her eyes disoriented. She blinked a few times. "Sometimes I hear snowmobiles in the night. Just kids having fun."

He looked back at the canvas because he suddenly couldn't stand the broken look in her eyes. In the dark, the painting looked muted, almost black and gray, precious few light areas with way too many shadows, the old man in the lower right quadrant lifeless and crumpled.

"It would be best if you told the truth," he said but didn't have it in him to really get up into her face again. The run and tackle out in the cold had taken the bluster out of him, as did her palpable misery.

He wanted the whole vision thing to turn out to be fake. Like he'd wanted the kid out there to be Blackwell. But if he wasn't strong enough to accept reality, he wouldn't be strong enough to catch the bastard. And reality was that she'd painted the image out of nothing. Reality was his cop instincts said she wasn't faking her emotions. His most basic instincts said she was real in every way. And as much as he resisted it with all the willpower he had, something inside him responded to her.

She is going to be a complication.

He didn't like the idea. He didn't like that someplace deep inside, he was softening toward her. He'd come for something completely different.

Her chin came up and she held his gaze, some of her fire coming back as she said, "You want the truth? The truth is, I'm going crazy."

Okay, not what he'd expected, but he considered the words for a second. He'd certainly seen his share of the mentally unbalanced in his years of working for various police forces. "People who are crazy usually insist that they're completely sane."

She didn't seem relieved. "Are you going to take this painting too?"

He didn't need it; he had the photos on his phone. He nodded anyway. "It's evidence." Although of what, he couldn't say.

And he wasn't sure whether he was taking the damned thing because part of him wanted to give her a break and he didn't like that so he felt the need to make sure he wouldn't give an inch. Or because it looked like the painting was hurting her and he felt some weird need to stop it.

He didn't do emotions.

He sure as hell didn't do mixed emotions.

"Don't leave town," he said, to make sure the both of them knew it.

Deathscape

Chapter Six

After a night that started pretty roughly, then continued with her tossing and turning, worrying about what Jack Sullivan would do with her paintings, Saturday morning came too early. Ashley lay in bed, the bedroom dim in the gray winter morning light.

She looked at her cell phone on the nightstand, dread and disappointment filling her little by little. She had to call her father and Maddie, let them know she couldn't come today.

Detective Sullivan had ordered her to stick around. On any other day, it wouldn't have been a problem. But today was the day she was supposed to show her father that she was making progress. She wanted to get into her car and try, even if her throat would close up when she reached I-95. Even if she would be gasping for air and swimming in cold sweat. Even if she had to pull over. Even if it took her all morning to make the two-hour drive.

She needed to face her fears. She couldn't give up, or she'd never have Maddie back.

She sat up in bed. She would not give up. She felt stronger now than last night. She would call Jack Sullivan and demand her freedom back. She hadn't committed any crimes, hadn't been charged with anything. He had no right to put her under house arrest or whatever he was doing.

She reached for her cell phone just as the sounds of a rumbling motor reached her from outside. A snowmobile. She hesitated. Maybe she should go and talk to those kids and warn them about the creek. Her property in the back was really becoming a mess.

Come spring, she would have to hire Eddie to clean it up a little. If one of those kids got hurt on her land...

She pushed to her feet and hurried to the closet, shrugged into the first set of clothes she put her hands on, jeans and a thick sweater. She shoved her phone into her pocket and hurried downstairs, combing her hair with her fingers as she ran. She wanted to catch those kids before they rode away.

She jumped into her boots and grabbed her coat, and could still hear the motor, coming closer, when she rounded the house. But as she reached the back, it was Eddie driving a snowmobile from the woods, pulling a log on a chain. And then she saw his beat-up pickup parked to the side.

"Did I wake you?" he asked with an apologetic smile as he stopped and turned off the engine. He wore his usual quilted flannel jacket and wool cap, lumberjack boots, and work gloves—he looked like someone out of a maple-syrup commercial.

"I needed to wake up. When did you get here?"

"About an hour ago. I've been looking around out back. Plenty of fallen branches. A couple of trees too. Water washed out the roots of a pretty big oak at the far end of the creek, probably when all that snow melted after Christmas."

"Take as much as you need." He was doing her a favor, really. He used most of the wood in his woodstove and the big stumps for chain-saw art he made and sold, proving her point that deep inside, everybody was an artist.

He opened his mouth to say something but then looked toward the road, and his eyes narrowed.

She followed his gaze. A black SUV slowed at her driveway and pulled in. The car rolled all the way up to her front door, and three men wearing dark suits spilled out. Her stomach sank as she recognized them: FBI.

"I better see what that's about." She stomped up front.

Were they ever going to leave her alone?

The tallest of the men—early thirties, crew-cut blond hair, cold eyes—reached into his pocket and pulled out his ID as she reached them. "Agent Hunter, FBI. We met a few weeks ago."

"What is this about?"

"We need you to come with us, ma'am."

Her heart rate picked up. Why now? They'd been out here and had looked over her land, had found nothing and left. Had something new come up? Suddenly, with a sinking heart, she realized what that might be.

Jack Sullivan had handed over her paintings.

She had no idea how she was going to talk her way out of this. Her throat tightened. "I need to lock up."

"Of course."

The agents followed her in when she went inside to get her keys. "Do you think I could have five minutes? I ran outside this morning without getting ready for the day."

"No problem."

But Agent Hunter went upstairs with her, checked out her bathroom before she went in. At least he let her close the door behind her. She took care of her morning needs, too nervous to do more than the bare minimum.

What would they make of her paintings? She brushed her teeth with jerky, frenetic movements. Did she need a lawyer?

She'd had one after the accident on the reservoir. She could call him again. She hesitated. Not yet. Lawyering up right now would just make her look guilty. Not to mention she didn't have the money. But she would definitely call if things got any worse.

On the way out to the car, she looked to the backyard, wanting to tell Eddie that she was leaving, but Eddie had gone back into the woods already. He wasn't the type to sit around; when he worked, he gave one hundred percent. One of the many reasons why the town kept him even with the budget cuts last fall.

Whatever maintenance personnel they had left now answered to him. The town trusted him with all kinds of things, even sent him to tradeshows out of state to check out new road-maintenance equipment they needed. He'd been proud of that.

"Are you getting some work done on the property?" Agent Hunter asked as he opened the back door of the SUV for her, looking at Eddie's pickup.

"Just giving away some firewood."

The agent watched her through narrowed eyes, a cold expression on his face, not looking like he believed her. Which didn't bode well for the upcoming questioning. She was innocent, had nothing to do with Brady Blackwell or Jack Sullivan's troubles. How did she end up getting pulled deeper and deeper into all this mess?

At the end of her driveway, the car turned onto the road toward Broslin. Cold sweat gathered on her forehead as she clasped her hands on her knees. And her phobias were the least of her problems.

She hated, absolutely hated Jack Sullivan for forcing her secret out, then doing this to her.

* * *

The fans on the ceiling whirled in a futile effort to evenly distribute the heat through the Broslin Police Station. The phones rang off the hook; the department's ancient copy machine grated on, giving everyone within ten feet an instant headache,

Nobody sat behind the front desk. Leila didn't work weekends. She kept office hours Monday through Friday. The rest of the time, the nearest person answered the phone. Whoever was unlucky to be on duty had to fend for himself.

"No, ma'am. We can't arrest your neighbor's dog for getting yours with puppies. I'm sorry, ma'am." Jack listened. "You'd have to go to court for, ah, puppy support; we don't do that either." He let the old woman rage at him for another minute before politely saying good-bye and hanging up.

And, miraculously, there wasn't another call immediately.

He sat at his desk and watched the closed door of the interrogation room. The news that the FBI had brought in Ashley Price was the first thing he'd heard when he'd come in for his exercise this morning. Okay, when he'd come in to talk Bing into letting him back on at least partial duty.

Then he caught sight of her through the half-closed blinds, and he chose to sit at his desk instead, from where he could keep an eye on her while surreptitiously signing into the database on his computer. Not that the data could hold his attention. Twice he'd come to his feet to barge in. Twice he'd sat himself back down.

Bing was in his office, talking on the phone but keeping an eye on him.

Joe and Chase were off duty. Mike was out on some call. Harper, Broslin's black sheep turned cop, was the only other person in the office.

"Want some coffee?" he asked Jack as he put down his phone and headed for the coffee machine.

"Had too much already. Hey," Jack called after him. "Any missing persons since I've been out?"

Harper poured his coffee, then strode back to him, tall and lean, a ladies' man, if the gossip was to be believed. To his credit, he didn't parade his women around the office like Joe. Harper liked to keep his private life private.

"No one's gone missing. A single murder all week, early this morning, not ours, over in West Grove. Looks like nephew kept his old-man uncle locked up in a closet, starved him to death while he spent the vic's social security checks."

"People are idiots." Jack reached for the mouse and brought up the crime-scene photos of the West Grove murder in the central database, dozens of shots of the old guy's closet, with and without the body.

The short hairs stood straight up at the back of his neck as he took in the spookily familiar images on his screen—an old man folded on the floor, stacks of boxes at his feet, clothes hanging above him. Exactly as in Ashley's painting.

"Remind me not to get old." Harper scanned the images.

"Neighbor called it in. They hadn't seen the old guy in a while. Hell of a thing is, if they'd called a day earlier, the poor geezer could have been saved."

Jack looked at TOD. Time of death was approximately eight p.m. last night. Just when Ashley had begun painting.

An unpleasant shiver ran down his spine as Harper saluted him with his coffee mug, then sauntered away.

If Ashley did have visions, if she wasn't pretending…

Whatever was happening to her was taking a damn heavy toll, he had seen that. Hell, he was a tough-ass cop, and he wasn't sure he could live with something like that.

Bing got off his phone at last and headed for him. "You're only supposed to come in to use the gym for your physical therapy."

"Reporting back to duty, sir." Jack winced when his side brushed against an open drawer.

"Like hell."

"I'm all healed."

"Bullshit."

"Healed enough."

Bing's gaze turned to steel. "I'm the captain. Keeping my men safe is my top priority. Go home."

"I could be useful on this case," he said reasonably.

"Like a screen door on a submarine. You were one of Brady's victims. Your sister was one of Brady's victims. Can you say conflict of interest?"

Frustration tightened his jaw. "You can't keep me on sick leave forever."

"I can try. I sure as hell am not gonna lose you again."

A few moments of charged silence passed between them.

Jack broke it first. "What happened to me wasn't your fault."

"One of my men went missing, and I couldn't find him." Bing dropped into Joe's empty chair at the next desk, the fight going out of him. "You still look like death chewed on you before spitting you out."

Which was exactly what had happened, come to think of it. And yet… "I can't sit at home. How about desk duty? Partial duty?"

The man gave an irritated huff. "You looked right into my goddamn eyes and lied. You hadn't come to Broslin for a job. You came to hunt Blackwell. And you didn't say a damn word about it. I thought we were friends."

The words made him feel like dirt. Technically, he hadn't lied. He just hadn't told Bing everything. But he was in the wrong, and he knew it, so he wasn't about to defend himself. "I want Blackwell," he said simply.

"You stay away from that bastard if you want your badge."

Tense silence stretched between them.

"She was my sister," Jack said after a while. "I can't let this go. Could you? If you had Stacy's killer within reach?"

Bing's wife had been killed two years before, during a home invasion, the killer never apprehended, zero leads.

His mouth narrowed into a thin line. "Don't you dare throw that into my face. I had let it go. You know why? Because I swore an oath to the citizens of this town to protect them. Not to pursue my own vengeance, dammit."

"You're a better man than I am," Jack said, and meant it. He had carried the darkness around inside him for too long. It had changed

him, he knew that. He didn't care. He was so close now, he just
wanted to see this to the end, wanted to see Blackwell finished.
"I can't sit around at home and do nothing. All I do is think about
Shannon and that bastard. It drives me crazy," he admitted. "Let
me come back."

Bing watched him.

The phone rang again. Harper answered it.

Bing shook his head after a couple of seconds. "Hell, maybe work
would keep you busy, keep you out of trouble. Desk duty only."
He scowled as he thought for another second. "On three
conditions. You pass the physical, you talk to the shrink, and you
stay away from the Blackwell case."

He leaned forward, into the I-mean-business pose they all used in
the interrogation room. "I catch you as much as looking at that
bastard's file from across the room, and you're going back on
leave. Is that clear?"

Jack scratched the back of his head and let the captain interpret it
whatever way he wanted.

Bing leaned back in the chair, his shoulders relaxing a little. "I
don't suppose you remembered anything new?"

Jack shook his head. He'd been in and out for those three days he'd
been missing, the details sketchy. The fact that he'd been
blindfolded complicated things. And so far he hadn't remembered
anything that could have given them a clue on where Blackwell
had taken him after tasing him at that abandoned farmhouse. "I
was in some kind of a workshop, that's all I remember. He had
plenty of tools handy. Somewhere in a basement, I think, cement
floor, a woodstove and fan, a metal chair he chained me to."

Bing winced. "It'll come back. You need to give yourself a chance
to recover."

"Feds said anything about why they brought Ashley Price in?" he
asked after a few seconds, reaching for his coffee cup, gesturing
toward the interrogation room with it. "She has nothing to do with
anything."

A bushy eyebrow rose. "Now you're defending her?"

"Swore to protect the innocent and all that."

"I'm sure they're not going to waterboard her in there."

Yeah, but they would push her, push her hard, and she had enough stress on her already. She needed somebody on her side. She needed a damn lawyer. Why the hell didn't she hire one?
For the hundredth time, he considered just marching in there. Trouble was, he wasn't sure if that would really help her.
Bing's eyes narrowed. "Ashley Price and the Feds are not your concern."
"What else is going on, then?" Better take the captain in another direction before he kicked him out of the station.
"Still the damn string of break-ins, a handful of shoplifters, two domestic violence cases, and a parole violation, none of which you'll touch. You're on desk duty. Try not to forget it."
The interrogation room door opened, and Agent Hunter stepped out, apparently to take a call. Jack caught a glimpse of Ashley through the gap in the door. He didn't like her distressed expression.
"Be back in a sec." He jumped up and strode forward. By the time he reached the agent, the man was putting his phone away.
Jack shoved his hands into his pockets. "Anything new?"
The man flashed him a cold look. "I'm not at liberty to say. However, I do need to see you, Detective Sullivan, as soon as we're finished here."
"Regarding?"
"I understand you've paid Miss Price several visits lately."
"She saved my life. I owed her a proper thank-you."
The agent quirked an eyebrow. "Then you wouldn't be, by any chance, investigating?"
"Interfering with an FBI investigation could cost me my badge," he deadpanned.
"Let's not forget that, Detective."

* * *

The interrogation room was small, drab gray, and oppressive. It made her anxious. Then again, what didn't? She couldn't remember the last time she'd been as far from her house as the police station.
Ashley steeled her spine. She refused to live the rest of her life in fear.
"When was the first time you met Detective Sullivan?" Agent Hunter asked.

"The night I found him."

"But you didn't know who he was at the time?"

"No. He was unconscious for the most part." Except when he'd forced her to drive back to her house.

"When was the first time you heard the name Brady Blackwell?"

"A few days later, when the police asked me about him."

The agent threw more questions at her, his voice becoming more clipped with each, his shoulders growing stiffer. In a way, she understood him. He wanted a solution, a bankable lead. He wanted a victory and probably the promotion that would come with it, and he didn't like that he wasn't getting what he needed from her.

She pulled her neck in and waited for the bomb to drop.

But as the questions kept coming, he didn't ask about her paintings. In fact, he sounded like they hadn't discovered any leads lately, which was why they were going back, covering old ground. So maybe Jack Sullivan hadn't betrayed her after all but kept her secret. She wasn't sure what to make of that.

"People say you keep to yourself. Why?" Agent Hunter kept pushing. He was like a robot. He was checking off checkboxes in his head, marching forward, going for the win.

Jack was just as determined but not as detached. The case was personal for him. Blackwell had put him in the grave.

"I work a lot," she answered the question.

"And you have no idea who might have buried Detective Sullivan on your land? You had nothing to do with it?"

"No." She'd said that over and over again. "Am I an official suspect?"

"Yes."

She closed her eyes for a second. A suspect. Not even just a "person of interest."

Agent Hunter was hungry for a win. Jack had a personal vendetta. Captain Bing hated her guts to start with… Her future looked bleaker with every passing minute.

The agent pinned her with a cold look. "You had opportunity. The grave is on your land."

"But I didn't put Jack Sullivan into that grave. He can tell you I didn't."

"You could have helped Blackwell after Detective Sullivan had lost consciousness."

She gritted her teeth. Painting her latest vignette of horror and Jack's interrogation the night before had left her drained. She didn't have enough for another fight. "What possible motive could I have?"

He waited, held out the silence. "Am I correct that your mother died in a mental institution?"

And craziness could be hereditary. Crazy people didn't need a motive. A chill ran through her. Was that what they were going to run with?

"That has nothing to do with me," she protested.

"Doesn't it?"

She stared at the man. Were they this desperate? Did they care more about the win than the facts? Maybe they did. It wasn't like the innocent had never been made to pay for crimes they didn't commit. She'd seen plenty of shows on TV about people who'd been wrongly convicted and were only recently released, saved by DNA. Some had been in prison for decades.

And if Agent Hunter won...

He wouldn't. She was going to beat the FBI, beat Jack Sullivan, return her life to normal, and get her daughter back. She wasn't going to lose Maddie over this. Whatever she had to do—

"I would like to call my attorney," she said, although she was no longer sure that would be enough.

But the possible solution that suddenly burst into her head scared her as much as the false accusations, maybe more. Her entire body went cold. She considered the idea anyway.

What if she didn't resist her visions?

What if she embraced them? Would she see more? Would she see how Sullivan had come to be in the grave? Would she see Blackwell? Could she lead the authorities to him to end this nightmare?

Did she dare willingly walk into the abyss? And what if she did and couldn't find her way back? Would she end up like her mother and lose everything?

She needed to think this over, needed to get out of here. "I want to call my lawyer," she repeated.

The agent closed his notebook and rose. "You're entitled to an attorney, but we're done for today."

She swallowed hard. "I was going to stay with my father in Philadelphia for a few days, if that's okay." If the Feds released her, Jack Sullivan couldn't do anything. She held her breath for the answer.

But the man shook his head. "I'd rather that you stuck around for the time being."

Disappointment washed over her. She'd talk to her lawyer about this too. She had to see Maddie.

She walked out to the main area of the police station, thinking about the lawyer and how she could force a vision somehow, if she could make that work. Her gaze caught on Jack Sullivan. He hadn't been in earlier. Now he was watching her from behind a desk, across the room.

He pushed to his feet. Then Captain Bing appeared at the door of his office, stared at Jack, and Jack sat back down with dark thunder on his face.

Ashley took advantage of the reprieve and hurried out, but came to a screeching halt in the parking lot. Agent Hunter had brought her in. She didn't have her car.

He appeared in the doorway behind her before she could turn back in. "I'll have one of the uniformed officers drive you home, Miss Price. Just give me a minute."

But before she could thank the man, Sullivan came hurrying around the building. He must have come out somewhere in the back.

"I'll take care of it."

"I need to talk to you," the agent told him with a scowl of disapproval.

He didn't look too concerned. "I'll be back in a couple of minutes."

"See that you are." Agent Hunter went back inside as Sullivan strode up to her.

"I'm not up for another interrogation, Detective. I'd just as soon call a cab." Ashley steeled herself for more accusations, but none came.

Instead, he said, "Call me Jack. No more interrogation today. Just a ride, I promise."

She flashed him a doubtful look.

"I could recommend a couple of decent lawyers," he said. He looked tired around the eyes. Maybe he had as much trouble with sleep as she did. "You shouldn't be alone when they question you."

She found the sudden concern suspicious. "You came to my house and badgered me when you had questions. I don't remember you recommending a lawyer then."

He didn't have a comeback for that.

"I have an attorney. I had to get one after the accident," she informed him as he walked to his black Crown Victoria and opened the passenger door.

She thought for a couple of seconds before she got in. Only because spending some time with Sullivan, Jack, now, might make bringing back the vision later easier.

"What did the FBI want?" he asked once he'd gone around and folded his lean frame behind the wheel.

"Same thing as you do, to prove me guilty." She closed her eyes for a second. "It'd be easiest for everyone."

"Yes."

"Except for me."

"Except for you," he agreed and drove out of the parking lot, pulling into traffic.

Since the town was old, the streets at the center of it were pretty narrow, made narrower yet by the cars parked on either side. Just as they crossed the first intersection, a truck stopped in front of them to make a delivery. Horns beeped as Jack maneuvered around it.

She grabbed the sides of her seat and held on tight. On the way to the police station, she'd sat in the back and closed her eyes for most of the trip. In the front seat, it was more difficult to ignore that she was out and about in town, away from her safe place. Sweat slicked her palms.

Jack glanced at her.

"So, weird thing the other day," he said conversationally as he turned his attention back to the traffic, none of his usual intensity in evidence for the time being. "Call comes in about an accident. Thirty-two-year-old guy fell out of the window of his pickup on Route 30 with his pants down."

That caught her attention. "How do you fall out of the window of your car while driving?"

He shook his head, one corner of his mouth tilting up into an almost smile. "Turns out one of his buddies was driving. Our genius was mooning the passing cars out the passenger-side window, squatting on the seat. His buddy swerved, and the idiot fell right out. Broke his shoulder and a leg, on top of some pretty nasty lacerations."

She stared at him, trying to picture the scene. "Nobody can be that dumb, can they?"

"Not the stupidest thing I've seen on the job, by far," he said and started into another outlandish tale.

He fell silent when they stopped at a red light, looking at the mushroom factory on the corner.

She followed his gaze. "What is it?"

"The boss's car is up front. I've been trying to catch him. I'll do it on the way back. After I drop you off."

"You can talk to him right now, if you want." If this had to do with Blackwell, the sooner they caught him and cleared her, the happier she was.

"Are you sure?"

She nodded, and when the light turned green, he pulled up in front of the place.

She went into the main office area with him, waited while he talked to the secretary, then while he went back to talk to the owner. More than a dozen paintings of various mushrooms hung on the walls. She walked around and checked those out. They were pretty good, actually.

"These weren't here last time I was here," Jack commented when he came back out.

"Greg Shatzkin," she said. "Local artist."

"He spent days here, taking hundreds of photos for those," the secretary put in proudly.

Jack went still. "When?"

"Oh, that'd be over a year ago now, I think." The woman smiled at him.

Oddly enough, Jack seemed to find the information captivating. "How would I reach him?"

"I'm not sure. We worked with him through the Lanius Gallery. Graham arranged everything."

"What was that about?" Ashley asked as they walked out. Maybe he had a thing for fungi.

He shook his head, lost in thought for a second before he answered. "Something that might or might not lead to something." Then he went right back to entertaining her with various cop stories as they drove away.

They were in her driveway before she knew it. She'd even forgotten to be scared to death. And as she watched his stark, masculine profile, she suddenly realized that had been his intention.

The sudden kindness unsettled her. She didn't know what to make of it. For the first time, she didn't find him threatening. And she didn't want to find him attractive. Which part of her did already. God, of all the stupid things she'd ever done…

"Thank you, Detective," she said, eager to see him driving away.

"Jack," he reminded her.

"So how does it work? The agoraphobia?" he asked, plunging straight into her most private business.

"It's not really agoraphobia." She jumped to defend herself. "I go to the store. I go to places. I just don't like to leave the house."

"It started after the accident?"

She hesitated for a moment, but then she nodded. All her craziness did. "I'm dealing with it."

"Hey, you drove out to save me. I'm grateful for that." This time, he sounded more sincere than the first time he'd thanked her. "It couldn't have been easy."

"Nothing's easy."

He held her gaze. His usual intensity was tempered with something softer today, something that made it hard for her to look away as he said, "No, nothing is, is it?"

She filled her lungs. "I'm going to get better."

"I have no doubt you will."

The way he said it, with full confidence, unsettled her. The support felt good, and for a moment, she almost liked him for giving her that. So she made a joke of it.

"Are you all right?"

He arched an eyebrow.

"We've been together for at least half an hour, and you haven't accused me of anything yet. Has crime stopped in Broslin?"

His lips curved into a half smile. "I was just getting to it."

He looked dangerously handsome when he smiled.

"So his name is Burt Johnson," he said.

"Who?"

"The guy in the closet you painted."

And just like that, the relaxed moment was gone from between them.

He went on to tell her about the old man and his nephew, the neighbors who called in that he'd been missing.

The stark reality of the story shook her. Always did.

The thought of another vision frightened her. The idea that she should try to force one on purpose made her question her own sanity. She needed to be alone. She needed to think. She needed to get away from him, even if talking like this wasn't too bad. Or maybe especially because of that. She refused to like him.

"I have to go. Thanks for the ride." She bolted from the car and practically ran for her front door.

She locked up behind her, slipped out of her boots and coat, listened to the sounds of his car driving away while pushing the images of that last body from her mind.

She would think about it, whether or not she could do what she needed to do, but later. Right now, she had to take care of something else first. She strode to the kitchen and poured a glass of water, looked at Maddie's drawings on her refrigerator.

When she regained some equilibrium, she pulled her cell phone and dialed her father.

A moment passed as Bertha answered the phone and passed it on to Mr. Price.

"Something came up. I can't come today," Ashley told him. "I'm really sorry."

Silence stretched on the other end before her father said, "She's been waiting by the window for the past half hour."

Her eyes burned. "It's not something I can help. Could you come out?"

"No, we can't. I called together a small dinner party with your old friends to celebrate your visit. If you're not here, at least I ought to be." Her father hung up on her before she had a chance to ask for Maddie.

She stood there, in the middle of the room, her jaw clenched. Moisture filled her eyes. She blinked hard. *No.* She was done with crying. She let the anger come, set her jaw, and marched up the stairs. She would do whatever she had to do. And do it as soon as possible.

She'd wanted to think more about the idea she'd had at the station, but suddenly she knew that if she thought too much, she might lose her nerve. She needed to be brave for once. She needed to leap. She needed to force a vision.

She grabbed her stained palette and squeezed crimson red in the middle, half a tube, then black, then brown, mixed a sick gray, mixed all the colors of decay. There.

"I want to see," she said to the empty room. Then shouted, "I want to see!"

She visualized Jack's face, the way he'd been wrapped into that shower curtain, the way he'd looked in the dark and cold grave. She wished she still had the original painting. It might have helped to remember the exact details.

She stared at the canvas so hard, all her muscles bunched, that she was giving herself a headache. She was so focused, when her doorbell rang, she nearly jumped out of her skin at the sharp ring. She set the palette down and went to the door, expecting it'd be Pete with some mail, or maybe Eddie, just letting her know he'd be out back. Either way, the interruption wouldn't take more than a minute.

But instead, Graham Lanius leered at her.

"I was in the neighborhood. I thought I'd pop in and see what you have for me."

The art dealer wore a crisp suit with a Van Gogh Starry Night tie. He'd come in an Audi, pristine despite the slush on the roads, quite a trick. He stood at the same height as Ashley, freshly cut hair, meticulously clean-shaven face that he stretched into a smile. "May I come in?"

She stepped back. Graham was the last person she wanted to see right now, but sending him away would have been inexcusably rude. The way her career was going, she probably couldn't afford to alienate anyone in the business.

"I don't really have the series ready."

He waved that off. "Even a small glimpse would make me happy. You know I've been an admirer of your art for a long time. I can't believe we keep missing connecting."

They didn't so much miss as were kept apart by Isabelle, who'd worked hard to get Ashley's work into the top New York galleries and refused to go backward by booking shows at smaller venues. Small venues usually went hand in hand with small prices, and a lot of patrons collected art as an investment. When they bought something from you for a certain price, they didn't want to see that a year later, your paintings were going for half that money somewhere. Made them question their judgment of your talent, which made them look for someone else who might be the next big thing.

Graham's gaze clamped on a canvas visible up in the loft, and he strode toward the staircase, then up before Ashley could stop him. "Oh, is that it?"

He made her uneasy, which probably had less to do with his overly exuberant behavior than the fact that she'd become a virtual shut-in lately, unused to too much company.

She followed him up and waited patiently as he examined her paintings.

"You have an excellent start." He rubbed his chin. "A few minor fixes, some lines adjusted..." He stepped from one picture to the next.

Annoyance bubbled up inside her. Her lines were exactly where she'd meant them to be.

"You do have amazing talent." He turned to her with a calculating look. "I'd be happy to mentor you. As busy as I am, I like finding time to help up-and-coming artists."

Okay, he definitely was pompous.

"That's a very generous offer. I wouldn't want to take up your valuable time."

He kept the smarmy smile on his face. "When do you think I could pick these up?"

"My agent schedules my shows," she told him, then started down the stairs, hoping he would take the hint.

He did follow her. "Of course. Your very young agent. How good of you to give her a start."

Which was a laugh. Isabelle might have been young, but she was absolutely brilliant and knew everyone in the business. She regularly put together shows that attracted celebrities and were covered by the New York Times. Ashley was lucky to have her. "I should leave you to your work. The sooner you're done, the sooner we can talk dates." He stopped at the front door. "Terrible business with that cop on your property. I hope you're all right." The absolute last thing she wanted to talk about. "It's over." "Is it? So they're not coming around anymore?" His look turned apologetic. "Mystery buff. Have you read the latest Konrath?" She shook her head. She painted enough dead bodies; she didn't want to read about more. "I wonder if the FBI made any progress in the case?" "They don't really keep me updated," she said as she opened the door for him. "Of course. I shouldn't have brought it up. It's just…well, fascinating. Not as if we have too much excitement in Broslin." He gave a quick laugh. "I should leave you to your creating. We'll talk again soon." She was relieved to be able to close the door behind him. But she didn't give herself much of a break. She marched right back upstairs, to the blank canvas that waited for her on the easel. If somehow she could figure out how to force open that dark door to hell, she was determined, no matter what it cost her, to take the trip.

Chapter Seven

The Broslin flea market flourished every Sunday in an old airplane hangar that had been once part of the county airport. The utilitarian space was now divided into about a hundred "shops" that vendors rented on a permanent basis. In the middle, several rows of folding tables lined up neatly. Those could be rented by anyone just for the day.

Jack stalked around for half an hour, observing the sellers, the buyers, the gawkers, the complete lack of security, before finally heading back to the last row of stalls to the man he'd come to see. He weaved in and out of the crowd. The place was packed, the usual Sunday crowd of gleaners.

As colorful as a gypsy caravan, he thought, and wondered if Ashley Price had ever painted it. He had Ashley on his mind entirely too much lately. She was a puzzle, and he was a cop. Cops liked puzzles. And yet, deep down, he knew there was more to it. Another time, another place...if he wasn't what he was. He forced his focus back on his surroundings.

He couldn't imagine the place brought much money to its owners, but then again, the upkeep too looked minimal. Conveniences were slim to none, save the two single-stall bathrooms at the end. A questionable-looking hot-dog cart that stood right by the entrance provided the only place to eat.

He stopped at the stall he'd come for, neat in comparison with some of the others, offering an impressive array of unrelated goods, anything from corn medication to old TVs and even a few used kitchen sinks, right next to a dozen brand-new, in-factory-packaging, luxury, touch-activated faucets.

"Cold enough out there for you?" the old guy behind the counter, Lenny, according to the beaten-up sign behind him asked with a friendly smile. He wore a KISS ME, I'M POLISH T-shirt that had seen better days. "You know what they say, in like a lamb, out like a lion."

Jack rifled through a selection of bootlegged DVDs.

"Looking for anything particular?"

He didn't want to bust the guy for the handful of movies. For the moment, he needed to keep the good will between them going.

"Actually"—he looked up—"I'm looking for a good shovel."

The smile slid off the old man's face. "No more shovels."

"You sold them all?"

"No sell, no more shovels." When the smile came back, it has become decidedly artificial. "I got very good socks."

He didn't have time for socks. Jack flashed his badge. "I'd like to know how many of those shovels you sold before you ran out.

The man gave up pretending to smile. "I talk to other police officer already."

"Tell me anyway."

"I don't like poor man was buried with one of my shovels. I think he wouldn't want me sell more."

Okay, so Mike had told the guy when he'd picked up his own shovel and questioned him. The trouble with rookies was they talked too much. They screwed up a couple of times, that was how they learned, Jack thought without heat. He'd done the same, more than once, before he'd learned better.

He put on his friendliest face. "I'm the poor man. All I want is talk."

Lenny's eyes widened. "Is he you? The one came back from the grave?" He made the sign of the cross as he glanced back at a faded poster of the Pope among a hodgepodge of signs on the pegboard behind him. Then he looked Jack over with a mix of horror, fascination, and respect. "Is he really you?"

Jack nodded, only because he hoped it'd make Lenny more talkative.

The old man reached under the counter, pulled out a shovel still in its plastic wrapping, and handed it over. "No charge." Then he picked a black bead rosary with a silver cross from a small cardboard box on the counter and held it out. "Gift for you."

But Jack barely heard him. He held the shovel, balanced in his hand, his fingers tightening on the folded-up tool until his knuckles went white.

For a second, he could feel the freezing dirt on his face, and everything inside him went dark. His lungs constricted. Then someone squeezing through the throng of people bumped into him from behind, jarring him back to the present. He relaxed his fingers with an effort, drew a full breath, and looked up at Lenny, who was still holding out the rosary.

He reached out his other hand and accepted it. "I'd like to talk to you, if you have a minute."

"Wish I could remember better." The man touched the side of his head. "But too many people come every Sunday. Lots of strangers. I only know the regulars. They good people."

He'd be the judge of that, Jack thought, but the twenty-minute chat that followed didn't net any new information. Lenny did brisk enough business that he couldn't possibly remember every single customer.

He did give a list of his regulars, although all he had were first names and descriptions. Still, a start. Jack could give the list to Leila, who'd grown up in town and knew pretty much everybody. She might be able to add last names to some of the people on the list.

The only person he recognized on the list was Eddie Gannon. Lenny knew him. Apparently, everybody knew Eddie. He had bought a shovel a few months back.

Time to catch up with the town handyman, Jack thought as he thanked Lenny. He left the man his phone number in case he remembered more, then took his shovel and rosary and walked back through the market.

Other than Ashley Price, the only clues they had were the shovel, the shoe print, and the shower curtain. He passed by another store like Lenny's that had shower curtains hanging up front, and he dug through the particleboard bin under the display. He didn't see one exactly like the see-through one he'd snuck in to see in the evidence room but found one that was pretty close, except with some polka dots.

He picked that up. He could compare size, material, and brand later. He also grabbed a flyer that listed three other stores the owner had in the area, shoved the slip of paper into his pocket, then stepped inside.

The store was packed. He looked for boots. If Blackwell had bought his shovel at the flea market, which was still a big if, who was to say his shower curtain and his boots didn't come from here too. Jack scanned the merchandise, didn't find what he was looking for, so he stepped to the end of the line in front of the counter with his shower curtain.

Everyone he saw paid cash, and so did he. He didn't even ask if they kept customer records.

If the shower curtain was a match, he'd come back. If not, there was no point in wasting his time here.

Shovel and shower curtain under his arm, rosary in his pocket, he walked through every single store, and found half a dozen that did sell footwear. He checked the treads of every boot the flea market had, wasting the rest of his morning. Not one of them was a match to the footprint cast on his cell phone.

Didn't look like Blackwell had done his one-stop shopping here after all. Would have been too easy. But easy or hard, he would catch the bastard.

He stopped in front of a booth that sold nothing but snow gear, including a variety of shovels. He picked up a sturdy one for Ashley. Only because she couldn't lead him to Blackwell if she broke her pretty neck, he tried to tell himself, then gave up pretending. Truth was, he liked Ashley. Not that it meant anything. Like or not, he wasn't going to start anything with her. He was definitely not the right man for her, and he was too far gone to change.

On his way out of the place, he grabbed a sorry-looking hot dog and a soft drink, forcing his thoughts from her. A normal life was out of his reach, but revenge wasn't. That was where he had to focus his energies.

He ate as he drove, spending the rest of the day checking out over a dozen mom-and-pop stores in Broslin and the surrounding small towns. He didn't find any other places that sold army-surplus shovels, which didn't mean Blackwell had gotten his from Lenny.

Could have ordered it online or could have picked one up far away from here, on a trip.

He also stopped by every place that sold boots, hoping he'd luck out with that, but found none with the kind of tread he was looking for.

Since he didn't consider shopping fun under the best of circumstances, his mood was pretty sour by the time he finished. Another day wasted without progress. And all this time, Blackwell was out there, laughing his ass off at him, possibly stalking his next victims.

When he spotted Bing's SUV in front of Main Street's most popular watering hole, he pulled over. Maybe they had trouble. He could have used a good bar fight, gotten his frustration out. He walked in with all kinds of hope for a need to restore order, into the din of a drunk crowd. A horribly terrible band played loud enough to raise the dead and make them run for a place that did have some of that eternal peace.

Instead of being engaged in some satisfying police work—like, say, knocking drunk heads together—Bing was quietly nursing a beer in the back.

For a moment, Jack considered turning around, if nothing else, to save his hearing. But Bing looked just as pissed as he felt, which appealed to him at the moment, the whole "misery loves company" thing. So he strode through the gyrating, sweaty crowd and joined the man. What the hell.

Bing's eyes narrowed as he looked up. "You better not be here investigating something." Even in the back, he had to shout to be heard over the din.

Jack lowered himself onto a chair across from him. "No." He was pretty much done for the day.

"Good. You should be at home resting."

"I was just getting to that." He grabbed a handful of peanuts and tossed them into his mouth that still tasted like mystery-meat hot dog.

The waitress came by, smiled at Jack, tilted her head, and gave him a flirty look. "Hey there, handsome." Her body language held all kinds of invitation.

At another time, even a few weeks ago, he would have taken her up on that. He wasn't relationship material, but he wasn't a monk either. On the occasions when he ran into someone who didn't want more than he could offer...

"I'll have what he's having," he said simply and turned back to Bing.

"I'll be right back." She gave some extra swish to her hips as she sashayed away.

The captain arched an eyebrow but didn't comment.

Jack pulled the basket of peanuts closer. "Rough day?"

The captain drank from his bottle. "Freaking FBI."

He leaned closer, instantly alert. "They got something?"

Bing shrugged. "They can't catch the bastard soon enough."

Amen to that. "He needs to be taken down," Jack agreed as the beer came, cold and perfect.

"Listen, I know your sister—"

"It goes beyond Shannon. Fifteen women." He shot his captain a hard look. "All young, pretty, between the ages of fifteen and thirty-five. They were abducted in batches. Three in one week, then nothing for another year. Then two women. Then a three-year pause. Then another three victims, within days of each other."

Normally, they wouldn't have discussed a case in public, but the music was loud enough so that nobody could have heard them unless he or she sat on the table between them.

"So he takes his victims in groups. Why?" Bing asked, getting into it. He was too much of a cop to ignore a good mystery. But he did shake his head after a minute. "Forget it. He almost killed you once. Let the FBI figure it out."

"To hell with the FBI." Jack fisted his hand on the table. "The women in each batch were taken on different days. But what remains were found indicate that each batch was killed at the same time. Why?"

Bing couldn't resist a guess. "Efficiency?"

"They were found in pieces, together, with various body parts missing. As if he took what he wanted and disposed of the leftovers. What did he do with the rest?"

The captain's face darkened. "Some sick ritual."

"Then there's me. I don't fit the victim profile. He had just me. Nobody else. And he didn't kill me and take me apart."

"He meant to kill you. You would have been dead if Ashley Price hadn't found you."

He stared at the bottle as he remembered, cold sweat breaking out on his back. "I was in the tunnel," he admitted for the first time. "I was walking toward the light."

Bing swore and took a swig. "Leave the evil son of a bitch alone."

"Wouldn't matter. He won't leave me alone now. I'm the one that got away. His ego can't take that. He wanted me, and I slipped away. He'd been waiting for me. He had a trap all set up."

"You got too close."

"Not close enough."

"Be grateful he changed his SOP."

He'd given that some thought in the last couple of weeks. "The women were his victims. I'm different, because I'm something else. I'm his opponent, like in a chess game. That's why he did things differently with me. Whatever he needed those women for, with me, he just wanted to prove that he'd beaten me, both intellectually and physically. And he buried me alive so I'd have a little extra time to think about that defeat."

"A stupid move. You survived."

He thought about that for a few seconds. "Yes. He was too cocky. He thinks he has hometown advantage here. He got overconfident." He shrugged. "Not unreasonably. If Ashley Price hadn't dug me up, I would be dead. He didn't count on that."

Bing swore. "How did you know he was here, in Broslin?"

He explained about the spores.

"You saw the mushroom company? Talked to the workers?"

"As soon as I got here. Nothing popped." He drank some.

"You told the FBI about this?"

He nodded. When they'd first interviewed him after he'd gotten out of the hospital. They were here now anyway. Agent Hunter didn't seem impressed by Jack's theory. He didn't think the spores meant anything. "The workers alibied out. One or two might have been on vacation when the murders had been committed, but not one has been missing on all the dates."

He was going to check on the artist next who'd done those mushroom paintings. The timing lined up nicely. He wasn't going to tell the FBI about that, not yet. "Hunter thinks Blackwell caught on that I was hunting him and came here to make me stop."

"I like that theory. I don't want to think that the bastard has something to do with Broslin."

"I feel it in my bones, Bing. This is his lair, right here."

Bing gave a dark scowl. "They'll get him. Let it go."

Because Bing was as close as he had to a friend in a long time, he told him the truth. "I can't."

"You're a good detective. Don't throw everything away on this."

"I have nothing but this."

"You could have more. Guy with your looks and your brain. You could have anything you wanted. Take the waitress home. She wants you to. She's a decent gal. Give yourself a break."

But he shook his head, even as raised voices at the bar drew his attention. Some slick guy seemed to be harassing one of the other waitresses.

He had his hand on her waist, a few inches too low, and seemed to be holding on when she was trying to pull away. Jack drained his beer and pushed to standing, slapping some money on the table in the process. "Better get going."

By the time he cut through the crowd, the asshole had jostled the waitress enough to spill some of the drinks on her tray.

Jack stopped next to them, his shoulders relaxed, his eyes on the guy. "You want to let her go."

The idiot swung his way with a sneer, his mouth opening to say something. Then his face suddenly pulled straight, his hands slipping off the waitress. Cold anger came into his eyes for a second, then disappeared.

"Go home, Graham," Bing told the guy from behind Jack. "You know you can't hold your liquor."

The man held his hands up and mouthed okay, okay, which was lost in the din. This close to the band, the decibels were flying in the triple digits. The waitress flashed a grateful smile at Jack, then hurried away.

"Who the hell was that?" Jack asked when both he and Bing were outside and could finally hear each other again.

"Graham Lanius. Thinks he's a big shot because he owns a gallery. Must make good money. Gives a big donation to the police department every year."

Jack glared back toward the door. Too bad money couldn't buy brains. He parted ways with Bing in the parking lot, each going on his way.

He had one more thing to do tonight. He kept that to himself.

He was willing to do whatever it took to take down Blackwell. If it meant something that would end his career, or even his life, so be it.

Which meant it was better to keep Bing at a distance. He was a good captain; his career shouldn't go down the drain.

* * *

He watched the detective through his binoculars, the landscape abandoned around them, the ice of the reservoir a shining sheet of diamonds in the moonlight, not a car on the road, as if they were the only two people on earth. They both had their quests. They both had their rituals.

Sullivan came to the grave every night.

He could almost hear the detective think across the distance. He wasn't giving up. He wasn't pulling back. Another thing they had in common. Neither was the type to walk away from a job until it was finished.

The FBI might have been making pests of themselves, going around town, asking questions, but Sullivan was the true threat—the only threat.

The FBI would give up after a while, move out. They had timetables and a strict budget.

Sullivan would stay and keep distracting him from his art, from his true calling. It pissed him off. Sullivan was nobody. The man had no idea what he was messing with.

Across the reservoir, the detective was staring into the dark hole of the grave.

The ground hadn't been able to hold him.

The water would, and the ice. New plans had been made. Soon, a new trap would be waiting.

* * *

Jack stood over his grave in the gathering dusk once again, yellow police tape flitting in the wind around him. Should have stayed at the bar where it was warm, gotten another beer. But he was here once again, at a place he hated yet couldn't walk away from.

He needed a new lead. He needed some progress, dammit. At least one step forward.

His lungs couldn't get enough air, and it had nothing to do with the freezing temperature. He felt like that every time here. He had come every day since he'd been released from the hospital, hoping the place would jog some forgotten detail loose in his memory that could lead him to Blackwell.

And also hoping that the bastard would return. Maybe he would come to the site of his only failed project to see what had gone wrong. Maybe the grave would draw him too. No sign of him so far, though. Jack hated to think that between the two of them, he was the only obsessed lunatic.

He looked away from the grave and toward the house he knew stood somewhere behind the trees.

Ashley Price.

Every time he thought about her painting the old man in the closet, the short hairs stood straight up on the back of his neck.

Her paintings had nothing to do with Blackwell. Except his.

She painted the dead, those who died violently, in relative proximity to her—about a twenty- or thirty-mile radius. What the hell did that mean?

The dead who had unfinished business reached out to her? Why? Because she'd come back from the dead? She'd been dead for twenty minutes under the ice. The emergency-response crew had brought her back. Did she want to return to life? Did part of her, feeling guilty about Dylan, want to stay with the kid? Did she still have some faint link to that other world?

Had she been the presence he'd felt when he'd been dying?

He didn't understand her, and he didn't like what he couldn't understand. She couldn't be pinned down, could not be classified. Probably the very reason why she was getting under his skin every possible way.

He'd even dreamed about her. Naked dreams. Just the thought gave a tug at his groin. Hell, the only thing he knew about her for sure was that his body, very inconveniently, lusted after hers.

The lust wasn't specific, he told himself. All it meant was that he hadn't gotten laid in too long a time. He could go back to the bar tonight, hook up with the blonde waitress, share a night of physical release: the perfect no-mess solution.

Yet he didn't find the prospect the least bit tempting.

So he walked out to the road and drove up to her house, even if he hadn't intended to visit Ashley tonight. The last time had been plenty enough, watching her paint, watching her fight against her jumble of emotions that had threatened to pull him in.

Her downstairs lights were on but not the upstairs. Good. She wasn't painting. He leaned the new shovel he'd bought next to her old one, then ran up the steps and rang the doorbell.

A few seconds passed before the key turned in the lock and the door cracked open a few inches.

"Unless you have an arrest warrant, go away." The dark circles around her eyes said she hadn't seen much sleep last night. She wore black slacks made of some soft material that clung to her long legs, and a long-sleeved fitted cotton shirt that showed off her curves.

Predictably, his body responded. The irony that he kept coming back to her like a lover in the night didn't escape him. He watched her for a long minute before words he hadn't meant to say came out of his mouth. "Let's say I believe you."

She still hesitated a long second before she finally stepped back to let him in.

He kicked off his snow-covered boots, hung his coat on one of the pegs by the door, and followed her into the living room. "Tell me again, how the...visions work."

She walked away from him, into the kitchen, then measured him up as if trying to make up her mind, running her teeth over her lower lip, looking conflicted. "I see a picture in my mind," she said at last, "and it makes me sick. I feel—I can't explain. And it doesn't go away until I get it out. I can't stop thinking about it until then."

He tried to understand how that might work, how that might feel. "And it all started after the accident on the reservoir?"

She nodded.

He sat on a kitchen chair and leaned back, taking as relaxed a pose as possible, putting himself lower to set her at ease. "Why don't you tell me about it?"

Again she moved away from him, to the counter to stare out the back window into the night. "We used to go ice skating every chance we got. And that time, Maddie wanted to bring Dylan."

"Dylan Miller, the neighbor's son." He'd read the file. Victim: Dylan Miller, age four, male. Currently, the Miller farm stood abandoned across the road. The family had moved away shortly after the accident.

"We fell through," she said, her voice brittle. "Maddie was closest to me. I pushed her out, onto the ice; then I tried to save Dylan, but I couldn't find him."

And she wouldn't get out without the boy. She'd stayed and searched until she'd gotten lost under the ice. She'd spent twenty minutes down there, her metabolism shut down by the cold. Dead. Her file had included interviews with the ER staff. Her rescue had been hailed as a miracle.

"One second he was there," she whispered, "the next he disappeared. His skates pulled him down."

He recognized the look in her eyes as she glanced at him, the soul-eating guilt. He knew what it meant to lose someone and carry the blame for it, to be utterly helpless to do anything to save them.

It had been fifteen years and he still wasn't over Shannon's death. Dylan had been lost only a year ago. All things considered, Ashley held herself together admirably well. His gaze strayed to the crayon art on the fridge. Her daughter, probably, had kept her sane, given her a reason for living. Everybody needed something.

He had his revenge.

"I think maybe part of you wanted to stay with him," he said.

She stared at him as she considered his words. "I did. What right did I have to live if I couldn't save Dylan?" she asked quietly then. "I was dead. They brought me back."

"They did that to you. You didn't choose it."

"So?"

"I think you still have some kind of a link to the other side." God, now he was talking crazy, but he said it anyway. "As if you'd left a little part of you behind."

She stared at him, paling. "So the dying can reach out to me," she whispered.

He nodded.

"I thought it was because I lost a life. I thought if I saved a life, the visions would go away. They didn't."

"I'm glad you came for me anyway." He couldn't imagine how hard that must have been for her.

She gave a wry smile. "Don't make me regret it."

"I'm afraid I might have already." He watched her. "But thank you. I mean that, Ashley."

She looked away, then back at him. "I wanted to thank you too, for not giving my paintings to the FBI."

"How do you know I haven't?"

"If they had the paintings, they would have said something."

He hated the agents who kept getting in his way. And he didn't want them messing with her either.

So he felt protective toward her. So what? She'd saved his life. She deserved something in return.

"Any new urges to paint?" He asked the question to prove to himself that he was here to investigate and not just to see her.

She shook her head as she stood in the middle of the kitchen, looking all alone and vulnerable and completely lost. And completely hot, regardless. She had barely a touch of makeup on, the simple black slacks and cotton shirt she wore hardly seductive. Her body didn't need enhancement—all curves and mile-long legs. She was a knockout, pretty much. The sight of her certainly knocked him back a pace every time he looked at her. But something deeper than her physical attributes drew him now, and he got his first inkling that he might be in trouble.

He needed to say good night here and go about his business. But when he stood, he walked to her instead of heading straight for the door. He stopped a couple of feet from her. "Does it always make you feel sick when you paint like that?"

She nodded but wouldn't look at him.

"Next time you feel it coming on, call me."

"There's nothing you can do."

"I can come over."

"I can handle it. I don't want…" She bit her lip.

But he knew what she'd been about to say. She didn't want anyone to see her like that. He got it. He wanted to be alone too, when the darkest of his rage got hold of him. "Call me anyway."

Her gaze came up, her eyes wide—that impossible shade of green that haunted his dreams. She blinked hard, fighting to be strong. But underneath it all, she was broken still on so many levels.

He didn't think at all before he stepped all the way up to her. His arms went around her, and he pulled her closer, tucked her against him. Every inch where they touched, his body came alive.

For a split second, she leaned into the offered comfort. Instant lust cut through him, the urge to have her mixing with the urge to protect her. But, before he could have done something stupid, she pulled away.

They stared at each other for a moment.

She's going to be a complication, he thought, not for the first time. He was a cop. Regardless of whether he thought her innocent or not, she was an FBI suspect. "I shouldn't have— This isn't why I came. I came—" He had no idea how to finish that sentence, so it was a good thing she cut him off.

"To soften me up and see if I spill something?" Hurt and betrayal rang in her voice.

The momentary truce was gone between them.

Her face hardened, and her chin came up. "I want my paintings back."

Of course. That was all she wanted from him. Not comfort, and not more than comfort, certainly. And he shouldn't want anything from her at all. Even if his entire body ached with the need to have her back in his arms.

To hell with that.

"No," he said.

She folded her arms. "What do you want from me, Jack?"

Just a few days ago, he would have known the answer: a confession. But he no longer thought she was really Blackwell's accomplice.

Except, then why was he here?

He had no right to want anything from her. She didn't even like him, and to be honest he couldn't blame her. He'd been a jackass to her from the moment they'd met.

His ringing phone saved him from having to answer her question. He took the call—Mike from the station.

"I'm not supposed to tell you this, but someone just reported bones in the woods out beyond Beckett Road."

He walked away from Ashley. "Who?"

"Some kids out looking for trouble, no doubt, or a quiet place to smoke weed."

"Anybody dispatched yet?" He stepped into his boots and grabbed his coat.

"Bing is going out."

But he was closer.

He looked back at Ashley, standing alone in the middle of her kitchen, her arms wrapped around her, her haunted green eyes watching him. The twinge of reluctance to leave her was something new and unexpected. It surprised him more than a little. Something else drew him in the opposite direction, something darker. He gave in to that, leaving her with a brief nod as he walked out the door. And then everything else fell away, his mind focused on Blackwell.

Anticipation hummed through him as he jumped into his car and slammed his foot on the gas. He wanted to be first on the scene. He reached the spot in five minutes, saw the snowmobiles' tracks, pulled over by the side of the road, and followed the tracks in. His boots crunched on the snow, his flashlight illuminating the path ahead. The trees stood silent, their barren branches scraping against him now and then. In a minute or two, he could see the bright headlights of the snowmobiles up ahead.

"Who are you?" One of the four teenagers standing around challenged him.

"Broslin PD." Jack turned his flashlight on the kids.

Four boys squinted at him, one familiar, the one he'd caught on Ashley's land. The kid recognized him too and hunched down in his jacket.

They were all around high school age, red-cheeked and wide-eyed, half scared, half excited.

"What are you doing here?"

"Just hanging out," the one who'd challenged him a second ago answered, sounding defensive, probably the gang leader. "The bones are over there." He pointed to a stand of bushes.

Jack panned the bleached bundle of bones scattered over the frozen ground. They'd been there for a while, probably since the summer. Predators had gotten at them. He didn't even have to bend over to make ID. The remains belonged to an unfortunate calf that had somehow wandered away from a nearby farm and gotten tangled in the bushes.

He kicked at the bones and swore under his breath as they scattered, all the tension and anticipation leaking out of him, leaving nothing but stark disappointment.

Through the leafless trees, in the silent night, he could hear Bing's car coming up the road, slowing.

"You stay right here," he snapped at the kids, then walked out to the road to meet his captain.

Bing was shaking his head as he got out of his cruiser and spotted Jack. "If I thought it would work, I'd come up with some trumped-up charge and put you under house arrest. I thought putting you back on admin duty would keep you out of my hair." He got his industrial-size flashlight from the trunk.

"I haven't started admin duty yet." He had to pass a physical and get a psych approval first, which he planned on doing first thing in the morning. He'd already scheduled his appointments.

"Smart-ass. What's going on here?"

"Some old bones from a stray calf. Couple of teenagers where they shouldn't be."

Bing gave a resigned groan as he headed for the bushes, Jack following. The captain panned the kids with his flashlight when they reached them, settling on the tallest. "Your father know you're out here, Bobby?"

"No, sir."

"You know them?" Jack asked.

Bing turned away from the boys. "One of them is the son of the high school principal; the other one's father is Jim Foster, a local councilman," he said under his breath as he shook his head. "Might as well have them turn out their pockets. Read them the riot act. They probably already tossed whatever weed they brought to smoke out here, but it won't hurt to put the fear of God in them a little."

It didn't happen that way. A call came in before he took two steps.

"Officer down," Mike said on the other end and rattled off an address.

"Harper." Bing ran for his car. "He went out on a domestic-violence call earlier."

Jack was right behind him, the boys already forgotten.

Chapter Eight

"I booked you at Maximilian's for the end of May," Isabelle said on the other end of the line as Ashley pulled her dinner from the microwave, General Tso's chicken.

At five o'clock Monday afternoon, this was probably the last call her agent would make for the day. Which meant there was more coming. Isabelle hated giving bad news to her artists. Good calls went out first thing in the morning. Rejections were left until the last minute, as she usually would work throughout the day to make another booking, secure a review in a top newspaper, or otherwise soften the blow.

So Ashley asked, "But?" and waited for her agent to tell her the rest.

A long moment of silence passed.

Ashley brushed her hair back from her face. "I'm a big girl. I can handle it."

"If it's not a sell-out show, I'm not sure if I can book you again. And you need to be here," Isabelle told her. "I'm sorry. With the economy… Galleries are losing money. I can't book shows like I used to. They want a sure thing. They want the big names, the heavy hitters."

She understood. The last two shows, not only had she not been able to send as many paintings as she'd promised, but she hadn't been able to force herself into making the trip. Her anxieties had turned her into a prisoner. Which would change. She would have to go this time. Too much was riding on the line.

She had to conquer her fears, as simple as that. And she had to get the FBI off her back. But forcing a vision hadn't worked. She had tried again after Jack had left after his brief but bewildering visit, tried until she'd nearly been in tears from frustration. Nothing happened.

The first time she'd seen him in the grave, he'd been on the brink of death. Did he reach out to her? His theory—as crazy as it sounded—made more sense than anything she'd come up with so far.

Maybe the reason why she hadn't been able to bring back that connection was because currently the man was very much alive. And messing with her head.

He knew her darkest secret. He believed her. He'd held her in his arms, and it'd felt so good she'd wanted to stay there forever. She needed to snap out of that foolishness.

Even if his strong arms around her felt better than anything in a long time. Even if he made her feel alive, whether with anger or awareness or need, but always alive. Even if part of her was beginning to wish for things that could never be.

She closed her eyes for a moment. *Forget Jack.* He was trouble with a capital T, at a time when she couldn't afford complications. "Graham Lanius stopped by," she said to channel her thoughts into another direction. "I told him he needs to talk to you."

"Good. We're a little concerned but not desperate yet. You need to be in better galleries than his. He might think he's some hotshot dealer, but he doesn't have the best of reputations at the art shows." She hesitated. "Maybe it's more about the money for him than the art. I'll deal with him if he calls." The sound of a keyboard clicking came from the other end. "Now the most important thing. About the pictures you sent this morning."

Ashley held her breath as she waited for the verdict. Even after all these years, this part never got easier.

"The raw pain is gone." Isabelle paused. "I'm glad you're feeling better. The accident wasn't your fault. You almost died trying to save that boy."

Isabelle could read artists from their paintings like Freud could read people from their dreams. And she could read clients from their clothes, the cars they drove, how they wore their makeup, how they spoke. She knew the perfect art for every gallery, for every client. She was amazing at what she did.

"There's something else going on here," she said now. "Some new tension. Want to talk about it?"

Ashley hesitated, not sure what to say. The FBI thinks I'm aiding and abetting a serial killer, didn't sound like something that would advance her career.

"All right. We'll talk when we meet," Isabelle said on the other end. "So about the paintings—the work is good, which is the most important thing. Very moody. I like it. Fantastic colors. Good negative space. Good everything. The rhythm of the brushstrokes is mesmerizing. I really like the new energy."

Ashley let out the breath she'd been holding.

"Maximilian will want titles. I don't suppose you changed your mind about that."

She didn't title her work, as a rule. She felt like it would be too much of an imposition on the viewer, getting in the way of letting the painting say whatever it wanted to say, which would be different from person to person.

"I want dialogue. Art shouldn't be a one-way conversation. Let the viewer decide what the painting means to them." A piece either spoke to you or it didn't. If it had to be explained, it wasn't worth bupkis.

"And you know I agree."

"You think it will be an issue?"

"You're the artist. They'll ask, but ultimately they'll respect your artistic vision." Another pause on Isabelle's end. "So about the last photo you sent this afternoon, the one with the unfinished work. Is this a new direction? That one has a different tone than the others. There's hope in it. And some kind of masculine energy. Is there a hot guy in the picture you neglected to mention?"

Ashley looked at the painting on the easel. Soaring swirls of blue dominated the canvas. She'd started it that morning. She had no idea where the image had come from, what it meant. Hope? No, she didn't think so. This one time, Isabelle had to be mistaken. Her ruling emotion when it came to Jack Sullivan was definitely confusion. "Staying away from men until I have other things straightened out."

So what if there was a certain attraction? So what if the blue in her painting matched his cerulean eyes exactly? She itched to paint those eyes, the shadows and pain at their depth, the planes of his face that often turned sharp and hard. A portrait of Jack Sullivan. Except, for a good portrait, the artist had to know the subject, know him truly and well, know what lived behind the eyes. And she knew precious little of Jack Sullivan. He had as many secrets as she did, or more, she was sure of that.

Did he really believe her? Or was it a ploy to get through her defenses, get her to let her guard down so he could find some dirt on her?

He'd said he believed her.

Did she dare believe that?

She wanted to. It would have been nice to have someone in her corner who knew the worst about her and accepted her regardless. He'd brought her a shovel, whatever that meant. At least, she was pretty sure he'd been the one to bring it. The man was a puzzle. "So, what's new with you?" she asked.

"I'll come down the last week of March. We'll catch up," Isabelle said. "If you could have a few more works finished by then, it would be great."

"I will." Unless something unforeseen came up, like the FBI arresting her. She didn't like the way Agent Hunter's interrogation had gone. But unless they found another lead, she would remain the focus of the investigation.

She had to give them a lead. Whatever it cost her. Her mind was full of fear of what that meant, as she said good-bye to Isabelle and hung up at last.

Simply wishing for another vision hadn't worked. How did other psychics control their dubious "gift"? The only thing she could think of was a documentary she'd recently watched about a psychic who visited crime scenes to help solve murder cases. Her visions seemed to have been triggered by some magical "vibes" violence left at the scene of the crime.

Ashley looked out into the twilight. If her "sensitivity" could be used the same way... She knew only one place connected to Blackwell, one place where the man had done something terrible. She thought of the shallow grave where Jack had been buried alive. What if some vibes had been left behind?

Maybe if she went out there, she could pick up something. The psychic on TV had talked about years and years of effort to develop her skill into what it was today. So if the "skill" could be developed, that meant Ashley might get better at it if she kept trying.

If she could bring back the vision, if she could expand it instead of fighting it... If she could see Blackwell put Jack into the grave, she could draw the man.

Tomorrow, said the voice of fear in her head.

It always said, tomorrow, whether it talked about going to the grocery store or starting a new painting. Tomorrow you'll be brave, fear whispered. Tomorrow you'll be normal. Just give me today.

That was how fear stole whole lives away.

But she had to stop letting fear win.

She had to do it for Maddie. Her daughter needed a real mother, not the shadow of one. She needed to reclaim her life. Starting right now. Because if she didn't do it right now, she might never do it, and she wasn't willing to lose her daughter over stupid cowardice.

So she dressed as warmly as she could, got into her car, and drove down Hadley Road, without looking once at the reservoir, pulled over at the exact same spot as she had before, and forced herself to step out of the car.

Fear, like the night, surrounded her completely. An owl hooted somewhere in the woods, making her jump. She almost got back into the car.

But then she thought of her daughter and marched forward.

Memories of the night she'd first come out here to search for the grave flooded her. She put one foot in front of the other mechanically, ignoring the bushes that tore at her pants. At least this time her legs and feet were covered.

Soon she could hear the creek up ahead. She pushed through a jumble of branches, and there loomed the solitary boulder twenty feet or so in front of her. A pretty impressive gravestone, she thought.

Finding the grave was easy, even in the dark. Police tape flitted all around it, pale moonlight reflecting off the yellow plastic.

She stopped outside the circle and drew a deep breath, looking up to the stars. Waited to feel something, see something. *Come on.* Nothing happened.

She looked down at the grave then and tried to think back to the time when she'd been on her knees next to it, clawing at the dirt with bare fingers. The images came back easily enough, but nothing else, nothing new.

Frustration battled with anxiety inside her.

She lifted the police tape and stepped under it, moving all the way to the grave, stared down into the black hole and shivered. She stared hard, trying to see shapes, movement, an image.

And she did get glimpses of a man, hidden by shadows, and Jack, but they did not feel true. They weren't like her visions. They were images her brain was making up because she was forcing it.

She tried to focus harder. Closed her eyes.

The hand settling on her shoulder made her scream into the night.

She spun around, her heart racing so hard she could barely catch her breath.

Not a hand, she realized, still on the verge of a heart attack. Just a branch dipping in the breeze.

She drew back, nearly falling into the grave, caught herself before she would have tumbled.

"Okay, enough craziness for one night," she said to herself and began walking back to her car, feeling like an utter failure.

No. She didn't fail until she gave up. And she wouldn't give up. Visiting "the scene of the crime" obviously didn't work for her. She had to find something that would.

She thought about that all the way back to her car, unaware that she was being observed from afar.

* * *

Jack came close to smiling as he drove back out to the old firehouse Tuesday morning. *Full, active duty.* Finest three words in the English language, he'd ever heard. He got a new service weapon and a new badge, and he swore he'd die before he'd let anyone take them away from him.

Harper was in the hospital with a bullet wound to the shoulder, the poor bastard. A jealous husband had clipped him. The idiot was currently cooling his heels at the county jail. Bing and Jack had taken him in.

The jerkwad was out of circulation and would be out for a long time, but the shooting left the department one man short, which meant Bing had to bring Jack back to active duty.

He'd passed his physical first thing Monday morning, then did whatever he had to so Dr. Beacon would sign the psych release. By noon, he'd been reinstated and was interviewing burglary suspects. He was in charge of that now, officially. And only him. Harper had Joe working with him, but Bing moved Joe over to looking for a runaway teen. The captain wanted to keep Jack busy enough so he'd stay out of the FBI's way.

So he'd read the burglary case files, then reinterviewed the victims. Then, since he was on that side of town, he decided to swing by to see the old firehouse again. It matched his criteria for location for the place where he'd been tortured. Maybe he'd missed some hidden basement entry before.

The place was connected to Eddie Gannon; he kept the big plow there. And Eddie Gannon spent time on Ashley's land. He would know the lay of the property, the best spot to hide a body. He went there for wood all the time. For a woodstove?

There'd been a woodstove in the torture chamber.

Jack pulled up in front of the building, his pulse kicking up as he noted the open door. He checked his gun down below the dashboard without being too obvious about it.

Eddie was coming outside by the time Jack pushed out of his car. The man held a tire iron by his side, but his expression was friendly enough. "Hey. Looking for me?"

They knew each other by sight but hadn't interacted much in the past.

"Running down some leads."

"Out here?"

"Looking for the place where I was kept."

Eddie turned somber. "That was a messed-up business. You think he's still around? They said on the news that he moves from state to state."

He shrugged, keeping his arms loose, making sure his weapon was in easy reach. "I hear you recently bought a shovel."

Eddie's face went blank, then surprised. "That's why you here?"

"Just running down some leads." He kept his tone neutral. "Mind if I come inside?"

"No, man." Eddie stepped aside immediately. "You look at whatever you want."

"After you." Jack gestured. He wasn't about to let Eddie get behind him with that tire iron.

The big plow was in the middle of the bay, some tools lying around the front tire. Eddie must have been working on that. He plodded back there now and dropped the tire iron next to the other tools. "I can get you the shovel."

"I'd appreciate that." Jack stared at the woodstove in the back. He hadn't seen that when he'd looked through the windows before. It had been covered by a partially open door.

But this was not the place where he'd been kept. The sound wasn't right, the echoes different as they walked and talked, the high ceiling affecting the sound.

He checked but couldn't find any place a basement entry could be hidden. He asked anyway, "Basement?"

Eddie shook his head as he brought him the shovel. "Old rock foundation. It's actually sinking a little at the east corner."

Still in the wrapping, the tool didn't have a speck of dirt on it. It had never been used, at least not out by the creek where the rocks would have scraped it some if it had been pushed into the ground.

Okay. The building and the shovel weren't a match. Jack moved on to the next item on his checklist. "Can you tell me where you were the first three days of this month? From the first to the third?"

The man had to walk over to his calendar to check. He scratched his head. "Right here. Working on Gerty." He glanced toward the big plow. "She had a few small problems. They were predicting some weather. Wanted to make sure she was ready for it."

"Day and night?"

"No, man, I went home to sleep."

"Alone?"

"Unfortunately." He gave a good-natured grin.

He lived in a one-bedroom apartment above the diner on Main Street. Jack had already checked into that. No basement there either. He made a mental note to ask the neighbors if they'd seen him coming and going during the three days he was interested in. Blackwell had stayed with him nearly the entire time in that basement.

One more question left. "Captain Bing said you were out there on the roads, down Hadley Road the evening of the third. Have you seen anything out of place?"

The man didn't strike him as Blackwell. He was too relaxed, too happy-go-lucky, even with Jack up in his face, in his business. Blackwell had plenty of piss and vinegar in him.

But even if Eddie wasn't Blackwell, he might be a witness.

"Nope. Thought about that a hundred times since. The FBI asked too. I'm sorry, man."

He thanked Eddie for his cooperation, then moved on to the next burglary victim, the Blackwell case always in the back of his mind, the puzzle pieces in constant shuffle.

The middle-aged shopkeeper he popped in on was missing some of his power tools. The next, an old woman, had her jewelry taken. Another guy had his entire DVD collection booted. The woman after that, her laptop. And it kept going like that. Relatively small items, items that could be easily sold online and shipped. Nothing terribly valuable, not even the jewelry. At a few places, the beer in the fridge and some smokes had also gone missing.

Didn't seem like a serious burglar with serious connections. Plenty of high-value items had been left behind. Harper had already lifted prints, but none of them were a hit in the police database.

When Jack went back to his car after the last home visit, he pulled out an old-fashioned map from the glove compartment and took a good look at the streets where houses had been picked. They were all over town and outside of town. If there was a pattern, he sure didn't see it.

But he did have a few hunches. The burglar was either a small-time crook, trying to support a drinking habit or a minor drug addiction, or... Those kids he'd seen twice now, out after dark in places they shouldn't be, came to mind.

Questioning them was going to be tricky. For one, they were minors. Two, the son of the high school principal as well as a councilman were on the team. There would be a lot of huffing and puffing on the parents' part, exactly the kind of small-town politics he hated.

Maybe he'd run his thoughts by Bing, see how the captain wanted to handle it.

But not tonight. Tonight, he still wanted to check out the grave site.

First he stopped by the diner to appease his growling stomach. He made a point of having a decent meal at least once a day. He wanted his full strength back for the inevitable face-off with Blackwell. He also wanted to see if Eddie had an alibi.

He did, according to the owner.

"Eddie has breakfast and dinner here every day, hasn't missed a meal this year yet," the round-faced woman told Jack, one hand on her hip, the other holding a dishrag. "I remember him being here the evening of the first, specifically, because one of the giant dishwashers in the back threw a hose and Eddie went back there to help us fix it."

"You're sure it was the first?"

"One hundred percent. There was some water damage, so I had to fill out stacks of insurance papers." She frowned. "I haven't yet seen a penny of that insurance money either."

Jack thanked her and, after he ate, he took the long way out to the reservoir, taking the back roads, some of which, technically, were closed for winter. Creedence played on the stereo, an old CD that skipped on track four, right in the middle of "Born on the Bayou." He'd taken to driving the back roads at night when he couldn't sleep. Hoping for what? That he'd catch Blackwell dragging some victim off into the bushes? But he had no leads, and anything was better than lying in bed, staring at the ceiling and obsessing.

Or worse, falling asleep and dreaming of Ashley in his arms, his hands on her breasts, his mouth crushing hers in a wild kiss. He was that far gone now.

His high beams caught an ancient Chevy pulled over to the side of the road, almost in the ditch. He was instantly alert, shoving his coat aside to make sure he'd have easy access to his weapon if needed. Then he recognized the car and grinned into the night.

He pulled up to the side of the parked car and shone his halogen onto the backseat, and looked away from the tangled mass of limbs scurrying for clothes.

He rolled his window down, thinking he recognized one of his neighbors who lived a few houses down from the small ranch house Jack rented. He didn't like apartments. He liked to be able to look out the windows in every direction and see what was coming.

"That you, Billy Pickett?"

"That you, Jack?" Billy, the fifty-something town mechanic was struggling into a white sweatshirt. With his head stuck somewhere shy of the opening, he looked like a cartoon ghost.

"Detective Sullivan, under the circumstances. And would that be Molly in there with you?" He risked another look. With one eye. Squinting.

"Hey, Jack," said the woman, now wrapped in a wool blanket, thankfully.

"Road's closed. You get stuck out here, good luck getting a tow."

"Jeanne moved back with the kids again." Billy's head finally emerged.

Jeanne was their oldest, with twins and a deadbeat boyfriend. When things turned rough from time to time, she moved back with Billy and Molly. Who also had the four younger kids still in the house, plus Molly's parents.

He didn't blame them for sneaking away for some private time, but he was the law in town. He supposed he had to say something. "Open lewdness is a misdemeanor of the third degree," he told them mildly. Then added on a more serious tone, "There could be dangerous people out in these parts."

"You should know. Shouldn't you be home, recovering?" Molly asked with feeling. "You let me know if you need help around the house."

Darndest thing about small towns. He hadn't thought he'd made friends here. He'd kept to himself as always. Yet after he'd gotten home from the hospital, Molly had come over to clean. Another neighbor had brought an entire lasagna that had lasted him a week. Bewildering stuff for a man who'd spent his whole life a loner.

"Seen anyone since you've been out here?" he asked.

Billy shook his head, but Molly said, "We did hear some snowmobiles."

Those kids again. He was going to have a talk with them and soon, get a feel for them.

"All right. Go home. Stay safe." He shut off the halogen, rolled up the window, and cranked the Creedence song as he pulled away.

As the old Chevy disappeared in his rearview mirror, for a moment he wondered what that would be like, having all that normalcy, having a good woman to love, family. Something weird tickled in the middle of his chest, something that felt irritatingly similar to longing.

He didn't have time to be lonely.

But he wondered if Ashley was, living out there by herself.

Whatever her problems were, she was a fine woman. Seemed insane that somebody hadn't snatched her up yet.

He was a morose bastard; that he was alone was to be expected. But Ashley needed more in her life than what she had now. She deserved more—her daughter back, a family, a man to stand by her, a house full of laughter.

For a second, he almost wished he was the kind of guy who could give her that. Then he gave a sour laugh. Jesus, he was going soft in the head.

He drove down the road, watching for tire tracks, keeping alert. Finally he came out of the woods and onto the paved road again. In five minutes or so, he was coming up on Ashley's place. Her downstairs windows were dark, only one light on in the house, upstairs but not the loft, probably her bedroom.

On an impulse, he gave her a ring. "Hey, it's Jack. Just wanted to check in. Painted anything today?"

"Finished a pretty good abstract."

"Nothing else?"

She hesitated on the other end.

"It's not an official inquiry."

He could hear her releasing her breath.

"No, not today."

Something inside him relaxed. "All right. Good night, then."

"Thank you for the shovel," she hurried to say.

He didn't want her to read anything into it. "You needed one," he said gruffly, then hung up on her.

The dark hole in the ground.

The light in Ashley's window.

There was a choice there, whether or not he wanted to admit it.

The light drew him. But he drove past her driveway and turned right on Hadley Road, toward the grave.

Chapter Nine

Ashley woke later than usual, cursing herself for missing the best morning light for painting. She shoved out of bed bleary-eyed. Since visiting the grave hadn't worked the night before, she'd convinced herself that her "visions" were brought on by anxiety, stress, and exhaustion, so she'd stayed up most of the night, trying to think of all the things she was scared of. A pretty miserable way to spend the time.

And nothing to show for it. She didn't "see" a thing.

But she had to. She had to figure out a way to get the FBI off her back. She would somehow carve out a normal life, for her and her daughter, no matter what she had to do to get there. She would paint; she would force a vision if it killed her; she would not give up.

At least she no longer had to fight Jack. She was grateful beyond words for that break. He made a bad enemy.

But if they were no longer enemies, what were they?

The way his arms felt around her came back in a rush, unbalancing her a little as she plodded down the stairs, unsure whether she had energy to make coffee.

The phone interrupted before she could reach the pot.

"I hope I'm not disturbing your work," her father said on the other end.

Her stomach clenched. "Is everything okay?"

"Some people I'm working with called a last-minute meeting in Baltimore. I'm going to drive down. Leaving right now, actually. I thought—"

"Yes," she said, suddenly wide awake. "Could you please bring Maddie? You could drop her off, then pick her up on your way back."

"All right. We'll be there then, shortly."

She said good-bye on autopilot, grinning at the sink, doing a little dance barefooted on the tile.

Maddie was coming. On a regular old Wednesday.

Then she thought, *oh God, I probably look like a zombie.* Never mind that. She had makeup, and she knew how to use it. She could fix herself up and pretend that everything was okay.

Then, with her eyes open a little wider now than a slit, she registered the living room. The mess was, well, artistic. Creative chaos. Okay, disorder on a monumental scale.

She'd been looking for a magazine article on psychic experiences in the middle of the night. Most of the contents of her magazine rack as well as her bookshelf—at one point she'd thought maybe she'd seen the topic in a book, after all—were spread all over the place.

She couldn't let her father see this mess. He'd think she was having some kind of breakdown. Forgetting coffee, she tackled the cleaning as if it was an Olympic event. She even put a batch of cookies into the oven. She just finished, and was halfway up the stairs to clean herself up when a car pulled up her driveway.

She finger combed her hair and straightened her clothes, wishing she had another ten minutes. Her father was big on personal hygiene. But instead of her father, Pete was waiting outside when she answered the door.

He handed over a stack of envelopes, then reached into the side pocket of his mail carrier bag and pulled out a wad of newspapers that held half a dozen brown lumps. "Paperwhites. You pot the bulbs up now, and in a few weeks it'll be like spring in here. Maybe you'll paint them." He gave a friendly grin.

He was big on indoor gardening. He grew everything from tulips to hyacinths, bringing the outside in. He'd gotten into it two years ago when his mother had breast cancer and had some pretty bad chemo all through winter.

He'd been a traveling trainer for the postal service before that, but he came back to town and took a lower-paying delivery job, moving in with his mother to take care of her, and brought her spring.

He was a decent guy. As far as she could tell, everybody in town liked him.

"Mother says to say hi. She'll be by next week to pick up donations for the club if you have anything."

"I'll find something." She always did. If nothing else, she did a quick sketch that the Broslin Women's Club could auction off at the benefit auction they held once a quarter.

A familiar SUV rolling down the road caught her eye. As the car came closer and turned into her driveway, she recognized the man in the driver seat. Agent Hunter. Her stomach sank. Was he coming to arrest her this time? God, she didn't want to do this in front of Pete.

"Looks like I have visitors. Thank you for the flower bulbs. Say hi to your mom for me." She gave a none too subtle hint for him to leave.

"Don't mention it." He gave her a big grin, casting a curious glance at the car. "I better get back to work. Say hi to Maddie for me."

Agent Hunter waited to get out until Pete climbed into the mail delivery van and drove away, rubbernecking but only a little.

Her insides twisted into a knot. Two other men came with the agent like before. Her face was so tight, her teeth ground together. They couldn't take her in today. Maddie was coming.

"Miss Price." The man's tone and the look in his eyes were all official. He pulled a sheet of paper from his coat pocket. "We have a search warrant for your home."

She didn't know whether to be relieved or furious. "On what probable cause?" They'd searched her property before but had left her house alone.

"Jack Sullivan was buried on your land. You knew where the grave was."

Nothing new, then. Jack was still keeping her macabre paintings and her secret. As much grief as he'd given her, she was grateful for at least that. And the call last night. It was strange that he would care enough to check up on her. Of course, last night she'd actually been hoping for a vision.

"This is what I keep coming back to, Miss Price." Agent Hunter handed her the search warrant. "How is it that you would be out there, in the middle of your hundred acres in the middle of the night, at exactly the right place?"

"It was barely twilight, not the middle of the night. I went out there to look for a new subject to paint." She needed to stick with that, keep her story straight.

She drew a deep breath to settle her nerves. It didn't work. "Go ahead." She gestured anyway, knowing fighting them would be futile. "I would appreciate if you hurried. I'm expecting company." With a little luck, they'd be out of here before her father came.

The agents passed by her, not looking like they gave a hoot for her company one way or the other. Of course, they didn't.

Perfect.

They made her so nervous she was about jumping out of her skin, so she grabbed her coat, put it on, and stayed outside. Her obvious nervousness would just arouse more suspicions. Better go with the whole "out of sight, out of mind" thing.

They would look. They would leave. Maddie was coming, she told herself. Nothing could ruin the day. She simply wouldn't allow it. She had a small house. The search lasted less than an hour. They took her shower curtain and gave her a receipt for it.

She grasped the stupid receipt as she went inside, then nearly cried when she looked around. Her furniture overturned, the carpet bunched up, the bookshelf's contents spilled to the floor. The house looked like a herd of elephants had stampeded through. Exhaustion dragged her down. Tears burned her throat. To hell with it. She scooped up the pillows and the blankets. She could do this. They weren't going to win. She threw herself into cleaning, forcing herself to think positive thoughts, nothing but how much fun she was going to have with her daughter today.

She wasn't quite finished when her father pulled up the driveway. "Mommy!" Maddie flew into her arms as soon as she opened the door.

She carried her baby inside, kissing the top of her head, then nuzzling cheeks.

"What happened here?" her father asked as he walked in behind them, looking at the sofa she hadn't had a chance yet to drag back into its place. "You look disheveled. Is everything all right?"

Her first impulse was to hide her troubles. But lying to her father wasn't progress. She had to be strong enough for the truth. So, as Maddie ran off to check out the cookies on the kitchen table, Ashley told him about the FBI.

"It's not a big deal. They can look all they want. They're grasping for straws. I have no connection to Blackwell, so it's not like they'll find anything."

He watched her for a long moment. "I happen to know the best criminal attorney in the state. I'll have him give you a call before the day is out."

"No," she said, then pulled back a little. She didn't want her father to keep solving her problems for her. "No, thank you. I have nothing to worry about. I didn't do anything other than save a man's life. I already contacted my old attorney. If they want to question me again, he'll be coming with me."

There, she stood up to her father. And, oddly, he didn't seem to mind. He accepted her decision with a look akin to approval.

"I might be late coming back tonight," he said.

And for the first time that week, she smiled. "Be as late as you like." She glanced back at her daughter, who was pouring a glass of milk and missing the glass here and there. Warmth spread through her chest.

"So you're feeling well." Her father's tone held a touch of concern. "This new thing didn't bring back any of the old depression?"

"No."

"How are you doing with the anxiety? If you're scared, you don't have to stay here alone."

Giving up her independence wasn't the answer. "Whatever happened, happened on the other side of the property. Over two weeks ago. The guy isn't sticking around. He's probably in another state by now. Yes, it's creepy, kind of, but I'm okay with it. Bad things happen, and then we move on, right? Life keeps going."

And she knew her father couldn't disagree with that. She was quoting his own words, after all, something he'd told her after her mother's death, a million years ago.

He gave her a brief nod and left them with a brisk, "See you later." She locked the door behind him, then skipped to Maddie with a grin.

* * *

135

Jack started his morning with calling the Lanius gallery and asking about how to reach the mushroom artist, Greg Shatzkin. The guy had been all around the mushroom houses. He could have been the one to track those spores onto the last Blackwell crime scene. He could be Blackwell.

But it didn't turn out that way. Shatzkin, when finally reached, claimed a solid alibi, teaching at a local college, which was confirmed by the admin office. Another dead lead.

After Jack finished grousing over that, he spent the morning online, checking eBay and Craigslist, checking local listings against the roster of stolen items he had from the burglaries. The work was tedious and not the case he wanted to work, but if this was the price he had to pay for being back on active duty, then so be it.

His hand paused over the mouse as a listing for a laptop came up, same model as on his stolen items list. The hard drive would be wiped clean by now, the laptop pretty much unidentifiable, but he made note of the username—topjockhere with numbers after it—then did a search for anything else that user might have listed.

The office buzzed around him, the usual business. He tuned that out as he scanned through some pictures.

He saw things that might or might not be the same as the items he was looking for. He also saw some snowmobile parts that user had traded recently. Made him think of the teens who rode their snowmobiles out around the reservoir.

"Hey, Joe," he said as Joe passed by his desk. He showed him the username he'd scribbled on a piece of paper. "What do you think of this?"

Joe shrugged. "Looks like my e-mail address."

"Decoded?"

"Position I played, and my number."

"If you had to guess, what position do you think this guy plays?"

"Captain."

"You know the captain of the local football team?"

"Sure. Sometimes the coach has me come in to give the kids a talk." He gave a cocky grin. "I'm considered very inspirational. I think Bobby Adamo is the captain now. Principal Adamo's oldest. Man used to bust me for everything back in the day. Then I played in a few championships, and now they have a separate display case for me in the hallway. Figures." He swaggered away with a sentimental look on his face.

Jack stood and walked over to Bing's office, and filled him in. "Not enough for a search warrant," the captain said from behind his desk with a scowl on his face. "Not with these kids. When we make that move, we have to be a hundred percent sure. Their parents will be asking for our badges. Get me more."

He would. He didn't need a warrant to talk to the kids. "And if I get more?"

"We take the little suckers down. Town politics or not, I took an oath to defend our citizenry from dipshits like this."

Exactly why he liked Bing. Jack was turning to leave when the captain called after him.

"I hear you've been asking about Eddie Gannon at the diner. Is he connected to this somehow?"

Right. Bing got his coffee there too, in the mornings.

Jack took a step back. "Not really."

"Are you investigating the Blackwell case?" Bing leaned forward in his chair. "Look at me. This is not my happy face."

He was right about that. "On the side," Jack admitted.

"Do you listen to anything I say? You're not to investigate that bastard. How many ways do I have to tell you? I hear you took Ashley Price home the other day."

"I ran into her in the parking lot. She didn't have a ride."

"Don't run into her again. I mean it. You have a serious conflict of interest. Even if you find something, you could mess up the whole case. If the FBI catches you meddling, they'll bring a shit storm down on us we won't want to see."

A moment of silence passed between them, tension rolling off both of them. On anything else, he could have backed down, but not on this.

The captain shot him a frustrated look. "I know it's difficult for you to stand back. I even understand it. But you have to do it anyway. I put you on sick leave. It didn't work. I put you on another case. It didn't work. I don't want to have to ask for your badge."

That brought Jack up short, both the words and the serious tone in which they'd been spoken. For too many years now, he'd been the badge. The badge was his life. That and Blackwell. "Listen—"

"Focus on the burglaries, dammit. You're obsessed. I'm beginning to wonder if you're not right in the head. You're crossing a line here. Stay away from Blackwell."

"Why?" he challenged. "What the hell is the FBI doing?"

"Following other leads. They're looking at Ashley Price again. I heard they got a warrant."

The wave of protectiveness rose swiftly. "They found anything?"

"Not that I know of."

He relaxed a little. "I was thinking too, actually—"

"Don't."

"Do you think Blackwell ever returns to her place? He's got an ego on him, fed by the fact that he hasn't been caught all this time."

"Tell me you haven't been back there by that creek." Bing glared. Jack was smart enough to keep his mouth shut.

"You've seen any evidence of him returning?"

Frustration tightened his jaw. "Nothing." Yet.

"The reason he hasn't been caught is because he isn't stupid. He's probably out of the state by now."

"Maybe." But his instincts said something else. He was almost sure that Blackwell was still around. He was meticulous in what he did. He didn't seem like the type to leave a job unfinished. The thought that the bastard might come for him filled Jack with anticipation instead of dread. In fact, he was counting on it.

Bing shoved a folder aside on his desk. "The cabin with all the guns has nothing to do with Blackwell, by the way. Just to set your mind at ease. It belongs to old Albert."

"Shoemaker?" He knew the guy, a retired mechanic who sometimes still worked on cars out of his garage at home.

"He's been watching some TV show about people preparing for the end of the world or whatever. The old man decided to buy a hunting camp and turn it into a survival bunker."

"Shouldn't he be stockpiling food?"

"He's got two hundred cans of kidney beans buried all around the cabin, apparently." Bing swore under his breath. "Him and his buddies have some kind of club. This is what happens when the city cuts funding for the senior center. Too much time on too many old geezers' hands. Like I needed something else to worry about. None of them can see worth a damn. Running around in the woods with guns." He closed his eyes for a second and rubbed his eyelids.

"Maybe we could offer bingo night here at the station." Jack tried to lighten the mood.

Bing looked up. "Maybe I can put you in charge of that without messing up."

"Not if Albert and his buddies eat all those beans."

The door to the conference room the FBI occupied banged open and the agents spilled out, just as he said the last word. They headed out the front door, Agent Hunter in the lead.

"Any news?" Jack hurried from the captain's office and called after them before Bing had a chance to call him back.

"Missing-person case up in New Jersey. Two, actually. Female, twenty-one and twenty-three. One kidnapped three days ago from her home, the other one this morning," the last of the junior agents said before the door swung shut behind him.

In batches. Jack's heart rate picked up.

"See? What did I say?" Bing came out of his office. "Blackwell moved on already. He was never from Broslin. He came here because of you. He tracked you down to stop you from following him."

No. "Maybe." He headed for the door.

"Where are you going?"

"Home to rest. My ribs are hurting."

"Bullshit. You never admit to anything hurting. I don't want you near the Feds."

"Roger that," he said, without promising anything, knowing he was risking both his friendship with Bing and his career over this case. And for a moment, just a moment, he wondered if he could toe the line this once, let the FBI bring Blackwell in.

As long as the man was brought to justice—

But no, he couldn't. For one, he didn't trust the FBI not to mess up. Two, this was too personal. He needed to personally see it finished. He'd gone too far to pull back. He had too much invested in this.

He strode out of the station, stepped into the falling darkness, and sucked in a sharp breath when the cold hit him. With everything he was, he wanted to drive to Jersey. But he didn't turn right out of the parking lot, toward Route 1 that would take him there. The crime scenes would be crawling with FBI tonight. He had to give them first look. He would drive over in the morning.

He turned left and drove by his house, packed Ashley's paintings into his trunk, except one—his. Then he headed toward the reservoir. He needed to think right now, and there was one place that never failed to bring his mind into sharp focus. He wanted to ponder what the new development in Jersey meant, if Blackwell had moved on. If the bastard did know that Jack had been after him all these years, would he expect Jack to move after him again? For the first time, he didn't want to. Broslin wasn't a bad town, better than many. And his sudden inclination to stay didn't have anything to do with Ashley Price, he told himself, even if he wasn't sure he believed it.

The victims circled in his mind, along with dozens of questions. But he reached no solution, gained no new insight by the time he pulled his car over on the side of the desolate stretch of road about three quarters of a mile from Ashley Price's house. He got out and started forward. The cold would do him good. It would wake up his brain.

Here he always felt as if Blackwell was right next to him, within reach. And, of course, Ashley was here, not far behind the trees. He hated Brady Blackwell with a passion that bordered on religious fanaticism. Yet he no longer spent every minute of every day thinking of him. Sometimes now, he thought of Ashley.

Not even the cold, bracing wind would clear her from his mind. The light at her core drew him, the light behind her palpable fears, especially when she spoke of her daughter. She loved that kid.

A million years ago, his father had said every man had two wolves in his heart, one representing love, the other hate, fighting for dominance. Which one wins? The one you feed. He'd made his choice, Jack thought. He'd been feeding hate for too long. He needed it to catch Blackwell.

His black, cap-toe boots crunched in the snow as he headed toward the creek. He saw the rock first, before he heard the water. It ran too fast to freeze over, even when the weather turned this cold. He slowed, watched, and listened for other noises. Nothing. He moved forward again, looking for footprints, any sign that someone had been out this way other than him.

He pulled his keychain from his pocket and the tactical light attached to it. He let the high-powered beam sweep the ground. He walked straight to the grave. Snow had filled the hole nearly to the top. Most of the yellow police tape was still waving from the nearby bushes where the wind had blown it.

Almost a month had passed since he'd been pulled from the damned grave, and not many new clues since. Maybe Blackwell *had* moved on to Jersey. Frustration tightened his muscles as he kicked the snow. Then he stilled as the short hairs stood straight up at his nape.

He was being watched. He felt it.

He turned slowly and reached for his weapon.

He couldn't see anyone, bushes and trees and the boulder obstructing his vision. The moon sat too pale in the sky for him to see much beyond the circle of his flashlight.

Yet he knew, without a doubt, with every cop instinct he had, that he wasn't alone in the woods.

A branch snapped somewhere to his right.

He whirled that way. "Hey! Who's there?"

No response came.

"Broslin PD. Step forward and identify yourself."

Nothing.

But a second later, he heard more rustling.

He moved forward, carefully, step by step, his weapon ready. When he reached the point where he thought the sounds came from, he panned the ground with his flashlight. The ground rose here, rocky, blown clear of snow, so he couldn't see footprints. The rocks led straight down to the creek.

He looked there too and kept looking, but he found no prints anywhere, and he didn't hear any suspicious noises again.

Had Blackwell come? Why? To recall fond memories of torture? To plan his next move? To say good-bye to a failed job before heading back to Jersey for a third victim?

Jack cast a last glance at the grave, then started off toward the house, through the woods, looking for evidence that Blackwell might have gone that way. He hurried.

Chapter Ten

He found no footprints as he moved forward, keeping a close eye on the ground, keeping his gun out, listening. The dark woods seemed endless suddenly, the frigid air menacing. He was pretty chilled through by the time he walked out of the woods.

He walked around the backyard, did find some shoe prints, but not the size and tread he was looking for. As he strode up to the front door, he could hear Ashley talking and laughing inside.

No extra car in her driveway but her own. Maybe she was on the phone.

Light poured out the windows. He glanced back at the woods that stood in dark silence. And darker yet, the grave.

He cursed, his breath visible in the air. He stabbed the doorbell before he could think more about it.

Then Ashley opened the door, with a black eye, and everything inside him stilled. Rage rose swiftly. Whoever touched her—

He hadn't come up to the house with any clear idea of what he wanted, and whatever little he'd prepared in his head now fled, replaced by hot, pumping anger. "Are you okay?"

Maddie peeked from behind her with wide green eyes and dimples in her cheeks. "Hi, Jack," she squeaked. "We're playing makeup. Want to come in?"

A second passed before he regained his balance. *Makeup.* She wasn't injured. "Sure."

Ashley stepped back to let him through, long-legged and curvy in jeans and a simple sweater. "Maddie is visiting today. My father is in Baltimore for the day. He'll be picking her up on his way back."

The little girl ran forward in a fluffy skirt made of rainbow silk. "I'm a princess." She had a sparkly purple magic wand in her hand.

Ashley watched her daughter with a smile, the first true smile he'd seen on her. It dazzled him more than it should have, so he turned to the kid. "Hi, Princess Maddie." He scrambled for something to say. "Uh... How is Princess Lillian?"

"She had a fight with Prince William. She wants to get earrings, and Prince William won't let her. And all her friends have them already."

Huh? And then he caught up. Man, he was slow tonight. Princess Lillian's latest drama was probably the reflection of a real-life earring issue Maddie was having with her grandfather.

Jewelry and body piercing in general were out of his realm of expertise. He had no idea what to say. He came up with, "True beauty needs no adornment," and was damn proud of himself for the quick thinking.

She looked at him as if he was talking Japanese.

"When you're the most beautiful princess already, all the extra stuff is just distracting," Ashley translated with a grateful glance at Jack. "Who needs it?"

Maddie's scrunched-up face eased into a smile as she lifted her doll. "She is the most beautiful already, isn't she?" She hugged the doll. "See? Jack says beauty doesn't need ornaments. 'Cept if you're a Christmas tree." She glanced up to her mother for confirmation, looking happy when her mother nodded.

He was about to extricate himself—he hadn't meant to intrude on a private moment, take up any of the precious time they had together—when Ashley said, "How about some coffee?"

An invitation to all the warmth and light and smiles the house held. He hadn't known, until just now, that a part of him, deep down, wanted something like this. He wasn't sure what he was going to do about that. But he kicked his snowy boots off and hung his coat on a peg. "That would be great."

"Do you want to play makeup?" Maddie's face transformed into a look that he was pretty sure one day would have kids and puppy dogs ruling the world. "I'm very good at it. Mommy let me. See how pretty she is?"

He looked at the dark blue eye shadow all over Ashley's cheekbone, held her gaze as he said, "She's very pretty." He wasn't lying.

Surprise crossed her face as she looked away. "I don't think Jack wants makeup, honey. How about we frost the last of the cookies?"

"Yay!" The kid danced around them, rainbow skirt flying, wand pumping in one hand, Princess Lillian in the other.

"I swear she lives for sugar." An apologetic smile hovered over Ashley's lips.

He moved toward the kitchen.

"Better get started before somebody loses an eye."

She already had coffee made, probably for her father to have a cup for the drive home. She poured him a cup; then they all focused on frosting and sprinkles. Maddie wanted to make a contest of it, so they did.

He figured the kid would lose interest in ten minutes—short-attention-span generation and all that. He hoped in vain. An hour passed before the contest ended, not before every last cookie was elaborately frosted. They had secret voting. Maddie came in first. The little girl pushed the biggest cookie toward him. "You get a condensation prize for trying."

He glanced at Ashley.

"Consolation prize," she translated.

"Can we play a board game?" Maddie beseeched, already squirming on her seat.

"I don't think we have time before Grandpa gets back, honey."

"Can I watch cartoons?"

"Sure."

The kid scampered off to the living room with her own frosted sweet, turned on the TV, and plopped down to watch a cartoon elephant doing cartwheels.

Ashley was wiping pink frosting off the tablecloth. "It's not as bad as you think. Oatmeal, and I used honey instead of refined sugar, substituted some of the oil in the recipe with applesauce. She loves her cookies, so I try to make them as healthy as possible."

He grabbed a sheet of paper towel and helped. "It must be difficult not to be able to see her every day."

The smile she'd been wearing all evening slid off her face.

He wished he hadn't said anything. He really liked the lighthearted, smiling Ashley. She was going through a hard time. And he had done nothing but make it worse, ever since they'd met. She needed these moments of lightness. She deserved them.

"I want to apologize for pushing you so hard before," he said. "I have your paintings in the trunk."

She looked more alarmed than relieved, probably because her daughter was there.

"I can come by again with them tomorrow," he offered.

She watched him with a wary expression. "Does this mean I'm completely cleared?"

"As far as I'm concerned."

"You came all the way out here to tell me that?"

"I came to make sure you were all right."

She took a moment to digest that. "Okay. Apology accepted."

Just like that. "You don't hold grudges."

"You do."

"Just the one."

A moment of silence passed between them before she asked, "So other than looking for Blackwell, what do you do all day?"

"Look for Blackwell."

Sympathy filled her eyes. That she could feel sorry for him, the man who'd wanted nothing more for the past weeks than to prove her a murderer's accomplice, spoke volumes for her heart and character. Not that he wanted anyone's pity. He was doing exactly what he wanted to be doing.

But she said, "Don't you see how sad that is? He couldn't kill you, but you give him your life anyway."

He didn't expect her to understand. He rose to go. He shouldn't have come. He had no right to bring all his darkness here, to her, when she had plenty of her own shadows to struggle with.

"I can put those paintings from my car into your garage, where your daughter won't see them." He glanced toward the living room.

Maddie was sprawled on a pillow on the floor, sound asleep. Ashley walked over there and picked up the kid, kissed her forehead, and lay her on the couch, covering her up.

"She's tuckered out. We've been playing in the snow all afternoon," she said as she came back to the kitchen. "I'm hoping she can move back home once school is out. I miss her too much when she's gone. You must think I'm a bad mother for letting someone else raise her."

"I think you're as good a mother as they come," he said sincerely. "You put her needs before yours. You want her with you, but you know it's better if you wait until you're fully back on your feet." And then she smiled at him, a true, full-on smile. For him. He tried not to think how many of his restless dreams she'd starred in lately.

The need that hit him was a punch to his gut. He cleared his throat and stepped back. "I should get those paintings."

"Maybe I shouldn't have them back. The FBI was here this morning with a search warrant. What if they come again?"

"They won't." He told her about the kidnappings in Jersey. He didn't like the thought of Agent Hunter and his men in her house, harassing her. Even if he'd done the same before. "They're moving on."

"Thank God. I thought they might frame me for it. Just so they have someone in the bag."

"I'd like to think I would have protested."

She looked at him as if she only half believed him. She opened her mouth as if to say something, but then closed it again.

"What is it?"

She glanced down at her hands. "I tried to force a vision. To see him. I thought if I could draw him…"

Everything inside him stilled. He held his breath. "Did you?"

"No. I even went out to the grave the other night. Scared myself silly."

He grabbed on to the back of his chair. "Don't do that. Ever. Don't go back out there, do you hear me?"

"That I can promise." She tilted her head. "So if Blackwell is in Jersey, why are you here instead of being there?"

"I'll drive over tomorrow."

"Why not let the FBI handle it? You could let it go. You're alive. You won."

He didn't want to talk about it. And then he did anyway. He'd never cared before if anyone thought him an obsessed lunatic. He shouldn't now. But he did.

"I had a sister. Six years older than me. She raised me, pretty much. Breast cancer took our mother in her twenties."

A dull pain throbbed to life in the middle of his chest. Then came the flood of guilt. "Our father was working the graveyard shift. I was a teenage brat, wanted pizza. We lived too far outside of town. The only pizza shop didn't deliver that far out. I begged her into it. I stayed home and played video games. She drove out for the pizza. She always tried to make up for the fact that I had to grow up without a mother. I was a spoiled little shit, pretty much."

"Jack—"

"Anyway, she never came back. They found..." He swallowed hard. "Parts of her, six months later." He searched her gaze, looking for blame. He didn't find any. "I grew up then."

"And followed Blackwell since?"

"I'll be following him until the day I catch him."

"Even if it takes the rest of your life?"

He shrugged. "Whatever it takes."

She came over and laid a slim hand on his arm. Heat shot through his body instantly at the slight touch. She was too close; he'd been holding himself in check for too long. She meant her gesture to be comforting, he was sure, but he wanted another kind of comfort.

She drew a slow breath. He didn't want to hear what else she had to say. She wanted him to walk away from his vengeance and be a better man. She wanted him to fight against the forces that kept pulling him back to his dark place, like she was fighting. He didn't want to hear it.

He reached for her and drew her to him. And then he kissed her. He brushed his lips across hers. Hadn't meant to do more than that. But he went back for another brush. Still too quick, still too unsatisfactory. She smelled like butterscotch frosting and tasted incredibly sweet. So he let his lips linger, then pressed a little harder, pulling her even closer. And again.

He was in complete control. And then he wasn't.

Raw need shot through him, so sharp as to be nearly painful. He had to make a conscious effort to gentle his hands, not to hold her too tightly. He pulled back before he could have given in to the urge and crushed her lips under his like he meant it.

She looked at him wide-eyed, stunned. And, God, so beautiful she took his breath away.

He should apologize, some long-buried decency inside him said. He should walk away from her. Instead, he bit back a curse and kissed her again.

Since he was never going to get into heaven, this was the closest thing he was going to get. He lowered his hands to her waist and anchored them there. And then he deepened the kiss.

* * *

She wanted so badly to think, but she couldn't. Those sculpted lips she'd thought about painting were over hers. Oh wow. The body she'd assessed with an artist's eye was now pressed against her, suddenly gaining another dimension. So much more interesting, so much better, so much…everything.

As an artist, she kept her subjects at arm's length. But now Jack was suddenly very, very close, her head reeling. Heat poured off him that threatened to set her on fire.

He was a ball of pain and hard man, a man on the edge, yet there was something heroic at the core of him, and at the same time something incredibly tragic. A complicated subject, layer upon layer, colors bleeding into each other, twisting. How on earth was she supposed to make sense of him?

She couldn't, not for the moment. Right now all she could do was feel. She hung on to his wide shoulders, because she wasn't sure how much longer her knees could hold her.

The passion that flared to life between them stunned her. There were parts of her that had been simply dead since the accident, most likely because of the depression and the pills she'd taken at the beginning. But suddenly everything came roaring back to life, passion as a swirl of vibrant colors. For the first time in a long time, she felt like a woman again. The fire was all-consuming, hotter and wilder than she'd ever felt before.

And it was all wrong.

He was the wrong guy for her, a drifter cop who was obsessed with a serial killer. He'd never put her and Maddie first, never.

She needed steady and normal. She wanted that more than anything. He was anything but. Yet she couldn't pull away. The weak whispers of reason were drowned out by the roaring drums of passion.

Her nipples puckered up under her bra, her breasts pressed against the muscles of his chest. When a soft sound escaped the back of

her throat, to her utter embarrassment, he was the one who first
pulled away.
They were both breathing hard, staring at each other.
He looked as stunned as she felt while he cleared his throat.
Silence stretched between them as her body and mind still reeled.
What on earth had just happened?
But then he pulled himself together and said, "You don't have to
come out into the cold. Just give me the garage-door opener, and
I'll set the paintings in there, cover them up."
What?
He was moving fast in another direction, while she was still stuck
on the kiss, her lips still tingling, her nipples still puckered.
He wanted to talk about paintings?
Of course. The haze in her mind began to clear; the heat
enveloping her dissipated. He probably wanted to get out of here.
Wanted to get an early start tomorrow to head to Jersey. Anger
swept through her swiftly.
She refused to show how much the kiss had shaken her. She kept it
together as she marched by him to the front door, grabbed the key
to the garage door from the laundry room, and held it out for him.
His gaze caught on the helium tank and the handful of boxes next
to the washer as he took the keys. "What's that?"
"Maddie's birthday is this weekend. We're having a party with her
little friends."
His face hardened immediately. "No."
She wrapped her arms around herself. "I'm afraid you don't get a
say in that."
"What if Blackwell comes back?"
Really? They were back to that? "But you just said Blackwell
moved on to Jersey."
"It's always smart to exercise caution. You should go and stay with
your father tonight. Stay with him for a couple of weeks."
She stared. "You notice the irony here? When I wanted to go, you
told me I couldn't. Anyway, Agent Hunter wants me to stay put."
"I'll clear it with him. Will you go with your father?" His tone
turned urgent. "Tonight?"
Her independence was the last thing she had left, and she'd fought
hard to be able to keep it. She wasn't giving that up now. "No."

149

His jaw clenched. "At least cancel the party." His intense gaze held hers. "I think he came back. I felt him back there tonight."
He was beyond reason, obsessed beyond the point of rational thought. He scared her a little now, which was such a contrast to what the kiss had been just a few seconds before.
A man of so many contrasts, he had some strange ability to set her head spinning. She struggled to understand him. One minute he could be gentle, and the next completely infuriating.
He proved that by saying, "I'm ordering you."
Her jaw clenched.
He stared her down. "As an officer of the law. No party."

Chapter Eleven

Jack tried not to think of Ashley or their kiss as he walked back to the locker room at the east end of the high school the next day. The team was gathering for a morning huddle about an upcoming game. He wanted to get this over with before he headed off to Jersey. He called out the players he needed, gathering them in the hallway.

"Is this about the bones?" Bobby Adamo asked, gripping a cup of coffee. "You guys took off. Nobody said we were supposed to wait around."

None of the four looked anything but cocky, feeling safe in numbers and on their home turf.

Jack watched their eyes, looking for the weakest link. Probably Tyler Foster, the councilman's son. He was the youngest, the one Jack had caught on Ashley's land before. He'd scared the boy when he'd tackled him.

"Actually, I'm here about a laptop you're selling online." Jack looked Bobby in the eye. "I wouldn't mind seeing it."

The surprise on the teenager's face was quickly masked. The others pulled closer to him.

"I don't know what you're talking about."

Jack pulled a piece of paper from his pocket and unfolded it, a printout of the website with the laptop, seller ID on top.

The coach loped up to them, sweatpants and T-shirt in team colors of blue and yellow, a trim man in his fifties, no hair, hard eyes. "Is there a problem here?" He was clearly protective of his players.

"Detective Sullivan, Broslin PD. I'm running down some leads on a couple of stolen items."

The man bristled. "I don't know if I feel comfortable with you interrogating these boys without their parents present."
"It's not a formal questioning. That would take place down at the station. I'm just asking for their help here," he said and stayed where he stood.
The coach shot him an aggravated glare, then walked away.
"So about the laptop?" Jack held up the paper.
"That's not my account," Bobby said.
"Are you sure? How about you?" He showed the sheet to each of the kids, giving them time to think about it.
The blank looks they gave him were a little too good to be convincing. Almost overdone, really.
He nodded as he put the paper away. "Here's the thing. Even online service providers have to hand over user data when confronted with a police warrant."
Tyler Foster twitched.
Jack was about to lean on him a little harder when Principal Adamo came rushing toward them with the coach. Jack knew the man from a teen drunk-driving accident a few months before that he'd handled. The principal hadn't been happy with him then and looked even more aggravated now.
"What is this about, Detective?" He put himself between Jack and the kids, exuding authority, while the coach headed into the locker room with a last disapproving glance at Jack.
"Following some leads on a stolen laptop and other things."
"I'm sure these athletes had nothing to do with it," he said, a tall man with an imposing attitude, dressed impeccably in a suit and tie.
"That's what I'm here to confirm."
The man glanced at his son, then the others.
"Dad, it's complete bullshit," Bobby complained, sullen and angry.
"Watch your language," Adamo snapped before turning to Jack.
"If you want to talk to them, you'll have to request a formal meeting with their parents and attorneys present. I'm sorry, Detective. My job is to protect these boys."
"I understand completely." Jack nodded without heat. "Tracking down some two-bit thieves is not the highlight of my career, believe me. The sooner it's over, the better."

He looked past the principal at the boys. "So here's the deal. First one who comes clean gets a free ride. Rest of them get a record and go to juvie." He turned on his heels, then walked away. He had more important things to do today. In Jersey.

* * *

Ashley blocked in the main areas of light and shadow, then set the brush down for a second as she thought about how she wanted to approach the rest.

And thought about Jack Sullivan.

She bit her lower lip, hating that it should tingle every time she thought of the stupid kiss. God, the man confused her. And turned her on. And infuriated her on a regular schedule.

There was good in him, although she wasn't sure if he knew it. He was too focused on other things. The past bound him. She could relate.

Worse, she could fall for him.

The whole package of masculine beauty, the edge of danger, the tragic past, the way he kissed... The attraction was there, despite her better judgment. Way too much attraction.

He could be thoughtful—bringing her a shovel, playing with her daughter—then unreasonably bossy, trying to tell her what to do, to move to Philly.

At least he'd left before her father arrived, so she didn't have to make any explanations why she had a man out at her house so late at night. Her father had been in a rush to get home. She hadn't mentioned the party cancellation; the time just didn't seem right. But she'd definitely tell him when they talked on the phone tonight.

She couldn't believe she was doing this, canceling something again because of Jack Sullivan.

When the doorbell rang, she was certain it was him and was preparing to give him a piece of her mind as she ran down the stairs. But when she opened the door, she found herself facing the mailman.

"Hey, Pete."

He gave his widest smile as always. "You got too many magazines to fit into your mailbox. Shouldn't have to walk all the way out there in this cold anyway."

"Thanks."

"Painting today?"

"All morning."

"You planted the flower bulbs?"

"Haven't had the time yet. But I will. I promise." He was such a nice guy, safe, stable. Why couldn't she feel the same spark now that she'd felt every time Jack came near her?

Pete hesitated on the doorstep. "I found a beaver dam on the creek when I was out hunting last week. Pretty small for now but neat." The first thing she thought was how much she would have liked to paint that.

And maybe Pete saw the gleam in her eyes, because he asked, "Would you come out there with me?"

She stared at him for a confused second. *Okay.* She'd kind of known for a while that Pete was sweet on her, but this was the most forward he'd ever been about it. A date.

And why not? Maybe it would get her mind off Jack, who was nothing but trouble. She didn't want to like a man whose entire life, first priority, was a murderer.

She wanted normal.

And it didn't get any more normal than Pete, even if he was maybe a bit old for her.

"Sure." She'd promised herself she would start getting out of the house more. A walk in the quiet woods with a friend was just the thing.

His face lit up. "Saturday, then?"

"Sorry, I have Maddie's party on Saturday." Well, she might. The FBI could catch Blackwell between now and then. She was going to keep her options open until the last minute, she decided suddenly.

"After the party would be perfect. It's not far from here. And the moonlight on the water around the dam is something to see," Pete said with enthusiasm.

With anyone else, she would have thought twice about it, but Pete was...Pete. She knew his mother too, pretty well. It wasn't as if she'd be going with a stranger. She'd been out at the grave in the middle of the night by herself. She could handle the beaver dam with Pete.

She'd done night landscapes before, had enjoyed the challenge of handling the light and colors. Maybe someday soon she would do another.

"Okay," she said and watched as Pete just about danced back to the mail truck.

He beeped the horn as he drove away.

She went back into the house, locked the door, and padded upstairs.

She was painting. And she was going on a date. Someday very soon, if she fought hard enough, she would have Maddie back. Her life would go back to normal.

All she had to do was not give up.

And forget Jack Sullivan.

* * *

By the time noon rolled around, Jack had gone back and forth between the two crime scenes in Jersey half a dozen times and had talked to everyone worth talking to. Yet he wasn't any closer to figuring out whether the two kidnappings were connected or whether Blackwell had been involved in them.

Agent Hunter gave him a hard time about being there, but tolerated him as they reinterviewed key people. That Jack might be able to identify Blackwell from his voice helped. But nobody they talked to rang a bell.

Jack drove back from Jersey in a foul mood, not all that much cheered when he got a call from the high school principal.

"Bobby is willing to talk to you." The man sounded grim and cold. "On the condition that he doesn't have to go to the station to be interviewed. And, of course, our family attorney will be present."

Jack was too distracted by the two missing persons in Jersey to point out to the man that the boy wasn't setting conditions here.

"Fine."

"My attorney can be here by four," Adamo said and gave his home address. "I'd appreciate it if you came alone. No uniformed officers and police cruisers. I have my standing in the community to consider."

He should have considered keeping a closer eye on his son, Jack thought but agreed. With Harper still out, they were understaffed at the station anyway. The case wasn't big enough to justify pulling one of the others off something else.

He glanced at the clock on the dashboard. He had time to go out to see Ashley and try to talk her into going someplace until he caught Blackwell.

He knew, with everything he had, that the bastard had been on her land the other night.

The fact that he'd put the grave there couldn't be a coincidence. At the beginning, Jack had thought it was because Ashley was involved with the man. Now he knew better.

But Blackwell could still be someone she knew, under another name. It might even be someone who liked her.

The more he thought about it, the more likely it seemed. Maybe he'd been some sick gift to her. A cop, the biggest thing Blackwell had taken down so far. Of course, Blackwell hadn't counted on her finding and saving Jack.

The mailman popped into his mind again. He'd looked at the man at the beginning, but Bing had talked him out of it, vouching for him. But this was too important to take someone else's word for it. So, on his way to Ashley's, he stopped by the post office.

He lucked out. Pete was just coming in.

The man wore hunting boots, Jack noted, and wasn't surprised when two minutes into their talk, the man's alibi for the days in questions came up as a solo hunting trip. No alibi at all.

"Would you mind lifting your foot?"

Pete looked at him as if he was crazy but did it.

Wrong treads, which didn't mean anything. If he had one pair of boots, he would have others.

"How about the day of the third, that Saturday? You said you came back from hunting in the morning."

"I was home with my mother. Then I went in to work for an hour in the evening to take over someone's truck who had to leave early."

Mother wasn't exactly the strongest alibi, Jack thought. He was definitely going to keep an eye on the man.

* * *

"You're so sweet," Mrs. Kentner said, holding the small paintings at arm's reach. "We really do appreciate your support." She put the paintings on the living room table and lifted her purse from the floor, taking out a small box wrapped in sparkling paper. She handed it to Ashley. "For Maddie. Pete said she's having her birthday party this weekend."

"Thank you. You really shouldn't have."

"Well, the way things are going…" Mrs. Kentner gave a smile and a wink.

Okay, so Pete told her mother about the date. Ashley felt a moment of embarrassment, then pushed it away.

"I'm so glad he came back home," the older woman said. "He deserves something good. The way he took care of me with the cancer…" Moisture glistened in the woman's eyes.

Ashley patted her hand. Pete did deserve something good, but was she it? A sudden wave of doubt rushed her. What was she doing with Pete? But then she thought, they were just going to look at the dam. They'd been friends for a long time. It didn't have to be more than that.

"I'll have him bring you some venison." Mrs. Kentner gathered herself. "He got a big one this fall. Dressed and butchered it by himself too. Gave half to the homeless shelter, but the freezer in the garage is still way too full. I can barely squeeze anything else in there."

"Thank you," she said politely, not having the vaguest idea what to do with venison. Then again, she had Internet. There should be some recipes there. For when she was alone. No way she could put dinner on the table and tell Maddie they were eating Bambi.

Mrs. Kentner stayed to chat for a while. Dusk was falling by the time she left. Ashley washed the few dishes in the sink, trying to decide whether to tell her father tonight that she wanted to cancel the party. She didn't want to cancel. She didn't think there was any danger.

She looked outside as she dried the silverware. More snow had fallen overnight, coating the trees, the woods pretty enough to paint. Not enough color left in the day, but still, even as a monochromatic work, the view from her kitchen window would have made a good composition.

As she scanned the trees, something caught her eye—a patch of value difference. If she wasn't so attuned, she probably wouldn't have noticed it. The patch moved. A bit of russet hair came into view.

Jack.

Aggravation and something else, something she wasn't willing to name, flashed through her in equal measure. The man didn't know when to give up. She dragged her coat on, stepped into her boots, then walked through the front door. His car wasn't in the driveway. Where had he come from? She had a good guess.

She strode around the house. "What are you doing back there?"

"I was walking through the woods." His face was drawn even more than usual, shadows all around him. He seemed to be in a dark mood, his coat open and flapping in the cold breeze. He didn't seem to care.

"Where's your car?"

"Back by the side of the road."

She'd been right. He'd been to the grave. Unease spread through her. She wished he could see what his obsession was doing to him. She wished they'd met at another time, under vastly different circumstances.

"How often do you go back there?"

"Every night."

He had good in him, at his core, that drew her to him. But he seemed inextricably mired in the past and in darkness. She didn't want to want him. If she was going to fall for anyone, she wanted simple. She couldn't live the rest of her life dancing on the edge of the precipice.

The cold seeped through her coat and made her shiver. She turned away from him and walked toward the house.

He followed. "I really do think Blackwell came back. Might be coming back all the time. I know I heard him last night."

"Did you see him?"

Silence.

"Did you see anything?"

He didn't respond.

A short bark of a laugh escaped her throat. "Teenagers hang out back by the creek sometimes. I told you they drive their snowmobiles all over the place. I found cigarette butts before. And empty beer bottles."

"It's him." He caught up with her and grabbed her by the arm to stop her. Turned her around. His gaze cut hard and cold. "Listen to me. This is serious. I think you know him. I think he might be

watching you. What if he didn't just come here because of the grave? What if he buried me on your land for a reason?"
For a second, fear stabbed through her, but she pushed it away. That was the old Ashley. She refused to live the rest of her life in fear. She watched his face, his gaze intent on hers. He believed, with everything he was, what he was saying. She didn't.
Regret washed over her. "I understand that you can't let go of Blackwell. I have my own issues in the letting-go department. But please leave me out of this."
"I can't."
"Why?"
His cerulean eyes looked nearly black in the twilight. His gaze held hers. "Because I care."
The quiet admission sent her for a spin.
Especially since, deep down, she cared about him too. She wished things were different, for both of them. She swallowed the lump in her throat. "How did this happen? How did we get here from anger and hate?"
His eyes gentled. "I never hated you. I was angry at you because you were supposed to be my straight line to Blackwell, but it was becoming obvious pretty fast you weren't. And I hated myself because I was attracted to you even back when I did think that you were in league with the bastard."
She stared at him. "I don't know what to say to that."
"Say that you'll keep yourself safe until this is over."
"Safe from what? From imaginary trouble? You know how long I've been doing that? You know how hard I've been fighting the anxiety. I'm making progress. I'm moving forward. I'm trying not to hide from my own fears. I can't start now to hide from yours. Don't ask me that."
One moment they were glaring at each other, and the next the heat was back, his gaze dipping to her lips. And, yes, part of her wanted him to kiss her again. Part of her wanted more than a kiss. But even as desire tingled across her skin, an ache grew inside her chest. Because she knew what little good it ever did to wish for impossible things.
He'd never want anyone half as much as he wanted Blackwell. So why did he have to mess with her? Why did he have to kiss her in

the middle of her damn kitchen where she would now think of that kiss every time she walked in there? Why did he-
She froze.
The cold wind slammed into her, but the ice that spread in her stomach was colder. *Oh God.*
Humiliation and a sense of betrayal washed over her. She scampered back. "Are you playing some kind of sick game? Did you kiss me in front of the window last night, with all the lights on, because you thought Blackwell was watching?" Her stomach turned. She was going to be sick.
He stared at her, his face darkening. But he didn't deny her words. Her eyes burned. He opened his mouth to say something, but she lifted a hand to stop him. The darkness he carried, the paranoia, was too much. She was already fighting her own demons. She couldn't take on his. "I don't want any of this, Jack."
"You might not have a choice. If he has an interest in you, like I think—"
"You need help." She turned on her heels and hurried away from him.
He called after her. "Have you canceled the party?"
She glanced back over her shoulder.
His hands shoved into his pockets, tension bracketed his mouth as he watched her.
Brady Blackwell's shadow had destroyed his entire life. But it wasn't going to destroy hers. "I'm sorry about your sister," she said. "I'm sorry what it did to you. But this is my life. And I'm going to live it." Then she ran up the steps.
She went inside and locked the door behind her, had no intention of letting him in if he came up and rang the bell. He didn't.
The ache in her chest deepened. She refused to cry as she took off her coat and kicked off her boots. For the first time in forever, here was the guy she could have been interested in, someone she actually had chemistry with.
He had strength, despite his deep, dangerous flaw. She was attracted to that strength—maybe because of her myriad weaknesses—but Jack's strength wasn't what she needed. She needed to find her own strength. She needed to stand on her own two feet. She needed to fight for what she wanted.

She moved to get the mop to deal with the mud she'd brought in, but the cell phone ringing on the coffee table stopped her. Her father's number flashed on the display.

"It's me," Maddie chirped on the other end.

"Hey, birthday girl. What's new in the big city?"

"Bertha took me shopping for a birthday dress. She said it's so pretty it would make princesses weep." Excitement poured through the line.

"I can't wait to see it."

"Am I getting a lot of presents?"

"You'll have to wait and see."

"Moooom!" A moment passed in disgruntled silence, then, "Grandpa would like to talk to you."

Her father picked up the line then, and they talked about what he should bring. Bertha had apparently baked up a storm already.

"About the birthday party tomorrow…" she began, thinking of Jack.

Her father waited.

"This weekend…" She couldn't say it. The phone conversation when she'd canceled her trip to the city still lived vividly in her mind.

"If you're having problems—" he said, his tone resigned.

Did he expect her to beg off again?

"No problem," she rushed to say. "I just wanted to let you know they're calling for snow. The kids will have nice, clean snow to build snowmen with. And I'll drag the old sleds out of the garage."

Jack Sullivan and his all-consuming obsession would not be allowed to ruin her relationship with her daughter. She was reclaiming her life. And she was starting it by driving into the best bakery in town and picking up their biggest cake.

* * *

"Did you kiss me in front of the window last night, with all the lights on, because you thought Blackwell was watching?"

Had he?

The question haunted Jack as he drove to his next meeting.

Had he kissed her to tick off Blackwell? Not consciously. But on some level…

Maybe, partially, yes. Get Blackwell angry. Get him to make a rushed move on Jack. Get him to make a mistake.

Had that been there, in the back of his mind?
He hated himself for the possibility as much as Ashley hated him
for it. She had every right.
He was crossing too many lines. But he didn't know how to stop
now, he thought as he drove to the Adamo residence to officially
interview Bobby.
While it was a generally acknowledged fact that teachers were
underpaid, some school administrators fared pretty well, he
thought as he pulled up in front of the largest house on the street, a
stone-covered colonial with giant banks of windows, three-bay
garage, and professional landscaping.
The principal himself opened the door when Jack rang the bell. He
looked even more unhappy now than at the school early that
morning, his tone clipped as he said, "Detective Sullivan. Come
in."
He guided Jack to the library that didn't quite rival William Price's
but was nevertheless impressive, with a conference table in the
middle. Bobby sat there, looking a lot less cocky now, next to his
pale-faced mother who was wringing her hands, and another man
Jack assumed to be their lawyer.
He sat as the introductions were made, then turned to Bobby, the
reason for his being here. He wanted to be done, to be able to close
this case that Bing had assigned to him only as a distraction in the
first place. "So have you remembered anything since we talked this
morning?"
The lawyer responded instead of the teenager. "Bobby is willing to
acknowledge that the Internet account in question is his, but he had
no idea the items listed were stolen."
"And where did he get these items he claims he doesn't know were
stolen?"
Bobby swallowed, looking at his father with resentment, but both
his father and the lawyer nodded, prodding him to go ahead.
And Bobby did, naming his friends one by one.
"Do you have any stolen items in your possession?"
"No," he immediately protested.
"You realize that since you confessed, I can get a warrant for this
house? You came clean about the listings. How about we do this
all the way?"

The principal glared; the lawyer said nothing. But Mrs. Adamo's quiet words, "Bobby, honey?" did the trick.

"Tyler gave me some stuff." The kid shifted on his seat, quickly adding, "I thought they were his. I don't know anything about any burglaries."

Jack nodded, even if he didn't believe a word. The kids were caught; the burglaries would stop. Bobby would get special consideration for turning on his friends. Life wasn't perfect, but progress had been made in the case. Bing would be happy.

"How about I take what you have in evidence right now and avoid the whole search-warrant thing?"

"Absolutely," the principal answered for his son, then snapped at him, "Bobby?"

The boy got up. "It's um... The stuff is in the basement."

They all followed him down to a fully furnished space that looked like a college-dorm rec room, complete with flat-screen TV, pool table, video games, even a full-size refrigerator for snacks. The space was as cluttered as a teenage boy's hangout would be, sports paraphernalia everywhere.

Bobby picked through the mess and handed over a laptop, a couple of phones, a Skilsaw, a dozen top-brand golf clubs, and a ratty old fan. "That's all I have here." He glanced at his father. "I swear."

Jack catalogued the items and gave the lawyer a receipt. "I want a full, written confession."

"I'll bring it to the station first thing in the morning," the lawyer promised.

"Why the fan?" Jack asked on the way up the stairs. "It can't be worth two bucks."

Bobby gave a sheepish shrug. "We plug it in when we hang down here, so nobody upstairs hears us talking."

While the kid's father chewed the boy out, Jack could only shake his head.

He couldn't believe Blackwell was out there while he was wasting his time on two-bit stuff like this. At least he was almost done with the case. Go back to the office, have the other kids and their parents called in, make the arrests. Maybe that would put him back into Bing's good graces again.

That would be nice, since he was about to redouble his efforts to find Blackwell. He'd already lost Ashley. Not that he ever really had her. Maybe under different circumstances, he could have. But he'd now lost even that remote chance. He had nothing else to lose. This was it, the endgame. He was on a collision course with Blackwell, and he had no intention of stopping until one of them was dead.

Chapter Twelve

He stood in the middle of his life's work, an installation that filled the entire top floor of one of the nicest buildings in Broslin. His soundproofed workshop was down in the basement. The downstairs he left as it had been when he'd bought the abandoned building. If anyone somehow peeked in through a boarded-up window, let them see nothing.

But the top floor, here he spent money. The space could have been part of a wing in the Louvre. Not that he ever wanted his art to be moved there. This was his hometown. His museum should be here, maybe with the town named after him eventually. Let the French come here if they wanted to see his work. He was proud to be an American.

The canvases that hung on the walls had been painted in living blood. They'd been his first true creations, the very thing that eventually led him onto the right path.

He'd been in North Carolina to pick up a car he'd bought online. He met a young woman at the hotel bar. She came back to his room with him.

And then she changed her mind, right when things were starting to get interesting.

He hadn't meant to kill her.

She shoved him first. He shoved her back, not that hard, really. But she'd had too much to drink, and she hit her head on the edge of the desk. There was blood, but his open suitcase on the floor caught most of it.

He didn't panic. He wrapped her head in a towel, pulled a plastic bag over that, got her out of his room in the middle of the night, drove her to the beach, near the rocks, removed the towel and bag, and dumped her in.

When they'd found her, her death had been ruled an accident. There'd been alcohol in her system. The police had said she'd slipped on the rocks, and the rising tide dragged in her body.

He didn't realize what he had until he came home and unpacked a white shirt that had blood all over it, the pattern amazing in its complexity, the color more real than anything he'd ever seen in a gallery.

And then he realized what he'd been doing wrong all these years he'd been trying to create art. He'd been missing the human element. So he went back to being an artist, this time using the most valuable media.

The women he took he honored with his choice. His art made them immortal.

He had a good selection of paintings now, even collages, but the centerpiece of his legacy was his three-dimensional works. He liked to walk up here, in his very own exhibit, literally walk through his art that represented death and life and resurrection. He created it all, and he would protect it.

He didn't like having to worry about his secret treasure. It interfered with his creative process. But he was ready to end the distraction at last.

Before the day was over, Jack Sullivan would be dead.

* * *

The birthday party was in full swing, Ashley's head spinning. But it was worth anything to see her daughter silly-giggles happy. Maddie and Jenny, one of her little friends, were going around the house with a bouquet of two dozen balloons in every color of the rainbow, letting them go one by one to float up to the ceiling for decoration. Heather, Jenny's mom, the first mom to arrive, provided assistance.

"You have some pretty good works up there." William Price came down the stairs from the loft, noiseless in his Italian-leather loafers.

"Thanks." Ashley smiled at her father, relaxing a little. She put out the sandwiches, all shaped like crowns or ponies or butterflies— with the help of Christmas cookie cutters. She had plenty of butterflies in her stomach too. She wanted everything to be perfect.

His gold watch glinted from under his shirtsleeve as he reached out to adjust a tray. "You think you have enough material for a show?" "Almost." She was doing well with time. Whether or not she could go all the way to New York for an opening was still a question. But she was working on it. This morning, she had driven to the town bakery to pick up the cake. She'd even done her grocery shopping during the daytime.

"I know I've been hard on you," her father said as she set out utensils and napkins that had colorful balloons on them, then added paper cups with the same pattern.

"After your mother's death..." He linked his hands together behind his back. "I just wanted everything to be normal. The rumors about the unfortunate affair with DaRosa—" His lips flattened for a second. "When a family has the kind of standing in society that ours does, there's a lot of pressure. One is tempted to keep up a façade even at a personal cost."

She busied herself with refolding the napkins, but she couldn't stop the memories from coming back. Her mother in that mental institution, the scandal of the high-society gatherings, all the guessing, all the digging for gruesome detail, then her death. Then, less than a year after Abigail Hastings Price's celebrity funeral, her teenage daughter falling pregnant and accusing a pillar of society, a man two decades her senior, of seducing her. DaRosa denied it. And her father kept her quiet, squelching the rumors as fast as they'd begun. He'd been in negotiations on a hundred-million-dollar business deal with DaRosa at the time.

"I don't suppose you read the business pages much?" he asked now.

She shook her head, then felt a little guilty. Whatever her father's faults were, he'd always taken an interest in her work, always supported it, always asked, kept track, sent friends and clients to her shows. But she'd shown very little interest in his company over the years. "How is business?"

"We've had some issues with DaRosa's branch. Some accounting discrepancies were discovered. He's been discredited to a great degree, I'm afraid. Well, ruined, according to the business analysts."

She stared at him. "Will that drag the whole company down?"

"Since he was ousted by the board of directors almost immediately and forced to sell his shares back at a discount, I think we retained credibility. Stock price took a dip, but for the past few days, it's been inching back steadily. Our stockholders seem convinced that we've made meaningful changes."

Something in his voice made her wonder if he'd somehow engineered DaRosa's bad luck personally, and there was more to the story than he was telling.

Then he said, "I'm sorry I didn't believe you back then."

She blinked. "Why believe me now?"

"Maddie looks like him," he said simply. "And I know now that you don't have any of your mother's flair for drama. Even in the face of insurmountable difficulties, you do whatever you have to and manage."

Her throat tightened.

"I'm not a man given to emotions. I'm more apt to criticize than to praise. But I want you to know that I'm proud of the choices you've made and the things you've achieved."

One of the tight knots inside her loosened. "About Maddie…"

"I'm only trying to help."

She drew a deep breath. "I know, but even while I know it, in the back of my mind I resent that you have her and I don't."

"School will be out in a few months."

She nodded.

She wanted to say more, but the rest of the guests were arriving. Maddie had wanted to invite both the friends she had in Broslin before the accident and the friends she'd made in the city since living with her grandfather. And as much as having a crowd in her house frazzled her, Ashley agreed. She would have done absolutely anything to make her daughter happy.

Soon the dozen kids were playing dress-up in the living room, half the contents of her closet scattered across the floor, hats and scarves and high-heeled shoes, fancy theatre purses, things she'd held on to from the past when she'd actually socialized. They got hold of her makeup case too. She would definitely have to clean up the girls before the parents came to take them home.

Her father was a great help. He'd always been busy with business, working late hours and always staying a little reserved when she'd been a child. But Ashley realized now how much age, and

Maddie's company for the past year, had softened the man. They were good for each other. Maddie got a positive male role model in her life, while William Price got some cheerful company in his lonely penthouse apartment.

As her father helped one of the little girls loop a silk scarf in a tie knot, Ashley relaxed at last and let herself enjoy the sound of Maddie's peals of laughter.

She was pulling it off. The party was a success.

She scanned the coffee table. Half the sandwiches were gone, and they were down to two juice boxes. She headed to the kitchen for more, but as she passed by the front window, she caught sight of an extra car in her driveway, a black Crown Victoria. Jack Sullivan's.

The man didn't know how to take no for an answer.

"I need to run outside for a minute," she told Heather, then grabbed her coat and headed out into the cold.

The car sat empty, but she found him as soon as she rounded the house. He was walking the edge of the tree line.

She shoved her hands into her pockets, frustration punching through her as she walked up to him. "What are you doing here?"

For a second, her gaze dipped from his eyes to his lips and a pleasant little shiver ran down her spine as she remembered their kiss. She shook that off immediately. God, how stupid was she to be still attracted to the man?

"Consider me free security."

"How about I consider you what you are? An enormous nuisance."

"Blackwell is still out there."

"You're the only person who thinks so. Let it go, Jack."

"I can't," he said, just as her father came outside.

He looked Jack over. "Ashley?"

She looked between the two men, wishing she knew what to say. That Jack was a deranged police detective, looking for a serial killer at her house, didn't seem like birthday-party conversation. Her father and she had just finally reestablished a real connection. She didn't want Jack's demons to upset that.

"Go away," she whispered.

But he was walking toward the house already, flashing a smile at her father. "Came to say happy birthday to Maddie."

"Not to investigate my daughter?"

Jack's smile never wavered. "She's been cleared. I'm glad for that. She saved my life." He pulled a small package from his coat pocket. "I take it the birthday girl is inside?"

He actually had a gift. *Huh*. Ashley shot him a questioning look, absolutely refusing to let any sort of warming happen around her heart.

"A DVD. Princesses and Puppy Dogs," he said.

Her father clapped him on the shoulder and laughed. "Can't go wrong with that."

What? They were best friends all of a sudden?

She ground her teeth but plastered a smile on her face. "I better go inside and put out some more juice boxes." Then she turned on her heels and left them in the cold to do whatever they wanted.

* * *

The sound and sight of a dozen little girls tearing through the house, screaming at the top of their lungs, left Jack immobilized for a second as he stepped inside behind Ashley's father. If there was a place on earth he didn't belong, this was it. He would stay anyway. He put his gift on the pile that took up most of the window seat.

William Price moved away to help one of Maddie's friends lift a box of dolls off a shelf.

Ashley stood in the middle of the melee, directing it like a general. She'd taken her coat off. Her light wool dress hugged her curves, falling to her knees. The sight distracted him for a minute as hot lust shot through him. That never seemed to change, whether they were on good terms or bad.

A woman in her thirties swept by him with a tray of sweets. "Hi, I'm Heather, Jenny's mom. Cupcakes?"

She probably assumed he was the father of one of the little terrors. He didn't correct her. "Jack. Maybe later. Thanks."

Ashley moved on to the kitchen, and he went after her. Then, when he caught up with her, he wasn't sure what to say. Her hair was all done up fancy, makeup accentuating her huge green eyes, a smattering of glitter drawing his attention to her lips. Her breasts looked practically gift wrapped in the pretty dress.

His fingertips tingled. He shoved his hands into his pockets.

"Need help?" he asked, hoping she would respond in the negative. Or give him a task like going out to the garage to guard the birthday cake in solitude and silence. That he could handle. Probably.

Then he caught sight of the birthday cake on the kitchen table behind her. The pink castle of sugar overdose was decorated with purple ponies.

"No thanks," she said in a cool tone. "Everything is under control." He glanced back at the living room, at the girl who was sliding down the banister with a tiara on her head, her frothy pink dress up around her neck, laughing like the devil. Another one was painting flowers on the landing with some finger paints. An angelic blonde was strutting from the laundry room, wearing an expensive blouse of Ashley's like a dress, bright red lipstick smeared all over her face.

"Let me know if things get out of control," he said weakly.

"Why?" She tilted her head, mystifyingly not bothered by the bedlam. "Are you going to jump in?"

"I'm going make a run for it. But when I'm in my car and at a safe distance to slow down, I'll call in the SWAT team."

Her lips twitched at that, her eyes softening a little.

His gaze caught on Graham Lanius, popping up in one of the corners where he'd been apparently helping a couple of kids finger-paint something.

"What's he doing here?"

Ashley made a face. "Ran into him at the bakery this morning when I was picking up Maddie's cake. He brought by a present. He's courting me for his gallery."

He didn't like the idea of him courting Ashley for anything, especially when he thought of the waitress the guy had grabbed at the bar. "I don't think you should work with him."

"My agent says the same." She grabbed an armful of juice boxes from the counter and pushed by him, then was immediately surrounded by a handful of hellhounds in pink as she entered the living room. They clamored for face painting.

With the kids, she was relaxed and carefree, a definite contrast to when she was with him. He didn't enjoy stressing her out, but he hated the thought of her in possible danger even more.

He padded up the stairs to escape the worst of the chaos, curious to see what she'd been working on since he'd last seen her work.

He'd never liked abstracts before, never understood them. He stepped closer to the first row of canvases leaning against the wall. As far as he could tell, any of the overactive ruffle-skirted little demons downstairs could paint something like these.

But when he moved to the middle of the loft to look around and take in the field of color as one, he found that one of the newest paintings in particular drew him. There was a calming quality to it, and he wasn't sure whether that emanated from the lines or the colors, but he liked looking at the weird swirly thing.

He turned to the next painting and let himself relax, trying to get the feel of it. Warmth, he thought after a minute. And love. A mother's love for her kid. A family. The longing that sliced through him took him by surprise, same as the other night when he'd held her in his arms. He'd been fifteen the last time he'd seen a semi happy family. He wouldn't have thought he'd still remember it.

A battle cry downstairs drew his attention, and he turned his back to the paintings to look down at the living room over the railing. A couple of the girls were playing tag and none too gently. Somehow he'd pictured the whole thing differently. He'd expected a dozen little ladies sitting demurely in a circle and combing their dolls' hair quietly. Or maybe having a tea party.

The only person sitting at the moment was Ashley. She was painting a little girl's face, not the least bothered by the noise and running. Heather was coming from the laundry room with a stack of board games; she looked up and waved at him. "Want to play Princess Magic?"

"Later," he lied through his teeth.

Heather laid the game out on the middle of the carpet, immediately attracting the attention of half a dozen girls who rushed up to her to see what she was doing.

Out of all of them, Maddie was the prettiest. Not that he was biased just because she looked like Ashley. Her tiara, sitting askew on a wavy mess of hair, was a little bigger than the others', and it was flashing. Who came up with these things?

She threw her arms around Ashley. "It's the best party ever. I love you, Mommy."

And there it was, that mood and sense of family again that tugged at him with invisible ropes, pulling him toward something he wasn't comfortable with. Yet he couldn't look away.

Then Maddie tore off to join the rest of the girls on the carpet. Heather divided the kids into groups and was handing out dice and cards and plastic board-game figures. Ashley raised her gaze to him and pushed to standing, wiped her hands on some paper towels, then walked up the stairs to him.

"You didn't come just to bring a present." She watched him warily.

"I want to protect you."

"How about you worry about yourself first? Figure out your own life before you start worrying about somebody else's."

Not bad advice, all considered. She was a smart woman, one of the many things he liked about her. "Can't. I'm a no-good, messed-up, obsessed cop." He quoted words she'd thrown at him a while back. "I'm sorry. About the other night... I would never do anything to put you in harm's way."

She watched him, conflicting emotions crossing her face.

"The chase has been my life for too long," he told her. "I never expected there to be more. This..." He made a frustrated gesture with his hand, indicating both of them. "This came completely unexpected. I don't know what to do with it."

She wrapped her arms around herself even as she swayed toward him. "I'm not going to fall for a man who's all wrong for me."

He wanted to kiss her so bad it hurt. "You shouldn't."

"When women fall for a guy with all the wrong kind of baggage, thinking they'll change him, it never works. I'm not going to be like that. I deserve better. So does Maddie."

His hands itched to touch her. "You do. I agree. I wish I could be the right guy. I do. Do you believe me?" He reached for her hand and took it, turning so it wouldn't be seen from below.

She let him.

There was something here, something so good and unexpected. Something he didn't deserve. If only he had the time to explore it. But he had a premonition he wasn't going to get the time.

Things with Blackwell would come to a head and soon. Every cop instinct he had was telling him that.

"Let it go," she asked quietly.

Three days of torture was nothing compared to how he felt as he said, "I can't."
And then, as if on cue, his phone vibrated in his pocket.
"Sorry," he said, looking at the display. "It's Bing."
She nodded as she pulled away, then walked downstairs, letting him take the call in private.
"The FBI got Blackwell in Jersey. They're bringing him back here to Broslin. They want you to come in and see if you can make positive ID."
A myriad of conflicting emotions swirled through him as he ran down the stairs. "Gotta go. They got Blackwell in Jersey," he told a startled Ashley as he sailed by her.
Then he was out the door, driving away from everything that could have been.

Chapter Thirteen

Everybody was at the police station. Since the FBI still had most of their things set up there, they were bringing Blackwell to Broslin, and nobody wanted to miss that. Even Leila came in, and Harper too, his arm in a sling. At first Jack had thought they'd come to see the monster. But as they clapped him on the back, one by one, Leila actually getting close enough for a hug, he realized they were here to support him.

"There. It's over now," Bing said gruffly. "They have him." Jack stood by the front desk, one eye always on the front door as he tried to figure out how the hell this happened. Apparently, he had friends.

He'd come to Broslin for Blackwell, and Blackwell alone. He didn't socialize; he didn't hang out; he didn't do the buddy thing. In his spare time, he either drove around town, trying to figure out where Blackwell might live, or sat at home going through the case files.

The FBI bursting through the door with their suspect in cuffs refocused him. Right age, right body type, right height.

Anger tore through Jack. Then hatred came and boiling darkness, his hands tightening into fists. He'd wanted to be the one to catch the bastard. Because he wouldn't have brought Blackwell in, he admitted to himself now. He didn't just want to end the chase, he wanted to end Blackwell too. Permanently.

The agents rushed the man toward the interrogation room, Hunter jerking his head at Jack to follow.

He hurried after them, blood rushing in his head. "Let me in there with him."

"In the viewing room." Hunter looked and sounded too damn self-satisfied. "Conflict of interest. We're going to put him away for good. No mistakes now."

Jack about gritted his teeth but went with it. He had no other choice at this stage. Blackwell had been caught. Somehow he was going to have to find peace in the thought that, at least, there'd never be another victim. He was looking through the two-way mirror by the time Hunter seated the bastard. He just stood and watched, even if he was tempted to go right through the damn glass, and let the chips fall where they may.

"State your name for the record."

The man shot a sullen look. "Jordy Myers."

"What is your relationship to Felicia Miller?" Hunter threw out the name of one of the kidnapped Jersey girls, then the other, but by that time, Jack was barely listening.

Wrong voice.

Although he couldn't remember Blackwell's voice perfectly, it was deep, not like this weird nasal tone.

The tension drained out of him, replaced by red-hot frustration as he kicked the chair in front of him.

"Not the right guy," he said when Hunter came over to ask him.

"It has to be him. Keep listening."

But the longer he listened to the interview, the more sure he was. Jordy had some questionable past with Felicia, but he seemed to have no knowledge of the other girl or any of Blackwell's previous victims.

He was so disappointed he walked back out and sank into his chair, uninterested in Hunter's display of various interrogation techniques.

"Not Blackwell," he told the people waiting.

Chase swore, his way of offering manly sympathy, then headed out. He had to be back for his shift first thing in the morning.

Harper went with him. Bing tried to talk Jack into a better mood, then gave up and headed out too.

Jack sat at his desk, paging through his folder. He couldn't stop looking at his notes, pictures, crime-scene lab results. He didn't know how to stop. There had to be something there, something he'd missed.

The agents brought Jordy out from interview, escorted him over to one of the station's handful of holding cells in the back. They were all empty.

"We'll transport him in the morning," Hunter said as they too headed back to their hotel, pleased with themselves as anything, patting each other on the back.

"It's not him," Jack said again, but they didn't even hear him.

Leila was just about to sneak out the door when Hunter caught her, handed her a stack of papers, asked her to scan them and e-mail them to him.

Joe and Mike stayed too. They had the night shift.

Jack slapped the folder closed and stood. Maybe Ashley was right and he was completely obsessed. In any case, if Blackwell hadn't been caught then he wanted to go back to her place, stay outside this time, guard her from afar.

"They're not the boss of me," Leila groused as she fanned herself with the paperwork up front, firing up the scanner that was temperamental at best. She'd be here for another hour, at least. Her cheeks were turning an interesting shade of red.

"You okay?" Mike asked.

"Hot flashes. Just started and I hate them already. I tell you this." She jabbed at him with the papers. "A woman's life is no picnic."

Mike seemed unprepared to discuss women's health at this level of intimacy. On any other day, the appalled look on his face would have made Jack laugh. Tonight, he was too drained to do anything but shake his head at the rookie.

"There's a fan back in the evidence room, if you want it," he told Leila.

Hope crossed her face. "You sure?"

"I doubt we'll ever get to present evidence on that case. We got a signed confession. Open-and-shut case. It'll never go to court. Kids will make a deal. No violence. No criminal history, good standing in the community. They'll get probation and community service. I'll get it for you."

He brought the thing up from the back, then plugged it in.

As the blades swung into motion, everything inside him went still.

Pain sliced through his ribs. Nausea rose up his throat as he straightened, and he almost lost the butterfly sandwich he'd eaten at Ashley's place, but somehow managed to keep it down, steeling his mind and body.

The fan's familiar grinding brought back images of torture in graphic detail he hadn't remembered until this moment.

"Jack?" Mike moved toward him.

"Don't touch the fan!" he ordered Leila as he stepped back, his mind clearing. "It's Blackwell's." He pointed at Mike. "Get it dusted for fingerprints." He ran for the door.

"Where are you going?" Joe called after him.

"Going to find out where those kids got this fan," he called back. "I'll let you know where to meet me. Be ready."

* * *

Maddie was sitting on the couch with a pink cupcake with the biggest birthday smile on her face one minute, lying down with the cupcake on the carpet the next.

"I'm tired. I don't want to go in the car. Can we sleep here? Please?"

Ashley looked at her father. "I have room for both of you."

"I have tennis first thing in the morning. It's a business meeting really. I've been trying to nail down this deal for months. I can't cancel. I'm sorry."

"She could stay." Ashley picked up the cupcake. "I could bring her to Philly tomorrow."

She wanted Maddie with her. The ride to Philly suddenly didn't scare her. She'd driven to town for the cake in the middle of the day. She'd pulled off a great party.

She felt stronger; she felt ready. She had stood up to both Jack and her father. Even Blackwell, which had been a nagging, if small, worry in the back of her mind, was in custody.

"All right," her father said. "You two should be fine here."

They said their good-byes, and she walked him out, watched as his taillights disappeared down the road. Another car came up from the opposite direction and turned into her driveway, an older-model family sedan. She didn't recognize the car, but she did recognize the man when he got out. He usually drove the mail truck.

Her stomach sank. With Jack having shown up unexpectedly and the excitement of Maddie staying the night, she'd completely forgotten about the date. Okay, so it was mostly Jack. Right or wrong, she responded to him on a whole other level. Pete was…a friend. She would have to make sure he knew that, an awkward conversation she wasn't looking forward to.

"Hi, Pete." She opened the door wider. Time to start apologizing and explaining.

"Come in."

Chapter Fourteen

Bobby Adamo didn't give up the information easily, keeping to his story that he didn't know anything he'd handed over was stolen, that he hadn't been present at the burglaries.

Jack had to turn the conversation serious. Principal Adamo had threatened charges, called his lawyer, called Bing.

Bing threatened back with a charge of obstruction of justice.

And then Bobby miraculously remembered the exact address in a split second. Jack called it in.

The old Broslin Bank on Main Street had stood empty for years. It was the most stately building in town, all brick and fancy masonry, recalling another era. The bank had shut down during the financial crises and now sat with its windows boarded. Still, it was an imposing presence, between one of the town's two dozen galleries on one side and the post office on the other.

According to Bobby, they'd gone in through the back, just in case there was some leftover money in the safe, but had found nothing but garbage. They had taken the fan as a souvenir.

Jack brought his car to a screeching halt in the back of the building, jumped out with his gun drawn, and went straight to the window Bobby had indicated, where the boys had pried the plywood off, then had just stuck it back in.

He didn't wait for backup. All senses on alert, he climbed in through the broken window behind the plywood pretty easily, then panned his flashlight around the place.

Adrenaline pumped through him. He was here at last. At Blackwell's lair.

Dust, dirt, overturned chairs; the bank's counters were still standing. Some construction material lay piled up in a corner. He tried a light switch. No power. But there would be power in the basement. The lights had been on the whole time he'd been tortured. He went from door to door, looking for the right one, and found the steel security door after a few minutes.

He shot the lock without overthinking it. Had to hit it just at the right spot, but he managed.

He flicked on the light, then eased down the stairs step by careful step, his muscles coiled. His stomach turned again as a familiar musty smell, mold mixed with paint, hit him.

This was it. The smell, the feel, the woodstove in the corner, instruments of torture mixed with instruments of art. His gaze settled on the walls—professionally soundproofed. That explained why nobody had heard him scream.

Unfinished canvases lay against the wall here and there, painted with a mixture of paint and blood, some probably his. He'd imagined himself finding Blackwell's lair a million times. But it hadn't been nearly as sick as this. Ashley's paintings were macabre, but this was something else entirely. This was all the way insane.

His gaze caught on a metal chair, the chair he'd been chained to for three endless days. Rage built inside him. He wanted Blackwell. He wanted to end the bastard. Where the hell was he?

"Jack?" Joe's voice came from above. "Jack? Are you down there?"

"Right here."

The rookie drummed down the stairs, his gun straight out in front of him, looked around, paled when he understood where he was standing.

"This is it?"

Jack nodded, suddenly suffocating. "Don't touch anything. But see if you can find something that would identify the bastard. Got a crime-scene kit?"

"Up in the car."

"Go get it." Jack ran up the stairs just as Mike was climbing in through the window they all used as an entrance.

"I want to know who owns this building," Jack told him, although he wasn't sure how helpful the information would be. Could be the bank still owned the place and Blackwell was squatting here, knowing nobody would notice, nobody would come looking.

He panned his flashlight, and the circle of light caught on the stairs leading up to the next level, another steel security door up there.

"That's some heavy-duty lock," Mike said.

Jack ran up the stairs. He didn't shoot the lock this time. He'd taken the chance of a ricocheting bullet when he'd been alone, but wouldn't now that he had Mike behind him.

He kicked to door, and again and again, using all his strength. He was close, so damn close. Nothing was going to stop him now.

And the door did bang open at last.

Did Blackwell live up here? He pushed through, weapon drawn, ready for anything. Nothing moved in the darkness in front of him. He sensed more than he saw a great open space as he ducked in, went low to the left. Mike rolled to the right in a move straight from the police academy.

"Lights."

Mike reached up to flick the switch. Light flooded the cavernous space.

"Jeezus," Mike groaned and lost his dinner where he stood.

Jack damn near followed his lead.

* * *

He stood at the top of the stairs in Ashley Price's house. He'd planned this moment carefully and would pull it off without a hitch. That was why he was a true master.

He walked softly into her bedroom, careful not to make a sound. A pretty room, lots of white linen, the sort of simple elegance he appreciated. She wasn't as great an artist as he, but she had taste. He had nothing against her. He'd even liked her. Of course, she thought her paintings were too good for the likes of him. He could smile now at the irony.

She slept the sleep of the exhausted—big party tonight. He picked up her cell phone from the nightstand, scrolled through her contacts, sent a text to Sullivan. Then he turned off the phone and dropped it into his pocket.

The police would find it at the bottom of the reservoir. Along with her body. And Sullivan's. The police report would say she committed suicide, her troubled mind snapping. Sullivan had tried to save her but got pulled down. The detective might even get some posthumous medal.

He reached for his gun, ready to wake her.

"Mommy?"

The sleepy voice behind him, coming from the doorway, nearly had him dropping the gun. He whirled around. What the hell was the kid still doing here?

* * *

"Where does he come in?" Jack asked, back on the main level. He could take only so much of the "exhibit" at the top of the stairs.

"What?" Mike looked shell-shocked still, but trying hard to pretend he wasn't, doing his best to suck it up.

Jack scanned the place. "Where does Blackwell come in here? The front door to the street is rusted shut. The back entrance the same. He isn't coming through a broken window every time, not with tools and supplies and those big canvases. He didn't carry me through a window. No way."

"A secret door?" Mike was snapping back to a straighter frame of mind, where he needed to be for this.

"Find it."

And they did, now that they knew what they were looking for, behind some heavy-looking scaffolding that actually rolled pretty easily out of the way on wheels.

Another door back there, painted the same dirty white as the wall, cleverly camouflaged. Jack sent a bullet through the lock just as his phone buzzed in his pocket with an incoming message. Probably Bing wanting to know what was going on. Leila would have called him.

Not now. Jack ignored the call as he stepped into the dark. A narrow passageway opened up in front of him, and he swore as his flashlight illuminated his service weapon and badge on the ground, tucked to the side, the originals Blackwell had taken off him.

He reached for them as Mike said, "They'll have to be dusted for fingerprints."

Whatever. He wasn't planning on Blackwell going to trial. But he moved forward, the light landing on a regulation army shovel and a pair of dirty boots. Straight ahead, at the end of the short passageway, stood yet another door, this one plain wood, no super security here.

He kicked it in on the first try.
And then they were in the gallery next door, Graham Lanius's life-size portrait the first thing his flashlight hit. And behind it, two familiar-looking mushroom paintings.
Suddenly, everything clicked into place.
Graham had recommended the artist for the commission. He'd probably gone out to the mushroom factory for the handover of the paintings. And had gotten spores on his shoes...
Jack turned on his heels and dashed back through the passageway, pushing Mike aside. "Ashley Price. Call it in!"
Then he ran as if his life depended on it.

* * *

"Mommy," the little girl cried again.
Fury swirled inside him. He didn't want the girl. He didn't need the girl.
He had plans, and nobody was going to ruin them. He gripped the gun hard. Then drew a deep breath and forced himself to think.
Fine. The kid was here. He would deal with it. He was smarter than the rest of them put together. Certainly smart enough to adjust his plan on the fly. He prided himself on creativity.
The story would have to change.
The evidence would show that Ashley Price snapped, went crazy. She took her own life and took her kid with her. Not that far a stretch, considering last year's accident on the reservoir.
When he was finished with them, after all three were dead, including Jack, he could come back to the house and type up a suicide note on her laptop. Spell it out, not leave the cops too much to think about.
He drew another deep breath. It would work. All right.
As the mother stirred, he backed out of the room and went for the kid.

* * *

Ashley woke from a dreamless sleep to her daughter's voice. But when she opened her eyes, instead of Maddie she saw a dark figure looming over her bed, his gun glinting in the dim light. With his other hand, the man held Maddie.
Her heart jumped into her throat, her sleep-fogged brain scrambling to think.

Then the man shifted, and the pale moonlight washed over his face.

Recognition shocked her. "What are you doing here? What do you want?"

"Get up." He backed away, and, as she slipped from the bed, thrust her daughter at her.

"Mommy."

"It's okay, honey." She gathered her trembling baby up into her arms. "It's okay, baby. It's okay."

"Down the stairs." Graham gestured with the gun.

"Please don't do this." Why? Her brain couldn't catch up with the moment. But she moved. He was clearly deranged. She didn't want to make him angry. "What do you want?"

"Outside," he said when they reached the bottom of the stairs.

"I'm sorry. I know I was rude to you. I didn't mean it. We can talk. I apologize."

His only response was a cold sneer as he shoved her from behind.

* * *

Jack dialed Ashley as he drove. She didn't pick up her cell and not her landline either.

And then at last he glanced at the message that had come in earlier, from Ashley's number. One heart-stopping word.

GOODBYE.

The bastard was setting her up. Another trap, Jack realized. A trap baited with something Blackwell knew Jack wouldn't be able to resist.

A trap he would willingly walk into this time. He didn't care if he died tonight, he didn't even care what happened to Blackwell—as long as Ashley lived.

He slammed his foot on the gas. Dark premonitions settled on him as he drove, filling his chest with lead. He was going so fast he nearly flipped the car over when he turned the last corner. But he reached her house in record time, didn't bother to shut off the engine as he ran for the door, banged on it. "Ashley? It's Jack."

Nobody answered.

"Police. Open up." He banged again, then swore and kicked the door in, weapon in hand.

He scanned the downstairs. Swore when he spotted Maddie's pink coat on the peg, her pink boots on the floor under it. Was she spending the night?

"Ashley? Maddie, honey?" He ran upstairs. Empty, though both their beds looked slept in.

He stood in the middle of Ashley's bedroom, fear and fury coursing through him as he scanned everything, desperate for a clue that would lead him to them. Then his gaze snapped to the window. The room was in the back of the house, the window looking over Hadley Road and the reservoir. Moonlight glinted off a vast expanse of white.

His eyes caught on the dark shapes moving across the ice.

* * *

Her feet were frozen, her bedroom slippers little protection against the snow. Ashley wrapped her arms around her daughter as best she could, trying to keep Maddie warm. Her own body shook, and not only because of the cold. Dark panic gripped her as she shuffled forward on the ice.

For the past year, she had barely been able to look at the reservoir. And now here she was, the place where Dylan had died, where she'd lost her life, then gained it back, thanks to the paramedics. Where she had nearly lost Maddie.

So much grief and guilt was tied up in this expanse of rough ice. She couldn't think here. All the fear of the past was getting mixed up with the panic of the present.

She forced her brain to focus. "Why are you doing this, Graham?" The man shoved her toward a dark hole hacked into the ice. Another kind of grave. She recognized her axe next to it, the handle painted pink. He must have taken it from her garage. Next to the axe, a large cement brick waited with a rope tied to it. He pointed to that. "Tie it around your waist."

She felt lightheaded, as if all her blood had left her body. "You can have the paintings. You can have whatever you want."

He gave a harsh laugh. "You think this is about your so-called art? You don't know what real art is. I didn't even mind. I liked you anyway. I could have taught you. I didn't plan it like this. But you chose him."

She couldn't think. She was too scared for her brain to work.

"You shouldn't have dug up Sullivan," he told her, his voice hard and filled with hate.

Her mind spun to process that, her throat tightening as she made sense of it at last. "You're Brady Blackwell?"

"I'm the Master," he snapped at her. "Someday, they'll all know that. Someday, when nobody even remembers your name, my art will be worshipped."

"Let Maddie go. Please," she begged. "She's just a child."

"Old enough to finger me." He shook his head. "I'm prepared to be misunderstood and persecuted for my genius. I won't be the first in history. But not yet. My work isn't finished."

He talked like a man possessed, his tone cold, his mind focused on his delusions of grandeur. And she understood at last that there was no reasoning with him.

He kicked the rope toward her. "Tie it around your waist."

She put Maddie down, pushed her daughter away when she wanted to cling to her leg. She bent as if to pick up the rope. She was scared of that hole in the ice. She was more scared of that dark, frigid water than she'd ever been of anything. But she lunged forward, her head ramming into Graham's midsection as she grabbed him and twisted with him, plunging both of them in.

"Run!" she yelled to Maddie with her last breath before she went under.

Since Graham had gone in first, he was under her for a second before he shoved her aside and clawed up for air. She broke the surface next to him.

Maddie still stood where she left her, crying. "Mommy!"

"Run!" Desperation gave strength to her voice even as the cold seeped into her bones.

"Stay!" Graham thundered, and Maddie froze in place.

Ashley held on to the edge of the ice that was crumbling under her fingers. She was already frozen through, to her soul. Graham was better dressed. He was bulkier. Stronger. If he made it out and she didn't…

She couldn't let anything happen to Maddie.

The rope lay on the ice next to her. She wrapped it around her arm, then grabbed the brick. She took one last look at her crying daughter then yanked in the brick and went under, grabbed

Graham's coat with her other hand, and pulled him away from the ledge, down into the deep darkness.

He might have had other advantages, but she'd died here once before. She had practice. And she wasn't afraid of dying again. Not if it saved Maddie.

He fought hard, but he couldn't counteract both her body weight and the weight of the brick. And he couldn't pry her off him either. He shot at her several times but missed in the churning, dark water. *Please, God, just keep Maddie safe.*

Her body was going numb fast. Her ears were ringing. Graham let go of the gun, or maybe it slipped from his cold fingers. It floated by her, but she couldn't grab it. She would let go of neither the brick nor Graham.

He tried to shove her away, panicking now, frantic, bubbles going up from his mouth, losing air as he struggled. She stayed calm and just hung on. There was peace down here, in the dark water, knowing she saved her daughter.

Then his grip grew weaker at last. His fingers slid off her arm. She was cold, so cold. She couldn't move. The brick anchored her to the bottom, the rope tangled around her arm and holding her in place even when her frozen fingers slipped off it. She had no strength left to free herself. Hypothermia. Her body was slowing. Over the past year, she'd thought more than once that maybe she should have died under the ice. She'd cheated death. So maybe this was right. Maybe this was her destiny.

For a second, she saw a mirage of Dylan's little face float in front of her. No anger in his eyes, no fear, no blame. He smiled at her with all the love only a child could give. He seemed so real.

He reached for her and touched the rope, which slid off her arm and disappeared in the deep.

Up, he mouthed, his blue little-boy eyes serene.

Yet, for a moment, staying seemed so tempting. Right here, she could lay down the guilt, the visions, the fear. Death was peaceful and all accepting.

But as Dylan's face faded away, she chose life anyway, gathering up the last of her strength and kicking her legs, shoving Graham out of her way.

She swallowed water, tried to go back up, but her head bumped into solid ice she couldn't break through. She'd floated away from the hole while she'd struggled with Graham. His body floated next to her, buoyed by the air trapped in his down jacket. Her lungs burned as she banged on the bottom of the ice with her fists. "Ashley!" the shout came from above, as if from a great distance, through the sound of rushing blood in her ears.

Jack.

But he was too late. Her vision dimmed; she choked down water as her lungs gasped for air. Then that strange, floating, fading feeling came, one she was familiar with.

When the axe burst through the ice next to her, she barely registered it. When Jack reached in for her, grabbing on to her shoulder, she could do nothing to help. Then her head finally broke out of the water, and she went up choking, coughing up water, trying painfully to gulp some air.

Jack lay on his stomach to distribute his weight evenly, dragging her to air and life, to safety.

"On your stomach," he ordered as he dragged her completely out. "Are you okay?"

All she could do was nod, sputtering.

And then she watched helplessly as he slipped into the water.

"Mommy? I'm scared." Her daughter was sobbing somewhere behind her.

"Stay where you are, honey." She crawled that way, away from the hole. She kept one eye on her daughter, another out for Jack, but he didn't pull back up above the water.

Her heart pounded hard in her ears, her entire body shaking. Then she reached Maddie, and at the same time, Jack came up, sputtering, dragging Graham up onto the ice with him. He began CPR the second they were clear, banging on the man's chest.

"Mommy." Maddie burrowed against her, the wet mess she was. "Jack said I had to stand right here. He said I couldn't move, and he would get you back." Her little lips were blue. "He saved you like a prince."

Ashley wanted to tell her how much she loved her, but she couldn't speak. She was crying, clutching her daughter, never wanting to let her go again.

Sirens sounded in the distance, then closer. Then the police were there and two ambulances. She was too frozen to talk to anyone. Bing came around. He helped her into the back of the ambulance and told the EMTs to take good care of her. Then he ran off toward Jack.

"Don't do anything stupid. FBI is on their way," he yelled.

Graham, a heap of soggy clothes, began coughing water out of his lungs. Jack knelt over the man, breathing hard, his face illuminated by the lights of the emergency vehicles. He didn't look at her. He didn't look at anyone. His world consisted of one man, the one before him. He was back in the world of darkness and vengeance he'd created and lived.

The stark rage on his face sent a shiver down Ashley's spine, the last thing she saw before one of the EMTs shut the door of the ambulance.

* * *

"Stay back," Jack warned his captain. "Everybody stay back." He held on to the edge of the precipice as he looked at the sputtering mess before him.

Good. The bastard hadn't drowned. Jack coughed up some water himself. He wanted to be looking into those soulless eyes when he pulled the trigger. He wanted the bastard to see death coming and know that it was coming from Jack Sullivan. He had his gun in his hand.

One bullet between the eyes.

He wanted it. He wanted his vengeance. He wanted blood on the ice. He wanted justice.

But would it be?

Or would it just be murder?

If he went over to the other side, could he come back again? Ashley and Maddie were in the back of the ambulance. They would hear the shot. They would know.

He held his gun, swore at the half-conscious man, and punched the ice next to his head so hard with his free hand he cracked it. He was just pulling back his bloodied fist when Bing reached him.

"Jack, dammit. Step back. That's an order."

But he gripped the gun. He couldn't release it.

* * *

Ashley sat in the back of the ambulance with Maddie, so cold that her teeth were chattering. She didn't think she'd ever feel warm again. They huddled in their blankets, Maddie holding her hand while the EMT took her vitals. They'd given Maddie a very mild sedative to calm her, to head off her going into shock from the stress and the cold.

"Is Jack okay?" she asked as she leaned against Ashley sleepily.

"Yes, sweety."

"Is the bad man going to hurt him?"

"No." Things would happen the other way around, she figured, and wondered if she would ever see Jack again.

If he put a bullet through Graham's brain, he'd be going off to jail. If he didn't, the FBI would carry off Graham, and Jack would probably leave too. He would have no more reason to stay in Broslin.

The pain that accompanied that thought was worse than almost drowning again. She didn't realize how much she'd come to care for him until she'd seen him disappear in that dark water.

Maddie fell asleep, her little body going limp.

The back door of the ambulance opened, but even that didn't wake her. Jack climbed in, got wrapped up, then put his arms around them without saying a word.

The ambulance was moving, going down the road by the time he asked, "Are you okay? Maddie?"

She blinked back her tears as she nodded.

He took her hand, held it between his.

She let him. "What happened?"

"I thought Blackwell was important." He drew a long breath, held her tighter. "Then I saw you go under with him as I was tearing down the road. It put things into perspective."

"You let Bing take him?"

"The FBI is here. They'll do what has to be done." He reached up and brushed the wet hair out of her face.

"Probably look like a drowned rat," she said, suddenly flustered.

"You look alive." He gave a lopsided smile. "I like that look on you. It's pretty damn fantastic."

They sat in silence. He held her gaze as Maddie slept on her lap.

"I'm a no-good, messed-up, obsessed cop," he said after a while. "You deserve better."

"Says who? I'm a freaked-out, loopy artist."

He gave a bark of a laugh and took her lips in a soft kiss.

Chapter Fifteen

He went with them to the hospital. They were all checked over for cuts and bruises as well as hypothermia. The doctor kept Maddie overnight for observation. Even though she hadn't been in the water, she was a slight little thing and chilled through pretty fast. Since she was sleeping peacefully, the nurse sent Ashley home for a hot shower and rest. Jack got them a cab and went with her. And stayed with her.

"Why don't you grab a couple of hours of sleep?" he asked once she came out of the bathroom, wearing her thickest sweater and pants.

She wrapped her arms around herself. She didn't think she would ever get warm again. "I should go in and wait for Maddie."

"The nurse said she won't be released until after the doctors make their rounds at eight in the morning." He'd been up in the loft, looking out into the night.

She looked past him, out through the windows. The emergency vehicles had left, darkness blanketing the reservoir again. He didn't ask if he could stay, but she would have said yes if he did. She didn't want to be alone tonight.

"Go to sleep," he said. "I'll wake you up at seven and take you in."

"You don't have to."

"She matters to me too."

She felt a smile tug at her lips. "She was pretty impressed with the rescue."

"Let's hope I'll never have to do that again."

"I'm sorry I didn't believe you about Blackwell," she said quietly. "You were right."

"Just because you're paranoid, it doesn't mean they're not out to get you, and all that." Humor glinted in his cerulean eyes, his tone and expression lighter than she'd ever seen it.

Her heart gave a hard thud. She wanted him to take her into his arms but didn't know how to ask. He'd just saved her life, hers and Maddie's. Didn't seem like she should be asking for more.

"Bathroom is yours. You can take the guest room after that," she told him as she walked into her bedroom. Then she pulled all the covers on top of her and let exhaustion claim her at last.

She woke a little before seven, shivering. She found him in her room in the armchair by the window, sleeping with his long legs stretched out in front of him. He wore his own clothes again, instead of what he'd been given at the hospital, and they were dry. Must have put them in the dryer at some point.

Moonlight poured in the window unobstructed, lighting his face, the hard edge of his jaw barely softened by sleep, the rough stubble testament to relentless days of hunting a killer. Her heart turned over. He was a mixture of warrior and protector and sheer exhaustion. And sexy.

Her gaze settled on those lips that had kissed her into near incoherence not that long ago.

He woke as she stirred. Blinked slowly. "Everything okay?"

"I'm freezing."

He pushed to his feet and came over to the bed. Waited. When she didn't object, he slipped in beside her and took her into his arms. This was nice. Okay, way more than nice. He tightened his hold on her, and she burrowed into his heat.

He kissed her forehead. Then the bridge of her nose. Then dipped his head lower to her mouth.

His lips were warm and gentle. And exactly what she needed. Heat suffused her as he caressed her lips with his own, then increased the pressure just a little until she opened up and let him in.

The heat built with every stroke of his tongue, then raced across her skin as he moved his hands over her body. It wasn't the kind of sexy seduction splashed across the silver screen by Hollywood. They were new to each other, unsure, awkward. They were both fully dressed.

Heck, she was dressed for the Iditarod.

Not for long. Because soon the heat became too much, and she reached for the hem of her sweater. He helped to remove it. Then the long-sleeved cotton shirt under that. He hesitated at the plain cotton bra.

She stifled a groan as he stared at her chest. Her first sexual encounter in years, and she was wearing grandma thermal underwear. He didn't look appalled. In fact, his gaze heated.

He claimed her lips again, his hand moving to her breast, outlining the bra, then cupping her gently. He trailed kisses down her neck, to the top of her breasts, his hands hesitating on the material as he fought with himself.

He looked up with a tortured look in his eyes. "You need rest."

"I need you," she said simply, and that was all the encouragement he needed.

The bra disappeared in the next second, and his seeking lips wrapped around her nipple. He nudged, nibbled, drew on the tight bud until her back arched, pleasure zinging through her, more heat gathering at the core of her.

She was falling for him, and she was helpless to stop it.

She was half out of her mind by the time he kissed his way down her abdomen. He stripped away her pants, trailing kisses down her legs, then up. She was more than ready for him, grabbing his shoulders and trying to urge him up, wanting him to line up their bodies at last.

"I don't have protection," he said in a strangled whisper.

Neither did she. It'd been forever since she'd been with a man. She groaned in frustration, shutting her eyes tightly. But her eyelids flew wide open when he touched his mouth to her core. He grabbed her legs by the ankles, pushed her knees up, opened her to him.

By the time she thought of protesting, she was flying high on pleasure, threshing her head on the pillow, calling out his name. Pleasure broke like a cresting wave as she called his name on a sob, and she sank into utter bliss, the whole world disappearing around them.

When she slowly returned to reality, he came up next to her and held her.

"I don't know how to be normal," he whispered into her hair.

"I'm okay with outstanding. Which this was, by the way." She smiled against his chest.

He pulled back enough to look into her eyes. "You know what I mean."

She did. He meant in life, in general. "Well, don't look at me for pointers."

She was smiling, but he stayed serious.

"I want this," he said. "I want you. For more than tonight. I'm the worst person to take a chance on, but I want you to anyway. I'm going to try my best. I swear."

"Yes," she said.

Epilogue

Spring came early and warm, the trees budding into a profusion of leaves. Ashley went to New York with Maddie and Jack and had a show opening that was the talk of the town. She sold half her paintings that first night and all the rest by the end of the week. She'd been uneasy with the travel but not scared. Having survived a second trip under the ice, having survived a serial killer, having faced her fears at last had changed something.

While in New York, as a surprise gift to Maddie, Jack had taken them to see a Disney musical. And, with a minimum of squirming, he sat through the long show of princess ballerinas in pastel tutus bouncing around the stage. After that, Maddie was pretty much in love with him.

When they returned home to Broslin, he also had a surprise for Ashley.

"Where are we going?" she asked as he led them out back, after making sure everyone was bundled up.

"A hike through the woods."

He took her hand.

Maddie bounded down the path in front of them in the twilight. Since she stopped to examine every ant and funny-looking leaf, she didn't get too far ahead.

Unease spread through Ashley. "We're not going back there, are we?"

Jack looked at her. "Trust me."

And she found that she did, so she followed him to the boulder by the creek. The hole in the ground was piled high with large, flat

packages. Her macabre paintings wrapped in construction paper—
she knew without him having to say anything.

"How about a bonfire?" he asked.

She looked at the heap and nodded, while Maddie squealed in the
kind of frenzied delight only six-year-olds could produce. Ashley
could barely catch her to press a kiss to the top of her head.

Jack took care of everything but let her throw the match. And as
the paper, then the oil in the paint caught on fire, she realized she'd
needed to do that.

Maddie skipped around the fire, tossing old acorns into the flames.
Jack went around and picked up whatever police tape still clung to
branches here and there and burned those. Then he came to stand
behind her and folded his arms around her. "Are you okay?"

"I haven't...seen anything lately." She stared into the flames,
feeling a tremendous weight lift with the smoke.

"You know my theory," he said quietly next to her ear. "When you
were in that coma, you knew you hadn't been able to save Dylan.
Guilt held you back. Maybe part of you that wasn't ready to return,
wasn't ready to let go of Dylan, didn't. And in this in-between
place, with unresolved emotions, others entering the place could
connect with you. Others who weren't ready to go screamed out
against the unfairness."

She thought about that for a long minute. "And this time I did
choose life. I chose it fully. Dylan was there. He wanted me to
come back."

"I'm glad. But I would have brought you back even if you
resisted." He nipped her ear.

Love welled up in her heart.

These past weeks had been crazy. Jack had stopped by often, and
spent the night when he could. All his darkness was falling away
from him, and, as attracted as she'd been to the old Jack, the new
one simply took her breath away. When they were together, she
felt more alive than she could remember ever feeling.

They were good for each other. They were healing together.

He held her, and they stayed like that, gazing at the bonfire and
Maddie, who buzzed around it like a mad hornet, now making
airplane noises.

When the fire died down, leaving nothing but ashes, Jack filled up
the hole with dirt. The ground lay flat again, no sign of all that had

happened there in the middle of winter. By summer, grass and weeds would grow over the scar in the earth, would make it as if nothing bad had ever happened there.

They walked back to the house, Maddie running up ahead again, excited because she had a play date with a little girl who lived across the road. A nice family with three kids had bought the farmhouse there. So Ashley and Jack walked Maddie over there, chatted for a few minutes, then came back home. Jack put on coffee.

"Any plans for later?" he asked.

"I think I'm going to paint."

"A landscape?"

She'd gone back to those again. "I think I'll paint you," she said on impulse. She'd been wanting to paint him for a while now.

"I have a better idea," he said as he came over to her and nuzzled her neck. "Let's do naked things."

"I could paint you naked."

The wolfish smile he shot her took her breath away. "I love you." Her heart skipped a beat. She reached up to unbutton his shirt, pulled it away from his skin. And smiled. She appreciated his body, both as an artist and as a woman. She felt happy with him. Happy and free.

When he was bare on top, he reached for her sweater and tugged it up, over her head.

"Hey," she protested without heat. "Customarily, the artist stays clothed."

"I strip, you strip." He laid down the law.

"Fine, if that's the kind of tit-for-tat guy you want to be."

Mirth lit up his eyes. "Actually, I'd prefer more tit than tat," he said and snatched her bra away. His gaze filled with naked heat. Pleasure tingled down her spine.

She reached for the buttons on his jeans, tugged his pants down, waited until he kicked them away, then reciprocated. She hooked a brazen finger into his boxer shorts. "These definitely have to go. The color clashes with the background I'm thinking about painting."

"I'm supportive of your art. You know that. I wouldn't want to mess up anything."

He stood still as she pulled his boxer shorts down inch by inch, kissing his body along the way as she squatted in front of him. He was hard and thick with wanting her, and it felt pretty amazing to be wanted with such unabashed need.

But he had his hands on her, pulling her up, before she could think too much about that. "My turn."

Her knees nearly gave out as he stripped her naked, drawing his long, seeking fingers over her hip bones and thighs, leaving kisses in their wake.

When she was sure she couldn't take more, he straightened and caught her up in his arms, heading off to the bedroom with her. "On second thought... I believe artists study their subjects before the actual painting process. I think we need a little more up-close studying."

She wasn't about to argue with him.

Not when the way he made love to her was art in itself.

He spoiled her rotten in bed. She tried to do the same to him, a resolution difficult to keep when she felt like her brain was melting.

Every touch, every kiss, every look took her higher, her body swimming in pleasure even as emotions filled her heart to the brim. "I want you," he whispered in a hoarse voice, his muscles tensing.

And he filled her, both body and heart, to bursting. "I want you now and forever."

She clung to him as the waves of pleasure crested.

"I love you. You have me," she told him.

"Forever?" He pulled back a little to watch her face for the answer. Now he wanted to be detail oriented? Now, when her brain and body were in shambles? "Forever. Obsessed cop."

"Loopy artist." The smile he flashed took her breath away. "My loopy artist." And then his lips descended on hers.

The End

Thank you so much for choosing my book to read! I really hope you enjoyed it. Authors live and die by their online reviews. Would you consider leaving a review on Amazon or Goodreads? Just your honest opinion. Even a single sentence would make a real difference to me. Thank you!!!!

Captain Bing's story is next. His wife was killed years ago, and they never caught her killer. This has been pretty hard on him, and he's done a pretty good job at shutting down. Oh, but there's already a woman on her way to Broslin who is about to change everything. If you'd like to be notified when their story is released, please visit my web site at **http://www.danamarton.com** and sign up for my newsletter. I only send out a one page note when I have a new book out, usually four times a year, so I promise not to overwhelm your email!

If you don't want to wait that long to read another romantic suspense story from me, check out AGENTS UNDER FIRE, a romantic suspense trilogy available now on Amazon. **http://www.amazon.com/Agents-Under-novella-trilogy-ebook/dp/B006Q2V2J4**

Please keep in touch! I'd love to hear you on Twitter and Facebook. **http://www.facebook.com/DanaMarton http://www.twitter.com/danamarton**

Acknowledgements

My sincere thanks to Linda and Toni for a fabulous edit, Kim Killion for the amazing cover, A.G. Devitt for his contribution to the novel, and my wonderful Facebook friends for reading the early version and giving me feedback. Thank you!!!

This book is a work of fiction. Names, characters, places and incidents are products of the author's imagination or are used fictitiously. Any resemblance to actual events or locales or persons, living or dead, is entirely coincidental.

First Edition: 2012

Excerpt from **AGENTS UNDER FIRE**
Book 1: GUARDIAN AGENT

Chapter One

Dark waters lapped the century-old palace's foundation, eager to claim the forgotten building on one of Venice's backstreet canals. At four in the February morning, tourists still partied on in the distance, drunk on love, youth and full-bodied Italian wine. Gabe Cannon could hear both the water and the faint beat of the music, but he couldn't hear the half dozen men in the building with him. His new commando team spread out like ghosts moving through the night.

"Target on the roof," the team leader's voice whispered in his earpiece.

He stole up the crumbling stairs, ready for the rogue soldier who needed to be brought in before he caused more damage. He'd known Jake Tekla ten years ago in the army--a decent guy back then, but war could change a person, could even twist a man's mind.

Static hissed in his earpiece before the words, "Kill order authorized. Repeat, authorized to shoot on sight."

His instincts prickled. Standard procedure called for an attempt to capture first, and see what information they could gain during interrogation. Usable intelligence trumped a quick kill, every time. Then again, he worked for a private security firm now: XO-ST. Xtreme Ops Shadow Teams. They did things differently than his previous employers, the U.S. Army and the FBI.

Gabe reached the roof. Plywood patches formed a psychedelic pattern in the moonlight—an unexpected break. Not having to sneak around on crumbling Mediterranean roof tiles would make this much easier. He stole forward and eased into the cover of a crooked chimney stack.

He caught a silent shadow at the door he'd come through--Troy, one of his teammates, joining him. Odd how Gabe had been last into the building, but first on the roof. Maybe the others had pulled back on purpose, testing the new guy. Another person might have been annoyed, but he'd expected this much. He wasn't afraid of having to earn his stripes.

Dormers, chimneys and ridges blocked visibility. Clouds kept drifting across the moon. Scan. Move forward. Take cover. A night game of hide and seek in a labyrinth, with a fair chance that the ramshackle roof could open up under his feet any minute.

Then he stole around a dormer and spotted the target at last. Jake Tekla blended into the night in black fatigues, similar to Gabe's, black ski mask in place. He looked much slighter than Gabe remembered. Being on the run had taken its toll on him. The man crept toward the edge of the roof, his focus on the jump he was considering.

No visible weapons.

Yet another thing that didn't add up. Not for a government-trained, seasoned soldier.

Gabe inched closer, watching for a trap. He flicked the safety off his gun. Come on. Turn. He moved another step closer then stopped with his feet apart, gun raised, silencer in place.

His target sensed him at last and spun around.

Oh, hell.

Gabe caught the curve of a breast in the moonlight, and his finger froze on the trigger as he stared at the woman.

She could be a trap--Tekla's accomplice or a decoy.

He had a kill order.

Most of the men he worked with squeezed the trigger each and every time, preferring to err on the safe side. He'd been like that once. A muscle jumped in his cheek. He pushed the North Village incident from his mind.

The woman stared at him for a moment, then her instincts kicked in and she ran. Or tried. He lunged after her, caught up in three leaps and brought her down hard. She was lean, yet soft, every inch unmistakably feminine. But none of that feminine softness showed in her fighting spirit. She shoved against him with all she had. She had to know she was conquered, yet she refused to yield, stirring some of his base instincts.

"Stop," he hissed the single word into her ear as he did his best to subdue her.

Plywood gave an ominous creak on the other side of the ridge--the team moving into position to cover the roof and inspect all its nooks and crannies. Something stopped Gabe from calling out even as the woman did her best to scratch his eyes out, fighting in silence. Enough small things about this op had triggered alarms in his mind for him to want to see what he had here before he called the rest of the team in.

He patted her down one-handed, although if she had a knife she would have probably used it on him by now. He kept his voice low. "Did Tekla send you?"

She tried to buck him off. He managed to hold her down with one hand and ripped her black mask off with the other. Wavy dark hair tumbled free, eyes going wide with panic even as her full lips snarled. Despite the semidarkness, he couldn't miss her beauty, or the fact that she had Tekla's eyes and nose.

"Who are you?" he asked, even as the answer was already forming in his mind.

The man had two sisters, the younger one a teenager and the other somewhat older. The one under Gabe now was all woman and then some. Definitely not the teenage sister. He'd met both once at the airport when he and Tekla had gone home on a short leave over Christmas, back in their army days. They didn't have parents, he remembered suddenly. Tekla had enlisted so he could support what was left of his family.

What in hell was his sister doing on the roof? No way his team's intel could be so bad on an op like this. They weren't fighting in the chaos of some distant battle field. The target's sisters were supposed to be living with a distant aunt in Arkansas, according to the op files.

His mind ran all the options as he pressed her down a little harder to keep her still. He wanted to believe that Brent Foley, the team leader, hadn't known who she was when he'd given the kill order, but being naïve didn't pay in this business.

But if Brent did know... Eliminating one of Tekla's sisters might push the guy over the edge, bring him out into the open as he came in for revenge. XO-ST's small army for hire consisted of ex-soldiers and ex-agents, conducting outsourced ops for the U.S. government and anyone else who could meet their price. Brent wrote the book on how to reach goals by whatever means necessary.

Except, Gabe hadn't signed on to kill innocent women, no matter how badly he needed the money. He motioned to her to stay down and stay quiet, then eased his body off her a little so she could breathe.

"Is he here?" he whispered.

After another spirited minute of resistance, her muscles went slack and she lay there, breathing hard, despair filling her eyes. She shook her head.

He pulled up all the way. Her gaze slid to his gun, and she swallowed, her body stiffening. Fear came onto her face, that wide-eyed look of people who know they are about to die. She didn't beg, nor did she offer her brother's life for her own. She simply met Gabe's gaze and lifted her chin.

She still looked impossibly young, although he figured she had to be around twenty-six or twenty-seven by now. Her slim body might have looked fragile next to his, but her eyes shone with defiance. That attitude wouldn't be enough, not with a kill order in place and a team of mercenaries spread out around them.

"I'll come back." He pulled a plastic cuff and, with one smooth move, secured her to the iron scroll that decorated the roof's edge. He switched on his mouthpiece as he turned from her, ignoring her silent struggle. "Target escaped the roof. East end."

He ran along the edge toward the other side where a six-foot gap separated the old palace from the next building. Dark shapes materialized from the shadows. He jumped without giving the steep drop below him much thought. As expected, his clear purpose and energy drew the rest of the team behind him.

He dashed forward as if he could see a man's disappearing back somewhere up ahead. He didn't slow for twenty minutes and several rooftops later. Then he braced against the edge of the roof as he stared down onto a dark, abandoned bridge below him. "Lost visual contact."

A four-letter word came through his headset, followed by, "Did he look hurt?"

"No."

"I could have sworn I clipped him before we lost him last week."

A moment of silence. "Spread out."

As the team scattered, Gabe made his way back to the old palace, trying to think of the woman's name, not expecting much after ten years, surprised when it did pop into his brain: Jasmine.

A simple plan formed in his mind as he walked. She was going to take him to Tekla.

He would bring the man in himself, making sure she didn't get hurt in the process. Things could get out of hand when a cornered person was confronted with an entire commando team.

For all he knew, the other sister was here, too. His jaw muscles tightened. He had no respect for a man who would use his sisters as a shield. Gabe vaulted from roof to roof, watching out for crumbling edges.

If he could complete the mission without bloodshed, he wanted to give it a try. Maybe saving a few lives, after having taken so many, would even the scales a little.

Except, he found the palace roof empty.

He stared at the sawed through plastic cuff next to a shattered roof tile and its sharp shards. He should have thought of that, dammit.

Anger coursed through him as he moved to look over the edge, not seeing her anywhere below.

A few hardy tourists strolled the sidewalks, out doing the whole 'Venice by starlight' thing. He considered going down among them, even as he knew it would be futile. She could be anywhere by now.

Closer to the city center, St. Mark's Square and the areas around the major hotels, would be even busier. A lot of visitors had arrived for the famous Carnival that would start next week. They enjoyed taking their fancy costumes out for a test drive. He would never find her tonight.

He'd underestimated her. She wouldn't be easily defeated. Of course, she was trying to protect her brother, which he respected, but he was going to bring Tekla in.

He needed the money badly. Lives depended on it.

…

Keep reading the AGENTS UNDER FIRE trilogy:
http://www.amazon.com/Agents-Under-novella-trilogy-ebook/dp/B006Q2V2J4

http://www.danamarton.com
First Edition: June 2011

ABOUT THE AUTHOR

--Dana Marton writes fast-paced action-adventure romances that take her readers all over the globe. She's a Rita Award finalist and the winner of the Daphne du Maurier Award of Excellence. She loves writing stories of intrigue, filled with dangerous plots that try her tough-as-nails heroes and the special women they fall in love with. Her 30 books have been translated into many languages and published all over the world.--

That sounds so good I almost impressed myself just typing it. LOL Well, a few shiny sentences can cover a lot of gritty truth. The above bio is my glamor version for press releases. My path to publication, on the other hand, was nothing if not unglamorous. I wrote for 13 years and completed 4 books (as well as writing a lot more that I didn't finish), before I finally received the call from a major NY editor. I was beginning to wonder if I was being tenacious or just too stupid to know when to quit.

When the editor called, I was so nervous, I was standing by the kitchen counter with the wall phone, my knees shaking. I sure wished for a chair. I sure wished for some paper and pen, too, to write down all the things she was throwing at me, like the possibility of pen names, deadlines and contract details. I listened to everything in a daze, hoping I'll remember half of it. After we hung up, I realized the phone was cordless. I could have gone and grabbed a piece of paper and sat down.

Everything worked out in the end. I looooove writing, and would spend all day doing it if I could only break my family of the pesky habit of wanting to wear clean clothes and eat. What's up with that? My wonderful assistant is Toby, a 6 mos old goldendoodle. If I have free time between books (I'm talking about a day here), I enjoy flea markets, gardening and going on long walks in the woods with my husband. But in my head, I'm always plotting. It's an occupational hazard.

Thank you for reading my books!
Dana Marton, Author

Made in the USA
Columbia, SC
12 December 2023

28137693R00115